PRAISE FOR
RIDING TEMPTATION

"A sexy, fast-action thrill ride!" —*Romantic Times*

"Full of intrigue, sexual tension, and exhilarating release. Definitely a must-read." —*Fresh Fiction*

"*Riding Temptation* has it all—action, suspense, romance, and sensuality, all wrapped up in a story that will keep you on the edge of your seat and have you clamoring for the next story in the Wild Riders series!" —*Wild On Books*

"Kudos to Ms. Burton for creating this exciting new series!" —*Romance Junkies*

RIDING WILD

"Forget about a cool glass of water; break out the ice! Each page will leave you panting for more." —*Romantic Times* Top Pick

"A wild ride is exactly what you will get with this steamy romantic caper. This sexy and sizzling-hot story will leave you breathless and wanting more." —*Fresh Fiction*

"A nonstop thrill ride from the first page to the last! Grab a copy of *Riding Wild* and take your own ride on the wild side of life!" —*Romance Junkies*

"What an exciting and wonderful book!" —*The Romance Studio*

"*Riding Wild* is a must-read for anyone who loves sexy romances filled with plenty of action and suspense." —*Kwips and Kritiques*

continued . . .

WILD, WICKED, & WANTON

"*Wild, Wicked, & Wanton* starts off with a bang and never lets up!"
—*Just Erotic Reviews*

"This is the best erotic novel I have ever read! I absolutely loved it!"
—*Fresh Fiction*

"Jaci Burton's *Wild, Wicked, & Wanton* is an invitation to every woman's wildest fantasies. And it's an invitation that can't be ignored."
—*Romance Junkies*

FURTHER PRAISE FOR THE WORK OF JACI BURTON

"Burton delivers it all in this hot story—strong characters, an exhilarating plot, and scorching sex—and it all moves at a breakneck pace. You'll be drawn so fully into her characters' world that you won't want to return to your own."
—*Romantic Times*

"Realistic dialogue, spicy bedroom scenes, and a spitfire heroine make this one to pick up and savor."
—*Publishers Weekly*

"Jaci Burton delivers." —*New York Times* bestselling author Cherry Adair

"Lively and funny . . . The sex is both intense and loving; you can feel the connection that both the hero and heroine want to deny in every word and touch between them. I cannot say enough good things about this book."
—*The Road to Romance*

RIDING ON INSTINCT

JACI BURTON

HEAT | NEW YORK

THE BERKLEY PUBLISHING GROUP
Published by the Penguin Group
Penguin Group (USA) Inc.
375 Hudson Street, New York, New York 10014, USA
Penguin Group (Canada), 90 Eglinton Avenue East, Suite 700, Toronto, Ontario M4P 2Y3, Canada
(a division of Pearson Penguin Canada Inc.)
Penguin Books Ltd., 80 Strand, London WC2R 0RL, England
Penguin Group Ireland, 25 St. Stephen's Green, Dublin 2, Ireland (a division of Penguin Books Ltd.)
Penguin Group (Australia), 250 Camberwell Road, Camberwell, Victoria 3124, Australia
(a division of Pearson Australia Group Pty. Ltd.)
Penguin Books India Pvt. Ltd., 11 Community Centre, Panchsheel Park, New Delhi—110 017, India
Penguin Group (NZ), 67 Apollo Drive, Rosedale, North Shore 0632, New Zealand
(a division of Pearson New Zealand Ltd.)
Penguin Books (South Africa) (Pty.) Ltd., 24 Sturdee Avenue, Rosebank, Johannesburg 2196,
South Africa

Penguin Books Ltd., Registered Offices: 80 Strand, London WC2R 0RL, England

This is an original publication of The Berkley Publishing Group.

This is a work of fiction. Names, characters, places, and incidents either are the product of the author's imagination or are used fictitiously, and any resemblance to actual persons, living or dead, business establishments, events, or locales is entirely coincidental. The publisher does not have any control over and does not assume any responsibility for author or third-party websites or their content.

PRINTING HISTORY
Heat trade paperback edition/April 2009

Library of Congress Cataloging-in-Publication Data

Burton, Jaci.
    Riding on instinct / Jaci Burton.
        p. cm.
    ISBN 978-0-425-22645-2
    I. Title.
    PS3602.U776R52   2009
    813'.6—dc22
                                                    2008046948

PRINTED IN THE UNITED STATES OF AMERICA

10 9 8 7 6 5 4 3 2 1

To my occasional coffee buddy—
you're someone I can always count on.
We need to do coffee more often.
I miss talking to you.

To Angie,
who's forced to listen to
my whining all day, every day,
who puts up with the constant chatter and ups
and downs and loves me anyway.
I love you back.

And to Charlie,
for dealing with me through the madness,
the hand-wringing, and the pacing.
Your patience is infinite. I love you, babe.

one

A STRIPPER? HER? NOT A CHANCE IN HELL.

Spencer King walked a circle around Agent Shadoe Grayson, shook his head, and decided that this assignment was going to fail.

"No way is anyone going to believe she's a stripper."

As he stopped in front of her, she arched one perfectly manicured brow and narrowed her brown eyes. She was pretty, but nothing about her screamed "stripper."

"Excuse me?"

"Sorry, darlin', but you're not the right man for the job."

She crossed her arms. "And why is that?"

"Well, look at you. Loose, dark pantsuit with God only knows what kind of body underneath it, hair in a bun without one strand out of place. Your face is pinched so tight you look like you have a stick shoved up your ass."

"Jesus, Spence, use some tact."

Spence glared at his boss, General Grange Lee. "When have I ever used tact?"

"Good point." Grange turned to Shadoe. "I'm sorry, Agent Grayson. The guys around here aren't polite."

"I don't need polite, General Lee. I'm just here to get the job done."

Spence leaned against the sofa arm and shook his head again. "You aren't gonna get it done looking like that. Strippers wear less clothes than that goin' to church on Sunday."

"This is regulation Department of Justice uniform . . . What is your name again, Mr.—"

"Spence. Just call me Spence." He directed his attention back to General Lee. "Grange, this isn't gonna work."

"It's going to have to. We've been given the assignment; we'll work it out."

Spence slid fully onto the couch and planted his booted feet on the coffee table. "Whatever. But who's going to teach the prim schoolteacher over there how to be sexy?"

"I am not a schoolteacher. I'm a trained field agent."

He grinned. "Yeah, but you ain't no stripper."

She pivoted and faced Grange. "Really, General Lee. This is ridiculous."

Spence thought so, too. He could think of a hundred women who would make better strippers than Miss Prim and Proper. Of course, those hundred women *were* strippers, so that was probably why. What dumbass in Washington thought up this colossal clusterfuck of an assignment?

"We have a DEA agent out there selling us out to the Colombians," Grange reminded him. "Our job is to find him and detain him, and if we're really lucky, intercept the next shipment so we can take down the drug smugglers. We'll make this work."

Spence shrugged. "Whatever you say, boss."

The others began to trail in—all part of the Wild Riders, a secret government organization charged with operating under the radar, assisting the government in less than legal ways. Spence loved his job. He got to steal and do illegal things that suddenly became—legal.

"So, another assignment?" Mac asked, his new wife, Lily, in tow. Jessie came with them. They piled up on the sofa, Lily pushing at Spencer to scoot over.

"So it seems," AJ said, coming in with Rick to stand behind the sofa.

Diaz and Paxton followed.

"Agent Shadoe Grayson of the Department of Justice. These are the Wild Riders." He made them all introduce themselves, then asked her to take a seat, motioning to a space left over on the sofa where Spencer sat.

Spence noted with some amusement that she took the vacant chair next to the sofa. Oh yeah, she was going to be all over the men at the strip club. She couldn't even stomach sitting close to one man. He resisted rolling his eyes, not in the mood for a lecture from Grange.

"I have new assignments for all of you, but we'll get to the reason Agent Grayson is here first," Grange said. "Here's the deal. For some time now, the DEA has been aware that every drug bust operation involving the Colombian cartel in the New Orleans area has been foiled, as if the Colombians have received advance knowledge. They know they have someone inside feeding them information, and every time the DEA tries to set up their own sting, the rogue is nowhere to be found. It's as if the Colombians are able to swing a ship into New Orleans, offload drugs, and move out without the government knowing anything about it. So someone is tipping off the Colombians about potential covert operations, and we think the rogue inside is in league with the Colombians."

"Probably because the agent knows everyone in his department, knows when he's being followed or if there's a plant," Mac suggested.

"Or *her*," Lily said.

"Exactly," Grange confirmed. "Which is why we've been brought in. The rogue doesn't know us."

"But wouldn't the rogue know Agent Grayson?" Lily asked.

"No. She's new."

"Great. A rookie," Spence mumbled.

Shadoe glared at him. Spence smiled.

"Agent Grayson might be new in the field, but she's very good at her job. Don't underestimate her. Plus, she has some . . . special talents that the department is thrilled to make use of."

"Such as?" Rick asked.

"I have a photographic memory," she answered.

"Oh, cool. So you can remember everything you read and hear?" Jessie asked.

Shadoe nodded.

"Bullshit." Spencer didn't believe anyone could have a photographic memory.

" 'No way in hell is anyone going to believe she's a stripper. Sorry, darlin', but you're not the right man for the job. Well, look at you. Loose, dark pantsuit with God only knows what kind of body underneath it, hair in a bun without one strand out of place. Your face is pinched so tight you look like you have a stick shoved up your ass' . . . Should I go on, Spence, or stop now?"

"Well, goddamn. She just repeated everything I said to her right before y'all came in."

"No shit?" AJ asked.

"No shit." Spence looked back at Shadoe with a nod of appreciation. "I stand corrected, darlin'. You've got the skills."

Those weren't her only skills, either. Because when her lips lifted in a hint of a smile, he saw a spark flash from her brown eyes that rocked his balls into a quiver of awareness. Damn she was pretty. Even with her severe clothing, without makeup, and with hair pulled back, there was definitely . . . something.

"Can we move on now, Spencer, or do you want to bullshit all day?"

Spence nodded, realizing he'd pissed off Grange. "Sorry, General."

"Okay. We have intelligence that a shipment will be coming in, and that the rogue will be there to meet with his . . . *or her* . . . Colombian contact in New Orleans sometime within the next couple of weeks. We don't know who either is, but with Agent Grayson's assistance, we hope to nab the rogue."

"What's the plan?" Lily asked.

"Agent Grayson and Spencer will be going undercover at the Wild Rose Club in the French Quarter. The tipoff is that transactions go down at the club, but the DEA has never been able to prove it or to set anyone up inside that the rogue can't make, so that's where we're going to plant our insiders."

"Hot damn! One of the finest strip clubs in the city," Rick said.

Grange nodded. "Agent Grayson will be undercover as a feature stripper, Spencer as her bodyguard. AJ and Pax will go along as backup."

"Oooh, can I strip?" Jessie asked.

"Oh, hell no," Diaz said.

Jessie affected a pout. "I never get to have any fun."

AJ snorted. "Your day will come, sweetheart. I'm sure there are thousands of guys out there who'd love to see you naked."

"Over my dead body," Diaz said.

Jessie grinned at that. Spencer shook his head. Jessie was the baby of the bunch. She'd been with the Wild Riders since Mac rescued her from a really bad situation when she was a teen. She was more little sister than partner to them, and they all protected her. She'd grown up, though, had finished her first assignment a few months back with Spence and Diaz. Jessie and Diaz had fallen in love on that case, making the two of them working together in the future a sticky situation. But since Mac and Lily managed it, Spence supposed Grange could work it out with Diaz and Jessie, too. Spence was just glad he didn't have to deal with those kinds of entanglements. Fucking was one thing. Love was something entirely different and not in his vocabulary.

"Anyway," Grange said, wrangling their attention again, "Agent Grayson will be the headliner at the club. Spence will be set up as her bodyguard, which provides her protection and they can back each other up, which gives them a good reason to stick close together. AJ and Pax will be vacationers who show up nightly and will interact with the crowds, in and out of the bar scene."

"Didn't you two luck out," Rick said, crossing his arms and shooting a glare at AJ and Pax.

AJ grinned. "Well, it's a tough job, but someone has to do it."

Grange cleared his throat and caught everyone's attention again. "Agent Grayson has memorized every single face in the DOJ's agent books. She's the only one who will be able to identify the rogue agent when he or she makes an appearance. Our job is to watch the agent when Shadoe identifies him or her, then see if we can break up this drug ring."

"After she learns to strip," Spence added.

Shadoe didn't even look at him, but tapped her fingernails on one crisp pant leg. He smiled at her irritation.

"I have an expert coming in to assist you with that, Agent Grayson," Grange said.

"Please, everyone, call me Shadoe. The 'agent' thing is too formal, and as Spence seems so fond of reminding me," she said, this time shooting a pointed look in his direction, "I need to loosen up."

He winked. She rolled her eyes.

This was going to be fun.

SHADOE UNPACKED, RATHER FURIOUSLY, JAMMING HER THINGS IN the two-drawer dresser in the tiny bedroom provided to her by General Lee. At least she could take out her frustrations on her clothing instead of the huge hulk of a man who'd infuriated her from the start.

Spencer. Why did he have to be the one she was going to work so closely with? The other guys seemed nice, at least. Spencer was an arrogant ass who'd apparently already determined she couldn't do the job. As if she hadn't come up against hundreds of guys just like him—starting with her father. She'd made the colossal sin of being born a girl and her father had never forgiven her for that.

She'd show him, and she'd show Spencer, too. She could do this assignment. And when she rose to the top of the ranks at the department, she'd tell her father to shove it, too. Her gender did not preclude her from becoming successful in law enforcement.

Just because all her father's brothers had been graced with sons and her father had managed to produce only one daughter did not make her a mistake, did not make her less than worthy to carry on the Grayson tradition of being prominent, decorated officers.

Her father was an ass. So was Spencer. She'd prove herself.

She'd parade down Bourbon Street stark naked if she had to, but she'd nab the rogue agent.

A knock at the door forced her to hurry and shove the last of her things in the drawer. She opened the door to find her new partner taking up most of the doorway.

God, Spencer was imposing. Impossibly tall, tan, stunningly

gorgeous, if she had to admit it. Brown hair cut razor short, and eyes the color of the ocean, with a square jaw that bore a hint of unshaven stubble. If she was the kind of woman to swoon over a good-looking man, she'd be a puddle on the floor by now.

Good thing her career took all her time and she didn't focus on men and sex.

Though her body was doing a pretty darn good imitation of libidinous longing at the moment. She ignored it. "Yes?"

"Your stripping instructor, Maria, was delayed. She won't be able to meet with you until tomorrow. But Jessie's offered to help loosen you up. She's waiting for you in the workout room."

"Okay."

"I'll show you the way."

"Fine."

"And I'd change into something less . . . anal-retentive . . . if I were you."

She rolled her eyes. Did he take her for an idiot? "Gee, thanks. I was planning on it." She waited. He didn't move.

"Do you mind?"

"No. Go ahead." He still didn't go away. Nor did he stop smiling. God, that was irritating.

"Geez, you're dense." She shut the door in his face, shook her head, and dug out a T-shirt and sweats, changing in a hurry. When she opened the door again, he arched a brow and gave her a tilted-head once-over, but didn't say a word.

Good, because she did know how to drop-kick a well-over-six-foot-tall giant, and she wouldn't at all mind giving him a demonstration right there in the hall. She was in a mood.

He took her down to the ground floor and into a good-sized gym.

Jessie was waiting for her in a back room, dressed in cropped workout pants and a tight T-shirt. And holy shit, did the girl have a body on her. Shadoe immediately felt inadequate.

Maybe Jessie should be the one stripping, because she was gorgeous. Platinum blond spiky hair, face of an angel, and a body made for sin.

"Hey!" Jessie said with enthusiasm when she spotted Shadoe. "I figured since Maria was going to be late, you'd want to loosen up a bit and maybe start working on some dance moves."

"Sure. Thanks for working with me."

"Are you kidding? I'm jealous as hell you get to strip. It sounds like a blast."

"Don't even think about it, Jess."

The deep baritone voice of Diaz came out as a warning, but Jessie only blew him a kiss and grinned.

"He belong to you?" Shadoe asked.

"Body and soul," she said. "But you can ignore him. He goes Neanderthal and jealous on me at times. It just means he loves me. And I'm still envious that you get this juicy assignment."

"Oh, right. Not exactly the best assignment I could have hoped for, but I'll live through the humiliation."

Jessie put her hands on her hips. "You're joking, right? Stripping is power, honey. You'll have men drooling at your feet, willing to do anything you say for the tiniest glimpse of skin. You'll be in utter control. Don't ever forget that."

"You know, for someone so young, you're very wise."

Jessie laughed. "I just know who holds the clout in that kind of situation. Growing up with all these guys, I've learned a lot."

Shadoe glanced at Spencer, who was leaning against the wall. His expression was noncommittal, but she could well imagine the protective instincts of all those men taking care of a teenaged Jessie. General Lee had given her cursory background information on all the Wild Riders. Impressive lot, all of them, having worked their way into their positions from nothing.

She supposed teaching the girl street smarts and learning about guys through living with them wasn't a bad thing at all. Shadoe wished someone had let her in on a few of those secrets, because as far as men were concerned, she was clueless. She'd dated them, had sex with them, but as far as understanding them, she was utterly in the dark.

"Let's stretch a bit, then we'll get to movements," Jessie said.

They got down on the floor and did some basic stretches. Shadoe was aware of Spencer still hovering near the door, but she tried her best to ignore him and concentrate on Jessie. She figured he'd get bored soon enough and leave for something more exciting, like wrestling on television. Or maybe a game on Xbox.

No such luck. By the time they had finished their stretching and Jessie went to put music on, not only had Spencer pulled up a chair, but two more of the guys had come in to watch.

"Hey, guys," Jessie said with a wave. "We're going to work on some dance moves. Want to join in?"

"I'd rather have the hair on my balls plucked out with tweezers," Paxton said with a grimace.

"Don't look at me," AJ said. "Two left feet, remember?"

Spence stayed silent.

"Pussies," Jessie replied, then laughed. "Let's get going." She turned to Shadoe. "Do you have dance experience?"

Shadoe nodded. "Years of it as a kid all the way through college. Mostly ballet though."

Jessie grinned. "Perfect. That'll help a lot. At least you know how to move your body."

"True enough, but I think ballet and stripping are two entirely different things."

Jessie laughed. "Dancing is dancing, honey. It's just a different type of movement. As long as you have rhythm, you've got a head start."

The music was slow and sexy, and Shadoe followed Jessie's lead. "First thing you have to do is relax your body. Breathe in and out," Jessie said, her chest rising and falling as she deeply inhaled and exhaled. "If your body isn't relaxed, you'll be out there dancing around like you have rigor mortis."

Shadoe snorted. "Good point." She did the deep breathing as Jessie instructed.

"Ignore the audience. Concentrate on the music and how it makes *you* feel. Because you're the only one who counts. It's just you and me dancing."

Shadoe focused on the music, relaxed, breathed, watched only Jessie. Jessie had a way with her body and the music, sliding her hips back and forth. Slight, but oh so sexy.

Ballet was all about certain moves, maintaining your body structure in certain positions. What Jessie did was nothing like that—it was all free-form movements. Shadoe was used to something entirely different and she tried to follow Jessie. She tried to concentrate, but knew she was failing miserably.

Jessie reached out and grabbed Shadoe's hips. "Honey, you are one tight ball of tension. Let it go. This is fun stuff. Loosen your hips and let them slide. Back and forth, back and forth. That's it. Now raise your arms over your head and swing your ass."

It was difficult for Shadoe to let go. Jessie was right. She was always tense, always on the job, always thinking, planning, plotting . . . working.

But . . . this *was* work, wasn't it? And her focus was on being the best. So she had to be the best at this.

"Come here," Jessie said, bringing herself up hip to hip with Shadoe and taking Shadoe's hands in hers. "Now, move your body in time with mine."

They were breast to breast, hip to hip. This made it much easier to follow Jessie, undulating her hips in a side-to-side rhythm. Oh, yeah, now she was getting it. She settled into the music, letting her body relax and flow along with Jessie's. Jessie pulled back, then Shadoe moved up close to her again until their breasts were touching. Then Shadoe would move back and Jessie would rock her hips against Shadoe.

"Oh yes, now you've got it. That's hot, babe," Jessie said. "Keep doing it."

This was fun. And Jessie was right. Dancing like this was hot, so much easier than the structured form of dance she was so used to.

When she turned to face the men, there were several sets of equally steamy eyes riveted on them, anticipation written all over their faces.

Jessie was right. There *was* power in this. And she hadn't even taken her clothes off yet.

"Fuck me, that's hot as hell," AJ said in a tight whisper.

"I don't think my dick's supposed to be getting hard, but it is," Paxton replied.

"You'd better all be staring at Shadoe or you're dead," Diaz said.

Spencer said nothing, but his throat was dry, his cock like steel, and his balls quivered. Watching Shadoe and Jessie dance together was one hell of an erotic scene. Though he wasn't focused on Jessie at all.

Now that she was out of her loose pantsuit, he realized Shadoe had a body. Not the knock-your-eyes-out-of-their-sockets body that Jessie had, but the woman definitely had curves. Nice breasts pressed against her snug-fitting T-shirt, an indented waist, and hips made for a man's hands. And legs. Long legs. He wanted to see those legs under the sweatpants she wore, dammit. A woman could have tits like mountains and he wouldn't care. He was a leg man.

And he was wrong—she could move. She learned quickly, and though he could tell she was a novice, once she was given instruction, she was a quick study. If Maria could teach her a few moves, she might make one hell of a stripper.

If she could actually handle it, and that was the key. Could she handle it? He'd have to find out before they put her up on stage.

He knew exactly how to do that.

He waited while she and Jessie practiced awhile longer. All the guys but Diaz left, obviously unable to stand the girl-on-girl torture any longer.

When Jessie finished up, Shadoe indicated she was going to hang out and practice for a while. Jessie winked at Diaz as she strolled by and left the gym. Diaz walked out right after her, but Spence hung back, watching. Shadoe was immersed in the music, clearly oblivious to his presence.

He stood and walked toward her. She rocked her hips back and forth in front of the mirror, her eyes open as he approached.

Maybe she wasn't oblivious, because she locked gazes with him, yet continued to move, raising her arms over her head. He stopped behind her.

"Stripping is more than just shaking your ass, you know," he said.

"I'm fully aware of that."

She continued to move. She had a really nice ass. His dick continued to pound. He didn't try to hide the fact he had an erection, either. He stepped beside her, and her gaze drifted down. She had to notice.

She did. Her gaze shot back up to his face.

"Yes, watching you and Jessie dance got my dick hard. Does that bother you?"

This time she stopped, turned to him, swallowed before answering. "No."

"Good. Because as a stripper you're going to be getting a lot of guys hard. Get used to it."

She grabbed a towel from the back of the chair and wiped her neck. "There are a lot of things I need to get used to. But I'm not innocent, Spence."

"Could have fooled me."

"I'm twenty-eight years old. I've had sex before."

"How many times?"

She stilled. "That's really none of your business."

He laughed. That answer told him a lot. "Oh, a woman of the world, are you?"

"You're an ass."

"Yes. But I need to be able to cover yours. And you need to be able to pull this off. So I'm not going to let you pretend to be something you're not. If you can't do this, you should stop now."

"I can do this."

"Prove it. Strip for me."

TWO

SHADOE BLINKED, UNABLE TO BELIEVE THE BULLSHIT SPENCE had just handed her. "What?"

"You heard me." He pulled the chair around and sat in it. "I'm a paying customer. Strip for me."

She wrapped her arms around herself like a blanket. "I most certainly will not."

"Babe, soon you'll be stripping for a hundred guys or more every night. And I'll be there every time. If you can't do it now, you'll never be able to."

"Screw you, Spencer."

"I didn't ask you to screw me. I just want you to strip for me."

Oh. Now she got it. He was challenging her. The first thing he'd said upon meeting her was that he didn't think she could do it. He was trying to prove his point right now. This was the academy all over again. Her father all over again. Every man who'd told her she wasn't good enough, that she'd never be able to do the assignment. That it was too hard. That she didn't have the guts for it.

Well, just fucking fine. She'd show him she could. Without embarrassment or hesitation. She threw the towel in the corner, marched over to the stereo and selected a song, then pushed the button. Sucking in a deep breath, she remembered what Jessie had told her.

When the music started, she had her back turned to Spence. She'd just pretend he wasn't in the room at all. Then again, this was her work, wasn't it? And Spencer was definitely all man. If she could turn him on—without Jessie there as the added allure—she could judge her adequacy as a stripper. Then she'd know whether she needed to make some adjustments or not. It would give her some advance knowledge for tomorrow when she met with Maria. She'd know what areas she needed to work on.

She let herself feel the music as it entered her body, remembering she had a "paying" customer watching her.

Think sexy, Shadoe. Be sexy. Of course she didn't have the right clothes on, but that didn't matter. Because underneath these sweats? Wait till he saw what she had on underneath.

The music was slow, jazzy, a beat that made her sway around the room. She took her time at first, not getting close to him at all, as if she were dancing only for herself. She kept her eyes closed, letting the music take hold and get her in the mood. After a few seconds, she started moving around the floor, gradually inching closer and closer, each step drawing her toward Spencer's chair.

The music slowed, the slow strains of the saxophone oh so sexy. She really felt it now, and it made her movements that much more fluid.

Spence's gaze followed her, and she teased him with a roll of her hip near his shoulder, barely grazing him. Emboldened by the sudden flash of heat in his eyes, she took it further, dragging the hem of her T-shirt up, baring the skin of her belly.

His eyes widened when he saw the diamond piercing her belly button.

"That doesn't look like government issue."

She smiled down at him, continued to roll her hips from side to side. "It's a transmitter and GPS unit. So it *is* government issue. You'll be able to track and hear me using this device."

His gaze slid up her body to her face, and his lips lifted. "Handy."

"I thought so. Sexy and functional."

"Guess you thought of everything."

"I try."

He followed every inch of flesh she revealed. With one hand she pulled the shirt up, and pushed the sweatpants down with the other, giving him a glimpse of her hips and the string of her thong.

Through half-lidded eyes she shot a smoldering gaze at Spencer, and was rewarded with his deep, slow swallow. His eyes were planted on her, never wavering. That encouraged her to move forward, lifting the T-shirt up, stopping short of her breasts. His heated gaze followed her movements, then locked on her face in expectation. She danced in front of him, fisting the shirt in both hands and rocking her hips back and forth, teasing him.

If he wanted it, he could damn well ask.

"Take it off," he said.

No, he hadn't quite asked, had he? He'd commanded it, and his gruff voice made her wet. That, she hadn't expected, but it helped her play the part, and she'd use anything she could to dig in to the persona of a stripper.

She stepped closer and lifted the shirt off, revealing the black lace demi-bra that barely contained her breasts.

His eyes nearly bugged out of his head.

Straitlaced and prim and proper, was she? *Choke on it, Spence.*

This was so exciting. God, she hoped she didn't look like a fool, but judging from Spencer's reaction, she didn't think so.

She tossed the shirt across the room and hooked her thumbs underneath the waistband of her sweats, just enough to tease. She might not be a professional stripper, but she knew when she had a man's interest. Her fingers splayed underneath just enough to taunt, to promise, tilting her pelvis in his direction as if offering herself to him. Then she turned around and swung her ass at him as she bent over, slowly inching the sweats down her legs.

Yes, that's right, Spence. Black lace thong panties. She might have to wear a hideous crisp pantsuit on the outside, but she loved her sexy underwear.

She stood, let the pants fall to her ankles, and kicked them off, then turned around, pointing a hip in his direction.

Spencer's gaze was hot, and when he licked his lips, she knew she had him. She took a step forward, spread her legs wide enough for him to zero in on the goods, and straddled his lap.

His brows went up. "Are you sure you've never done this before?"

"Never." She was operating purely on instinct and what she wanted. And right now she wanted to touch him, to feel his body under hers. She grabbed his shoulders and rocked against him, tilting her head back and arcing forward, letting him look. His deep breathing told her all she needed to know. And dear God it was exhilarating.

Truthfully, she'd never been bold like this before, especially with a man. Even her sexual experiences in the past had been in the dark and under the covers. She had no idea where this wild sexual side of herself had come from. She could tell herself she was doing this because it was her job, but she sensed it was more than that. She *felt* more than that.

Her body was alive, surging with tingles and pulses and wetness and need, all directed at the man whose lap she sat on. And, oh my, he was rock-hard all over, from the bulging muscles of his shoulders that flexed under her hands, to the wall of rock under her thighs.

As she inched closer, ever closer, she felt another hardness, one that compelled her need to explore. His cock was outlined against his jeans, thick and inviting, and she wanted to unzip his pants and slide her hands inside to wrap her fingers around him. Would he be as hot and pulsing as she was?

She was wet. He was hard.

She wanted to fuck him, impale her pussy on his cock until she came in a blistering, satisfying orgasm. Her clit quivered at the visuals slamming at her nonstop. Her gaze shot to his, and the message was clear in the heat of his eyes.

She could barely breathe.

"Do it, Shadoe."

This had suddenly become less about work and much more personal, because she wanted to. She really wanted to. Her nipples were hard and throbbing, and it wouldn't take much pressure on her clit before she went off like a rocket into a shuddering climax. Her panties were already soaked—probably through to his jeans.

But this wasn't part of the job description.

Shit.

Like a cold bucket of water had been tossed over her, training and protocol and everything she'd been taught about mixing business and pleasure—or rather *not* mixing them—slapped her back into reality. She shook her head and backed off Spence's lap, mortification mixed with regret, because for a moment there, she wished she wasn't on assignment. She grabbed her clothes and turned off the music, sucked in air, slowed down her breathing, and forced a calm she didn't feel. By the time she climbed back into her sweatpants, she was relaxed and smiling. "I think we've done enough for the day."

He stood, his erection still prominent, as was the frown on his face. "You haven't finished."

"What do you mean?"

"You haven't stripped."

No, she hadn't. Not completely anyway. She still wanted to. What would happen if she stood naked before him? Would he touch her? Do more than that? The thought of it made her weak in the knees.

She couldn't go there. She inhaled, then moved toward him, pulling her T-shirt over her head like armor. When she stopped in front of him, she felt more herself again. "I don't need to." She slid her gaze down to his cock, then back up again. "You're hard; you wanted me. I think I did a pretty decent job for my first day. I'll call that good enough."

She strolled past him and out of the room, hoping her legs didn't give out from under her.

By the time she got to her room and shut the door behind her, she was shaking, sweaty, and her heart was pounding.

"Stupid, stupid, stupid." She hadn't had control of the situation, and control was everything in her line of work. She'd let it get personal. Had she learned nothing at the academy?

She'd really like to blame Spencer for that debacle, but it wasn't his fault. She could have said no when he'd told her to strip, but honestly, she'd needed the practice. He was right. How could she hope to get naked in front of a roomful of hundreds of men if she couldn't do it in front of one? And frankly, doing it for him had helped her self-confidence. Oh, man, had it ever helped. She had no idea how sexual an experience it could be.

But was that stripping itself, or the man she'd stripped for? There was no doubt about it: she might find Spence arrogant and irritating, but there was also chemistry between them. Serious, combustible chemistry. Even now she could recall the feel of his skin under her hands, the way his rigid thighs felt under hers. She'd never been with a more commanding, sexual man in her entire life.

She'd wanted him to touch her.

"Good God, Shadoe, what's wrong with you?" She pushed off the door and flung herself on the twin bed, staring up at the lazily twirling blades of the ceiling fan. Which, by the way, was not cooling her body down at all. She lifted her hips and jerked the sweats off, then discarded her T-shirt, too.

Even clad in just her bra and panties, she was still hot. And she knew why.

That *was* Spence's fault, indirectly at least. He'd gotten her turned on, and she needed an orgasm. She could have rocked against his leg and gotten off if she'd lingered there long enough. *That* visual only made her body steamier. She laid her hand against her belly, feeling the heat of her skin there, then let her fingers slide lower, under the lace, to palm her sex. It was damp, still clinging with the heat and moisture churned up by her sexy encounter with Spence.

Oh, yes. Using her other hand, she undid the front clasp of her bra and pulled the cups apart, letting her breasts spill free. The cool air of the fan blew over them, her nipples spiking into tight, hard points.

Right now she'd love to have Spencer loom over her and fit his lips over her nipples—suck and lick them, tease them with his teeth.

"Mercy," she whispered, lifting her hips against her palm and wriggling her fingers. She plucked her nipple while her other hand cascaded lower, sliding down over her clit. She gasped at the sensation, the tight bundle of nerves swollen and wet with her pussy juices.

"I need to come," she said to no one in particular, but one man's face crept before her. She tried to block it from her mind, but he kept coming into focus again. Him, and only him. Finally, she relented and let him in.

"I need to come, Spence." She let the fantasy take over, and her fingers became his—his would be much larger, rougher, and would feel so good. She imagined the feel of them as she caressed her sex, then dipped lower to plunge two fingers inside her moist cavern.

"Oh, God, yes!" she said, then bit her lip as she realized she was too loud and had no idea who might be in the room next to hers. She lifted off the bed again, eager for release but still wanting to hold back.

She pinched her nipple between her fingers, needed that extra painful pleasure while she fucked her fingers in and out of her pussy. She was so wet, her juices ran down her ass. She loved it, reveled in every exquisite sensation.

The buildup increased and she had to fight back loud moans. She may not have a ton of sexual experience, but she knew how to pleasure herself. She did it often and she was a damn expert at it, bringing herself to the height of explosive orgasm within minutes.

She was there, at the precipice, ready to fall. The walls of her pussy gripped her fingers and she felt the contractions as her climax hovered. But still, she lifted the heel of her hand off her clit and hesitated, teasing herself just as she'd want Spence to tease her. She could see his tight, smiling face above her.

"Ask me for it," he'd say.

She shook her head and pinched her nipple harder.

"Beg me."

Finally, she couldn't wait. "Damn you. Please make me come."

She ground the heel of her hand against her clit, buried her fingers inside, and splintered, letting out that moan she'd tried so hard to hold in. Oh, it was so good, a rush of heat and wetness and such wild pleasure she bucked her ass off the bed, seeking more of the devilish bliss that soared through her body.

Aftershocks made her tremble as she slowly floated back to the mattress. Once she caught her breath, she stood on shaky legs and headed into her bathroom to turn on the shower, pausing to stare at herself in the mirror.

"You're a mass of contradictions, Shadoe Grayson," she said to herself. "Hot and cold, stiff and melty. But damn anyone who thinks you aren't sexual enough to do this job."

Because she could. And she was going to be very, very good at it.

SPENCE LEANED AGAINST THE WALL OF HIS ROOM, LISTENING TO the shower running in Shadoe's bathroom. Now it was his turn to let out a loud groan. He jammed his fingers through his hair and cursed.

What the hell possessed Grange to put her in the room next to his? The walls were thin and Spence had good hearing. He'd heard every one of Shadoe's moans, heard her talking to herself, and knew damn well what she'd been doing after her semi–strip show in the gym.

She'd been getting herself off. And all he could do was listen against the wall like some horny twelve-year-old voyeur and visualize what she was doing, how she looked as she came, and wish he was in there doing it to her.

Okay, so he might have been wrong about her. He'd thought she was a buttoned-up tightass. Turned out she had a tight ass all right, but not in the way he'd originally thought. He'd seen that sweet, perfectly formed rear end of hers in the gym. Who knew underneath those regulation clothes lurked a Victoria's Secret model?

He palmed his cock. Christ. He was still hard. And more than irritated that she'd managed to tie his balls up in knots. She might have given him a raging hard-on, but he'd be damned if he was going to take his dick in hand and jack off like a teenager. There were plenty of women in town more than eager to help him get his rocks off.

The problem was, his mind was occupied with a certain brunette with chocolate brown eyes and perfectly shaped long legs. *She'd* gotten him hard. Now he wanted *her* to get him off.

The way she'd eagerly slid onto his lap in the gym, the way her eyes had gone all soft and melted with desire and need? Oh, yeah. She wanted. Especially after listening to her masturbate in her room.

The woman was A-number-one sexual. There was nothing prim and proper about Agent Shadoe Grayson. The problem was, Spence knew better than to mix pleasure with business. And Shadoe was business. Concentrating on his dick meant he wasn't concentrating on the job, and that wasn't good for the Wild Riders.

Shit. Maybe he would have to head to town for some relief. Because working around the innocent seductress was going to be a painful experience. And Spence didn't do pain.

He also didn't do denial. Which meant he hoped Shadoe had more self-control than he did, because if she said yes, there was no way he was going to say no.

This was going to be one hell of an assignment.

THREE

Maria, the stripper Shadoe met with the next day, was a tall, statuesque, raven-haired beauty with long, long legs and huge breasts. Shadoe felt like a short, mousy midget standing next to her. But Maria was also very nice, so Shadoe had a hard time hating her, even though she really wanted to.

They met at a dance studio in a very ritzy section of Dallas, one that Maria said she used frequently when working out new routines.

Maria apparently knew Grange well, and was discreet, according to Grange. Shadoe had no idea how much of Grange's or the Wild Riders' business Maria understood, and they didn't discuss it. Grange just told her that Maria would be happy to show her some moves, and wouldn't ask questions.

Good enough for her.

Shadoe hadn't seen Spence all morning. Not that she'd gone

looking for him. He wasn't needed for this part of the assignment anyway. Grange had sent her to meet with Maria alone, which was fine with her.

Maybe Spence was avoiding her. Maybe he'd had enough yesterday after her impromptu private striptease. Shadoe released a triumphant smile at that thought, though she was pretty sure he just didn't care to watch again today.

Introductions out of the way, Shadoe and Maria set to work. Or rather, Maria took charge and Shadoe followed along.

Maria had dressed in a short turquoise miniskirt and a body-hugging midriff top, covered by a sheer blouse. She wore heels that Shadoe had no hope in hell of ever being able to walk in, though Maria assured her she'd get used to them over time since high heels were a required part of any stripper's uniform.

Shadoe didn't think there was enough time in the world to get used to six-inch heels. When Maria discussed a stripper's wardrobe, Shadoe realized she was going to have to go shopping. Maria gave her the name of her favorite trendy off-the-wall store where she could get some sexy stage clothes and shoes, then offered to go with her. Shadoe was grateful for any help she could get. Gun shopping she could do. Stripper clothes? Totally out of her league.

She thought they'd start dancing right away, but Maria was all business, discussing the philosophy and psychology of stripping. Maria took her job seriously, from what customers looked for all the way to how to please herself, to make sure she looked and felt her best, because if she didn't look and feel good, her customers would know it.

The woman was thorough. Then again, so was Shadoe. She took her job just as seriously, so she admired Maria's dedication to her craft. No wonder she was a headliner. This wasn't just a get-in-and-make-a-quick-buck-until-the-real-thing-came-along type of job for Maria. This was her career. Her eyes simply glowed when she talked about stripping. Shadoe could tell that Maria loved what she did, that she enjoyed being the center of attention, loved dancing and playing to a packed house.

And when Maria finally turned the music on, pointed to a chair, and had Shadoe sit while Maria went through one of her routines, Shadoe was mesmerized.

Not only was Maria beautiful, she was captivating. There was nothing crass about the woman. Sensuality oozed from Maria's body as she went through her moves, subtly removing each item of clothing—not too fast, not so slow as to make the audience lose interest—and the way she caught the eyes of her audience, let them know she loved what she was doing, like she was really there, as opposed to just counting down the minutes until her show was over and she could be somewhere else. It was magic and Shadoe felt utterly seduced.

And stripped down to just her thong, Maria was unashamed of her body, using every curve to her advantage as she gyrated around the room, completely in tune with the music.

When she finished, her body glistening with sweat, she grinned and Shadoe jumped from the chair and applauded.

"That was incredible," Shadoe said, moving toward Maria as Maria turned off the music.

Maria grinned. "Thanks. I'm glad you liked it. You can do the same thing."

Shadoe laughed. "Oh, I don't think so. You obviously had quite a bit of training."

Maria grabbed a towel and wiped the back of her neck, then unscrewed the top off a bottle of water. "Mainly it comes from on-the-job training. You learn a lot of tricks up there on the stage, and from watching the other dancers. You'll pick it up in no time at all."

Dancers. Maria constantly referred to herself and the other girls she worked with as dancers, not strippers. She'd have to remember that.

"I'll do my best, but I have to tell you I've never done this before."

Maria shrugged and pulled up a chair, seemingly not bothered at all by her near nudity. "Some girls step onto that stage and go at it like they've been doing it their whole lives. Others can dance for years and years and still look like amateurs. You'll either have it, or you won't, and no amount of training will help you with that."

"Have what?"

"*It*, honey. The magic. You either have a calling for entertaining, or you don't. Some are born to perform, to seduce men with their bodies and their eyes. Others just climb on the stage to make a quick buck, but they're never really into it. And it shows."

"Really?"

"Yes." Maria grinned, showing off perfect white teeth. "There are various levels of strippers, Shadoe. You have your seedy joints, with part-time strippers who are also hookers, or the drug-addicted ones out to make fast money for their next fix. Really low-class stuff. They look worn down, or bored, and you can tell right away that their hearts are not in it. Then there are the ritzier clubs, where you'll be. Those are the places where the headliners perform, where the owners are choosy about which girls get the privilege of dancing there. They hire only the high-class dancers. Believe me, there's a huge difference, and you can tell right away between the two."

Shadoe nodded. She had a lot to learn. "You're obviously high-class."

"Well, thanks for that. I like to think so. I've worked hard for the past ten years to get where I am today."

Shadoe leaned back and studied the beautiful woman. "How does someone get into a field like this? I don't mean to be rude, but it's not like stripping is something every little girl dreams of doing someday."

Maria laughed. "It's okay. I get asked that question a lot. I majored in theater in college, but I got bored and antsy easily, and though I loved performing, I found I lacked the patience for all the classroom work. I loved doing the shows, enjoyed the performance aspect, but didn't like taking the time to study the craft. Bad me. So I took some sideline jobs as a singing waitress and dancing at a few clubs—not stripping just yet—and then I got a great offer to strip at a high-class club because of my dance skills, so I decided to give it a try."

"Kind of scary for someone brand-new to that kind of lifestyle, I imagine."

Maria laughed. "You have no idea. The first night my knees knocked together so hard I was afraid I'd fall right off my shoes. But the customers were all encouraging and I fell madly in love with the spotlight. I never left after that. School just wasn't for me. I had found my calling and stayed there. It's a kick and a half and I love my life."

Shadoe nodded. "Life's too short not to do something you love."

"Isn't that the truth?" Maria stood and placed her hands on her hips. "So let's turn you into a stripper."

Shadoe stood, too, and swallowed past the dry lump in her throat. "You're kind of a tough act to follow."

Maria let out a throaty laugh. "Honey, you don't have to be me. You just have to be yourself. And eventually you'll figure out your own routine."

As Maria took her hand and led her to the middle of the floor, Shadoe slanted her a wide-eyed look. "I need a routine?"

"Of course. Every headliner needs an angle. Something that sets you apart from the other girls."

"You mean I can't just step on the stage, take my clothes off, wiggle my ass, and be done with it?"

Maria snorted. "Hardly. It's more than just stripping. It's a whole act, with music and costumes and choreography. You'll need a theme."

A theme? Good God. What kind of theme? Like GI Jane or Wonder Woman or Betty Boop, or something equally heinous or ridiculous? She pictured feather boas, sequins, and fishnet stockings, and those hideous chunky platform boots. Or maybe something in all bubblegum pink. She looked horrible in pink. Gag. So not her at all. Then again, was any of this?

"Don't worry about it. We'll get you a routine going in no time. I'll help. First you need moves. Let's see what you've got."

Maria hit the music, and like Jessie had done with her the day before, stood with Shadoe, helped her move and showed her what to do, which made it so much easier to get the hang of things.

Though Shadoe didn't think she'd ever be able to dance with the same fluid grace as Maria, who made stripping look like ballet. Elegant and refined, not at all blundering or tacky. No wonder she was a headliner. She was mesmerizing, and Shadoe felt inept and clunky in her attempts to mirror Maria's movements. For someone who'd studied ballet since she was a child, she was shocked at how she couldn't seem to make stripping seem as elegant as Maria did.

"Quit trying to be like me," Maria finally said after several minutes of dancing. "Watch how I do it, but don't do it just like me. Feel the music, then interpret it how you see fit."

Okay, that made more sense, because she was never going to be able to do what Maria did. She finally backed away, closed her eyes, and let the music take over. When the song shifted from softer R&B to something more hard rock, Shadoe smiled.

Yes. This was definitely more like it, more like her. Harder, deeper. She really got into the music then, feeling it seep into her bones, into her very soul. Moving became easy then, like second nature, and she lost herself in the song, in the lyrics, moving around the room, imagining herself up on the stage, knowing exactly what she wanted to do.

She'd always liked modern dance classes, had rebelled against ballet, even though she'd taken the classes because her father thought she should.

She grinned, realizing this was an awesome way to rebel.

She lifted her shirt, picturing a hundred men hungry for a glimpse of her skin.

"That's it, honey," Maria said, pulling up a chair. "But not too fast. Make them wait for it. Make them beg for it—with their money."

She nodded, this time teasing with the edge of her shirt, baring only her belly, then her ribs, swiveling around to show the audience—Maria—her back.

"Perfect. Now give them more. You want to hold their attention, keep them captivated and throwing money your way. With each item you strip off, you make more money. Remember, by the time you're down to the G-string, all that's left is the gyrating around and getting your skin close to them. By then they've pretty much seen it all, so draw it out as long as you can."

She did, following Maria's instructions until she was down to her thong. She made it through two songs, ending on her knees at Maria's feet.

With a satisfied smile, Maria reached over and turned off the music. "Well done."

Shadoe smiled and stood, grabbing her clothes and getting dressed. Surprisingly, she felt no inhibitions once she let the music take over. Besides, she figured getting naked in front of Maria was a no-brainer. She had nothing Maria hadn't already seen a thousand times before.

But could she do it in a public venue in front of all those men? In front of Spence? Well, technically she'd already done it in front of Spence, but not "officially."

She grabbed a bottle of water and took a couple of long swallows, then turned to Maria. "Stripping makes you thirsty."

"I'll say. I drink about a dozen bottles of water a night. Never drink too much alcohol. If a customer wants to buy you a drink, do one or two at most, then switch to club soda. Alcohol will make you sweat like a pig and dehydrate you, and trust me, that's so not pretty on the stage."

"I can imagine."

"Now," Maria said, standing in front of her with hands on her hips. "You were great."

Shadoe couldn't hide her smile. "Really?"

"Yes, really. You have a natural seductive ability, especially when the right songs came up."

"Thank you." That meant a lot coming from a pro like Maria.

"You still have a lot to work on. Don't be afraid to really let go. Touch yourself, pleasure yourself—within limits, of course. It really drives the customers crazy. Anything you can do to put the focus on your own sexuality will boost your tips and make the club owners happy as hell. And happy club owners mean more bookings for you."

"Okay." Shadoe's photographic memory kept track of the vital information she'd need later.

Maria pressed one finger to her lips and cocked her head to the side. "Now we need to figure out who you're going to be."

"Who?"

"Sure. Your theme. You don't go out there with your real name, honey. You need an identity. Your theme, remember? We can't go shopping for your ensemble until we figure out who you are."

"Oh, yeah."

The sounds of motorcycle engines firing up outside drew Shadoe's attention momentarily.

But then her lips curled in a wide smile, and she turned to Maria.

"I've got it."

"You do?"

"Yes. And it's absolutely perfect."

THE REST OF THE DAY PASSED QUICKLY. MARIA GAVE SHADOE training on the pole for several hours. Dancing around the pole wasn't easy to master, but was it ever fun. Many years of dance lessons had helped, as had field training at the academy; it meant she was coordinated enough, and had the upper body strength to lift herself up the pole and slide around. She found that part exhilarating, and the pole served as a useful prop, giving her something to do other than just stand on stage and gyrate around.

After a brief break for lunch, Maria took her shopping and Shadoe bought several outrageous outfits—plus shoes and scandalous lingerie. Even thinking about parading around on stage in the clothes she'd purchased made her blush, but Maria told her she'd have customers drooling.

As long as Shadoe could act convincingly enough as a stripper, she'd be happy. But she had a lot of practicing to do before she premiered at the club in New Orleans. She could hardly call herself a headliner if she tripped on stage or blushed all over with embarrassment.

So when Maria offered to let her take a practice run at the club in Dallas where she was headlining, Shadoe jumped at the chance. She knew she'd never think herself ready enough, but with Maria there to help point out her mistakes and give her moral support, she'd feel a lot better about her solo act in New Orleans.

She headed back to Wild Riders' headquarters much more confident than when she'd left. Grange met her at the elevator.

"How did it go today?" he asked.

"Great." She set her bags and boxes down on the floor. "Maria is wonderful."

Grange's lips lifted. "Yeah, she is. I figured she could help you out."

Shadoe wondered just how well Grange knew Maria, but it wasn't her place to pry into his personal business. "I'm going to do a practice run at the club where she's headlining."

Grange cocked a brow. "Really. When?"

"Tonight. I'll go on after Maria's first set. That way she can give me some advice on what I do well and what I need to work on before I head to New Orleans."

"Good idea."

"What's a good idea?"

Shadoe turned to see Spence walking into the entryway, along with AJ and Pax.

"Shadoe is going to do a dry run of her show at Maria's club tonight."

"Cool," AJ said with a wide smile. "We'll all go watch."

"We can critique your performance," Pax added, waggling his brows.

Oh, God. The heat of embarrassment crept up her neck.

"I don't think so," Grange said. "She doesn't need an audience of guys she already knows watching her strip."

Thank you, Grange.

"Just Spence will go with her."

Oh, shit. "Really, General, I think it would be best if I just did this one on my own."

"I can't advise that. If you're going to be out there with this alias in New Orleans as a headliner, you might as well get started going with your bodyguard now. Spence will accompany you."

She cast a desperate gaze to Spencer, who just shrugged and looked her up and down. "I guess I'll see you tonight. All of you."

FOUR

Spence muscled his way past the packed crowd of mostly men at the Angel's Gate strip club. After ten P.M. on a Saturday night, it was standing room only, especially with a headlining act like Maria's in town.

Beer was flowing, served by the three bartenders manning the long black bar. Half-naked women were everywhere offering lap dances, and dancers occupied two cages adjacent to the dance floor, topless and gyrating to the loud, heart-thumping beat the deejay had set for the night.

Eye candy everywhere, though Spence had his eye on only one woman, and that woman was nowhere to be seen. She'd headed out before him tonight, claiming she had to meet with Maria early to get some last-minute advice and she didn't need him to tag along.

Whatever. Fine with him. He didn't even want to be here

tonight. This wasn't part of the assignment, and the assignment was all he was interested in.

Though hanging out at the club had its advantages, namely beer and women—two of his favorite things. He bought a beer and moved his way to the front row of the stage where Steve, his friend and favorite bouncer, had left him a seat. The girls were in between acts right now, and the warm-up girls—basically the new girls— were still performing, which meant the more experienced girls—the ones everyone really came to see—hadn't been out yet.

Most of the action at a strip club never really started before ten or eleven at night. He got comfortable, easy enough with a table to himself, and nursed his beer, watching the girls in the cages on either side of the stage. Pretty things, though kind of young. Then again, it wasn't his place to judge anyone for their choice of profession. He of all people knew that circumstance could put anyone in a predicament. He'd also dated a lot of strippers, and many of them were hardly down on their luck, instead choosing to strip because it paid well and the hours were good. A lot of them were college students, some post-graduate, and very smart women who knew how to make money and get ahead, especially in a nice club like Angel's Gate. The seedier clubs in some of the bad parts of town—now that was a different story. He stayed away from those, preferring the clientele at a place like this. Beautiful women with a decent level of intelligence where he could watch them dance, he could drink his beer, and the criminal element stayed out, mainly due to the four beefy bouncers Jack Renshaw, the owner of Angel's Gate, kept on hand at all times.

That was why Angel's Gate stayed so popular.

The lights went down on stage, and the music kicked up. The deejay's voice came on strong, announcing a few of the Angel's Gate featured dancers—a triplet act called the Oreos—two black girls, one white.

Spence smiled. He'd seen Candy, Veronica, and Jane dance before. They were good. They lined up side by side and came down the long walkway, strutting their stuff in their stilettos like they owned the place, then drove the guys wild by sandwiching up together and rubbing oil all over their bodies. Every man's fantasy, girl on girl on girl action, though it was all simulated entertainment. All the girls had boyfriends; in fact, Spence spotted two of them in the audience tonight, cheering their girls on and waving money, trying to get the other customers to do the same.

He grinned and shook his head. It was all a gimmick, but it worked well. Money flew onto the stage and by the time the girls were down to their G-strings and slithering across the floor, money littered the stage. They raked it up, waved to the crowd, and blew kisses on their way backstage.

As soon as those girls went off, another girl came on, and so it went. Had to keep the customers happy by keeping girls on stage at all times. And in between their acts the strippers wandered around the crowd, offering up lap dances or just spending time with the customers.

About an hour later, it was time for the headliner—Maria. Spence had refilled his beer and had his feet propped up on a nearby chair, much to the irritation of the standing-room-only crowd.

Like he cared.

Maria's music was more up-tempo—more sax, grinding and hot and sexy. Colorful lights swirled all around the stage, and a spotlight hit the entryway.

"Ladies and gentlemen," the deejay said in a booming voice, "give it up for the one, the only, the dynamite seductress of the night, Vixen!"

Spence let out a laugh. Vixen was Maria's stage name. It fit her really well as she burst through the doorway, larger than life in a skintight white bra and boy shorts, a matching white jacket and leather hat, and white calf-high boots. She was a vision, with her tanned skin and dark, flowing hair a contrast to all that virginal white, which he supposed was the idea. As Maria moved center stage, she grabbed the pole and swung around, at the same time peeling off her jacket and flinging it to the floor. She had generous breasts that spilled over the top of a very small bra, and as she worked the pole, she reached behind her and unfastened the bra, letting the back loose but not removing the top.

The crowd went crazy, whistling for her to remove the top. By now she was at the bottom of the pole, riding it between her legs, and tantalizing the crowd by holding on to the cups of her bra. When she let it go, releasing her enormous breasts, the sound of cheering was deafening. She stayed on her knees and undulated around the floor, letting her voluptuous body and long legs do the talking, playing up to the guys at the edge of the stage, crooking her finger to invite them up close and personal to her breasts, and after they paid homage with their money, using her killer shoes to push them away. She had bodyguards to protect her in case anyone got out of hand, but it was all playful fun and the guys knew the rules. They wanted to stay right where they were and unless someone was stone-cold drunk on their ass, they wouldn't risk getting tossed from the club. Because once you got thrown out of Angel's Gate, you weren't allowed back in. Ever.

Besides, Maria had pretty much mesmerized the guys from the front row to the back of the bar with her smooth, sexy moves. Money was flying over Spence's head and onto the stage, men pushing at his back for a chance to tuck money into her G-string.

Yeah, she knew how to work it, all right.

She was on the stage for about three minutes, and bills covered the floor and her G-string by the time she was done.

The lights came back up and the deejay started spinning dance tunes. Girls climbed into the cages to gyrate and entertain, the next stripper came on to strut her stuff, and customers went to refill beers and stretch their legs.

Maria was good. Damn good. She was going to be a tough act to follow. The only thing that would work in Shadoe's benefit was that the night was growing later, alcohol flowed, the crowd was fired up and getting hammered, which meant they'd probably be oblivious to any mistakes she made. As long as she got naked and moved around the stage, they'd be happy. After all, guys came in to see naked women.

And he'd be there to keep an eye out in case anyone decided to get rowdy. Not that he expected to be needed. There were plenty of bouncers to keep the women safe.

Still, Shadoe *was* different. She wasn't an actual employee of the club, had no experience with this slice of life. He'd snuck into Grange's office today and taken a quick look at Agent Grayson's file. She was clean-cut middle-class with a by-the-rules military daddy. Parents divorced when Shadoe was twelve, and mother gave up custody. As far as he could tell, she'd never made contact with Shadoe again. What woman would do that?

Then again, Spence shouldn't be surprised. He knew all about worthless parents.

Shadoe had gone to an all-girls Catholic school from kindergarten through high school. He could well imagine how strict her father had been, how sheltered she'd been at private school. From there she'd attended a small, very exclusive college, got her master's after that, and entered the academy.

She'd had her entire life mapped out for her, no doubt by her father.

This assignment must be hell for her.

Then again, it was good to step outside your comfort zone. Shadoe had been sheltered too long. She'd never survive in her job with the department living in a cave. Might as well start with a good trial by fire like this assignment. If she survived this one, she could do anything.

Though he did feel kind of sorry for her being thrust into this atmosphere right out of the gate. And surrounded by guys like him as partners. He smiled. Yeah, trial by fire was right.

The lights went down and the deejay came on again.

"Ladies and gentlemen, we have a special treat tonight. A brand-new act, coming to you under the wing of our very own Vixen. Vixen thinks this hot babe has some serious talent, and she wants you all to pay close attention. Now let's give it up for Desi!"

Desi? Spence snorted. Of course she wouldn't use her real name. None of the girls ever did.

Instead of music, Spence heard a low, throaty rumble that sounded all too familiar, followed by the loud roar of pipes.

Motorcycle.

He smiled at the sound of revving engines. White smoke filled the walkway, and the music of Steppenwolf's "Born to Be Wild" cranked up loud and heavy, as purple black-light lit up the stage.

Shadoe wasn't tentative as she stepped through all that smoke, twirled around in a circle, and continued to march forward with all the confidence in the world.

Spence's tongue nearly dropped to the floor as Shadoe strutted down the walkway dressed in a black fringed vest cut down to her navel, revealing just a hint of cleavage. The vest stopped midway down, revealing her narrow waist and iron-flat stomach, the diamond piercing glittering in all the lights. She was darkly tanned, much more than she had been before. Her legs were covered in black leather chaps. As she turned around to grab the pole and do a quick twirl around it, he realized they were authentic chaps, the kind you wore on a bike. The butt of the chaps was cut out, revealing her nice, tight ass encased in only a G-string.

Holy shit. That was one sexy outfit. A biker's dream, guaranteed instant hard-on.

To hell with a biker's dream. Every guy's dream, evidenced by guys launching to their feet and going crazy, waving money and cheering her on. Shadoe seemed to love every minute of it, her dark eyes sparkling as she threw off attitude while she twirled around on the pole, pulling off the chaps to the rowdy catcalls of the customers, then slowly unzipping the leather vest. She wore knee-high leather boots with a spiky high heel, and walked on them like she knew what the hell she was doing.

Desi, a dream in black leather. A biker babe guaranteed to make every man in the place drool. As she finished unzipping the vest, she teased the crowd, holding the edges of the vest together and walking the stage, giving them just a hint of the inner swells of her breasts. She showed no nervousness at all, acting like she'd done this hundreds of times before. She let the vest slip off her shoulders and turned around, giving them all a glimpse of her gorgeous back. And as the music continued to pound and thrum, she dropped the vest and rocked her hips back and forth, showcasing the firmness of her ass, no doubt making every guy itch for a handful.

He'd been to strip clubs thousands of times, had sat back, drank beers, watched naked women parade before him for hours on end, women who had tons more experience than Shadoe, who knew the tricks of their sexuality and used them to their fullest extent.

Not once had any of them gotten him hard.

Until now.

As Shadoe turned around, her hands covering her breasts, her gaze shot to his and her lips lifted in a knowing smile. She moved toward him, raised her hands over her head, and revealed her breasts, dusky nipples hard and thrusting out as she bounced around the stage. When she crouched down in front of him, spreading her knees apart in a provocative pose, she gave him a look that shot straight to his balls.

He tried to remain nonchalant, like she wasn't affecting him, but it was damn hard.

Damn, was it ever hard.

She moved away to work the crowd clamoring near the edge of the stage and the money went flying. Spence gripped the edge of his chair as she scooted her hip to the edge of the stage while she danced, crouching down low enough to give all the guys a close look. No touching was allowed, but when their hair started brushing across her breasts while they slid money into her G-string, Spence found his fingers clenching into a fist. Especially since Shadoe seemed to be very, very popular. But no sooner would some guy nuzzle close to her breasts than she'd smile down at him and move away to the other side of the stage to give the guys there some attention.

When her dance was over and she blew kisses to the crowd, they cheered, long after she disappeared through the stage opening.

Spence exhaled.

Shadoe might not be an experienced stripper, but she had a natural, smoldering sexuality that surfaced once she hit the stage. He'd seen a glimpse of it yesterday when she'd danced for him, and she'd blasted it full force tonight. She'd rocked his cock into full awareness, something not easy to do since he was pretty much jaded to these sorts of events.

Or so he'd thought.

Now he was hard and throbbing and cranky as hell about it. He had to wait a few minutes, down the rest of his beer, and think about anything other than hot, naked Shadoe in black leather before he could get up from his seat and move around. He stepped outside to get some air, though the hot flash of Dallas humidity didn't help cool him down.

Why the hell did she get to him like that? He knew the stripper shtick. It was all an act, a performance and nothing more. Only morons and drunks fell for it, and he was neither, yet one shake of her hips and a wink and she had him drooling, dick in hand, eager for more.

Maybe he was a moron after all.

No. He wasn't. He just liked hot chicks in leather. Shadoe had played to his fantasies perfectly. But it was by accident. She had no idea what turned him on.

He'd been totally off base about her. She could move, she could strip, and she could play to the crowd. Maybe in her regulation uniform she was a pinched tightass, but put her in sexy gear and she was one hell of an actress who could play the part of stripper perfectly.

He turned around and went back inside, fetched a beer from the bartender, and leaned against the cushioned edge of the bar, watching one of the girls swirl around the pole. He'd lost his seat at the front of the stage, but didn't care. He'd seen all he needed. Now that Shadoe had danced he could leave if he wanted to, but figured he'd stick around for a while longer.

He searched the bar, but didn't see Shadoe anywhere. Typically after the strippers did their thing on the stage, they mingled around the crowds, stopping at the tables to encourage the customers to buy drinks, or to offer up lap dances. He smiled at that thought. Would Shadoe be willing to do a lap dance for a guy? Probably not, though most of the club owners would require it. Then again, if she was going to be billed as a feature stripper, they didn't have to do lap dances. They were there strictly to dance on stage, maybe mill around and talk to the customers, but no lap dances. Feature strippers were VIPs.

He finally spotted her, walking through the side door with Maria beside her. All eyes in the place turned to them as they strolled confidently among the clients, smiling and stopping along the way to chat.

Spence couldn't get over how hot she looked dressed again in her leather getup, with her hair curled and sweeping in long waves over her shoulders, nothing like the way it had looked yesterday, pulled back severely against her head.

He sank back into the darkness and watched her while she worked the crowd. She didn't stick so close to Maria that she looked unsure of herself. Instead, she branched out on her own and talked to the guys, tilted her head back and laughed when someone said something to her.

She was charming. And the more she wandered around and talked, the more guys followed her.

His stomach churned at the way the men leered at her. What were they thinking, that she was going to take one of them home with her?

Now there were some morons.

What he did notice was that the club's bodyguards hung close to Maria, making sure the overly large group of men didn't get too close to her. Which left Shadoe unguarded. And the cluster of guys surrounding her thickened in one corner. She had no way out now.

Spence pushed off the bar and stalked toward the throng, pushing his way through, receiving curse words in return.

Shadoe's back was to the wall and she was starting to look nervous and wide-eyed, until she caught sight of him. Then her shoulders relaxed and her smile returned.

Spence slid his arm around her waist and felt the tension holding her rigid as steel. Obviously she hadn't been as in control as he'd thought.

Fuck. He should have been at her side as soon as she'd come

through the door. Anger shot through him and he leveled a glare at the men pressing in on her.

"Back off. The lady can't breathe."

"Who the fuck are you?" one guy asked, his brows knit in a deep frown. He challenged Spence by taking a step forward.

Spence knew that level calm was the key, even though he felt anything but. "Desi's bodyguard." He reiterated his point just enough by reaching around his back. Any sane man would have to know he had a gun tucked into the waistband of his pants. "Now give her some room and we'll set up a space back here where you all can talk to her. But if you start pushing on her, I'm not gonna like it. Clear?"

The crowd moved back enough for Spence to do just that. He looked down at Shadoe. "You okay?"

She gave a quick nod. "I'm fine." She laid her palm against his chest. "Thank you."

The look of utter innocence in her eyes tore him apart. He cleared his throat and stared daggers at her male fan club. "Be nice," he warned, then pulled out a chair for Shadoe and moved behind her. She took a seat and the guys hovered, keeping a watchful eye on Spence the entire time.

Who knew she'd be so popular? The entire night she'd surprised the hell out of him. Watching her with these guys, she did even more, captivating them with her ability to converse, never leading them on, but keeping them talking, mostly about themselves instead of her, constantly stroking their egos. No wonder they liked her so much. He stood back and let her set the pace. He figured his place was just to stand there with his arms crossed and look imposing. No one even touched Shadoe or said anything inappropriate to her, so he must have done a decent job of it.

When the crowd began to thin out, Spence decided to take charge. "Time to go, Desi," he said.

She looked up. "Oh, okay. Sorry guys, I have to leave."

They made way for her, and Spence escorted her to the back room where all the women changed for their performances.

"How did you know it was time to go?" she asked while she pulled her street clothes from her locker.

"Group was starting to thin out. You always want to leave when you still have a crowd around you, rather than waiting until you're standing around with no one left."

"Oh. Good point."

She placed one booted foot on a chair and began to unlace it.

"I'll wait outside the door for you."

She nodded and he left the room, running into Maria as she was coming in.

"Your girl did good," Maria said. "Very good."

"Yeah, she did."

"She's going to do a fine job as a stripper. You have nothing to worry about."

"I wasn't worried."

Maria smiled. "You two look good together."

Spence choked out a laugh. "I'm just her bodyguard."

Maria arched a brow. "Sure you are, honey." She patted his cheek and slid by him and through the doorway into the changing room.

What the hell was that about?

He needed another beer.

But in a few minutes, Shadoe was out the door with her bag in hand. "You didn't need to wait for me. I can catch a cab."

He took her bag. "You can ride with me."

"Okay."

They walked out the front door and Spence was conscious of many sets of eyes following them. He was glad he had his gun. Who knew guys would be jealous of him leaving with Shadoe?

His Harley was parked right outside the front door. He secured Shadoe's bag, then climbed on. She followed, getting on behind him.

"You ever ride before?" he asked.

"Yes, a few times, but not in a while."

Good enough. He started up the bike and took off out of the parking lot. When he hit the main road, Shadoe leaned forward and wrapped her arms around him.

Her breasts pillowed against his back, her arms locked tight around his middle. Her body was warm.

He concentrated on the wind in his face, the roar of the bike beneath him, and the road in front of him, not the soft woman nestled close behind him.

It was a long damn ride home. Shadoe shifted every now and then, rubbing her breasts against him as she did, her thighs nestled against his. And every time he pulled to a stop, he could smell her. Her hair, the scent of her soap, a very faint vanilla scent.

She was quiet. It would have been easier on him if she chattered on nonstop. Quiet allowed him to think, to visualize, to remember what she looked like on stage in chaps, her sweet ass cheeks outlined against the black leather.

His dick pounded in agony. He was never happier to see the gates of the Wild Riders' compound and get the warm, sweet-smelling woman off the back of his bike. If he wasn't already sure it would arouse suspicion, he would have hopped off the bike and run into the house. Instead, he took his time, parked the bike in the garage, and calmly went inside, though he was seething with pent-up anxiety.

He needed to get laid. That would solve a lot of his problems. What he needed was a tension release. It had been too long since he'd been with a woman, that's all. Spending a few hours riding between the thighs of some hot, willing woman would take care of what ailed him. It had nothing to do with the woman silently riding up in the elevator with him.

Though it was late, almost all the others were in the oversized living room when the elevator doors whooshed open.

"How did it go?" Jessie asked.

"Shouldn't you and Diaz be humping each other at your apartment?" Spence shot back.

Jessie snorted. "Plenty of time for that. I wanted to find out how Shadoe's night at the club went."

Shadoe set her bag down and walked into the room. "Pretty good, I think. I made money. Maria said I did a great job." She half-turned to Spence.

Did she expect him to weigh in on her performance? She had to be kidding. He shrugged. "She looked good naked and she can shake her tits just fine."

Jessie rolled her eyes. "Spoken like a true man."

Shadoe's lips curled. "Well, thanks. I think."

"Trust me, that's a compliment," AJ said.

Pax nodded. "Practically a declaration of love coming from Spence."

"Fuck you," Spence said, deciding to ignore them all. He headed into the kitchen to grab a beer.

"Did I do something to upset you?"

He closed the refrigerator door and turned to face Shadoe. "No. Why?"

"You've been quiet all night."

"I did my job as bodyguard. I didn't know small talk was a requirement."

She folded her arms in front of her. "No, it isn't. But I would like some feedback."

He leaned against the counter and took a long swallow from

the bottle, letting the cool liquid slide down his dry throat. "I don't critique strippers."

"But you do frequent strip clubs. You have some experience watching women dance."

"Yes."

"So you're in a pretty good position to tell me whether I blend in or not."

"You did okay."

"That's not helpful."

"Maria gave you a critique, didn't she?"

"Yes."

"That should be good enough." He moved past her and out of the room.

She followed. "We're supposed to be partners on this case. We're going to have to talk to each other."

He took another drink, then plopped down on a chair in the living room. "When there's something related to the case to talk about, we'll talk. Until then, I don't see any reason for us to have a conversation."

She stood next to his chair. "It would be nice for you to weigh in about the dancing."

"Not exactly my field of expertise, darlin'."

"But you are going to be my bodyguard."

He tilted his head up. "Bodyguard. Exactly. I won't be up on the stage stripping with you. Get your feedback from someone else. My job is to act as a guard, not your freakin' dance instructor."

She sighed. "Are you always this much of an asshole?"

"Yes," said Jessie.

"Yes," said AJ.

"Yes," Pax added.

"Oh, hell yeah," said Diaz.

"Almost always," said Rick.

Spence ignored them, turned his attention to the television, and downed the rest of his beer.

"I'm going to take a shower and go to bed. Good night, everyone."

They all said their good-nights. Spence didn't, but he felt all eyes on him and not on the movie.

Dammit, what did they expect? For him to become Shadoe's best friend? He finally turned to them.

"What?"

"You're a dick," Diaz said.

"Yeah, and you're fucking Prince Charming," Spence said.

"Would it kill you to be nice to her, Spence?" Jessie asked. "It's so unlike you. You typically love women."

"Yeah, man," AJ said. "What's up with you, anyway? You need to get laid or something?"

That was exactly what was up with him. And he intended to rectify that problem as soon as possible.

FIVE

SHADOE WAS HAPPY TO SPEND THE NEXT DAY OUT OF WILD Riders' headquarters and away from Spence, who apparently didn't want to spend any time around her, either. When she came downstairs to breakfast everyone was present again, except Spence. Grange said he'd left early that morning to take his bike in for some maintenance.

She figured that was just an excuse to avoid her, which was fine with her. She wasn't looking for a repeat performance of last night, so she was relieved to find him already gone.

She'd made arrangements with Maria to work on her routine again, so they spent the day at the studio perfecting some of Shadoe's moves.

Maria told Shadoe she'd done a good job the previous night. Better than even Maria had expected for a first-timer. Shadoe thanked her years of dance training and the performing she'd had to do at recitals. Though none of those had been done naked. She'd simply blocked the nudity part out of her mind and just danced. At least she hadn't been completely naked. Playing to the crowd had been easy. Parading around mostly naked in front of eager men waving money was pretty much like playing to a captive audience. Unless you were a total dimwit and ignored the guys or moved like a stick, you could do the job. All you had to do was pretend to like it, to like them, to really get into what you were doing. And since she enjoyed dancing and acting, it had gone well.

Though she'd been petrified. Maria had forced her to take two shots of tequila prior to going on stage, told her it would help the jitters. Though Shadoe had initially objected, the liquor had helped calm her nerves. Stripping wasn't, after all, her actual profession. It was only an undercover assignment. Once finished, she could move on in her career and never have to do it again.

She danced all day long, breaking only for lunch. Maria really put her through her paces, but she appreciated the attention. There was nothing better than learning from a pro, and she knew this would be their last session together. Maria had a gig out of town the next day, and she and Spence were leaving for New Orleans the following day.

It was early evening by the time she got back to Wild Riders' headquarters. Every muscle in her body was stiff. She intended to eat dinner, relax, then maybe go for a run later in the evening after the sun went down to help her unwind before bed. But right now she was starving, and thankfully the guys had grilled steak for dinner. She resisted muscling them all out of the way to dive into the food, but dancing all day long worked up an appetite. She slid into her chair and tried not to tear at the steak like she hadn't eaten in days.

"So where were you off to all day?" AJ asked in between large mouthfuls.

"I worked with Maria again today." She tried to keep the conversation short. Really, all she wanted to do was eat, then maybe pass out for a quick nap.

"How did that go?" Grange asked.

She took a couple quick gulps of water before answering. "Really well. She's been wonderful to work with, and showed me a few things to help with my act so I'll look more experienced."

"Yeah, because drunk guys can totally tell the difference between a pro and a novice," Spence mumbled.

Grange shot him a look, but Spence was busy cutting his steak and didn't notice. Instead, Grange asked, "You think you'll be comfortable enough once you hit the Wild Rose in New Orleans?"

She nodded. "I'll be just fine."

Spence waved his fork at her. "The customers there expect only the best, you know."

She wasn't going to rise to the bait, nor tell him he'd just contradicted his previous statement. Clearly he was looking for an argument and she wasn't going to play. Instead, she smiled. "I'm sure I can handle it."

"It's a pretty high-class club."

What was he getting at? "Maria has played there before. She's prepared me for what to expect."

Spence shrugged. "Then maybe Maria should have been the one doing this job."

Grange tossed his napkin on the table. "Goddammit, Spence. What crawled up your ass?"

Spencer leveled a stare at General Lee. "Nothing. Just stating the facts."

"Bullshit. You have some gripe about Agent Grayson, let's bring it out in the open now."

"No gripe at all, General."

"He's cranky as hell, Grange," Diaz said, shooting Spence a glare.

"We think he needs to get laid in the worst way," AJ added.

Grange stared Spence down for a few seconds. "Then why don't you? Because your attitude sucks. You owe Agent Grayson an apology."

Oh, shit. The last thing she wanted was to cause dissension among the Wild Riders. "General Lee, really, there's no problem here."

"The hell there isn't. He's been on your ass since you got here and for no damn good reason. So if you have an itch you need to scratch before the assignment begins, Spence, then for the love of God go scratch it and get it over with. I need you and Shadoe working as a team, not at each other's throats once you go undercover."

Spence pushed his chair back and stood, wiped his mouth, and grabbed his plate. "Maybe I'll do that." He turned and went into the kitchen. Shadoe heard water running and the clanging of dishes, then Spencer returned to the living room and punched the elevator button. It opened, he walked in, and he pushed the button to close the door. In all that time he never looked at her—at any of them.

"Well, that was unpleasant," Jessie said. "Something must be bothering him."

"Something. Or someone," Diaz said.

Shadoe snapped her gaze to Diaz, who had been looking at her. "Me? What did I do?"

Diaz's lips curled in a very sexy smile. No wonder Jessie was so crazy about him. The man could make any woman's toes curl. "You didn't do a damn thing, honey. You didn't have to."

"I have no idea what you're talking about."

Then they all smiled in some weird, secretive way. And she was completely lost. Maybe it was a Wild Riders inside joke or something she wasn't privy to. Fortunately, with Spence's exit the conversation around the dinner table resumed to normal, she ate in peace, and helped clean up afterward. Then she watched television and played pool with everyone for a while until she grew too tired. She went upstairs and relaxed for a few hours, read, and took a shower, then thought about going to bed, but when she lay down she found herself staring at the ceiling.

It was one in the morning and Spence hadn't come back yet. Maybe he'd taken everyone's advice and had gone out, found a woman, and was at this moment fucking her.

Good for him. He probably needed it, the cranky bastard. Some men got tense if they didn't have sex, couldn't go without for long. Maybe Spence was one of those kinds of guys. She could imagine he probably was, one of those overly sexual types who had to have it every other day or something.

Hmph. It just figured she'd get stuck with a partner on testosterone overload. Great. Would she have to endure this throughout the entire assignment? It was worse than dealing with a woman in the throes of PMS. She couldn't care less if he screwed some random woman. They had no relationship other than a working one. In fact, she realized she didn't even like Spence. He was her partner on this assignment. That was it. She didn't have to like him to work with him. But maybe he could lighten up a bit after he got laid. Hopefully he'd have a lot of sex, too. Judging from his attitude, he needed it.

She shifted onto her side and stared at the dark wall, trying to shut out visuals of Spence naked, thrusting between the legs of some faceless woman. She tried to think of the academy, of the gun range, of terrorist training, the horrible hours she'd spent crawling through mud holes, anything to take her mind off Spence.

Nothing worked. All she could see was his body, his broad

shoulders, his penetrating blue eyes, the sharp angles of his cheek-bones, and the wicked way he smiled. All of that loomed over her and suddenly she was the woman underneath him while he thrust with deep determination, feeling his chest brush against her nipples with every upward sweep of his body. She could feel his cock inside her, and her pussy dampened with desire, her clit twitching with urgent need. Her skin felt on fire, prickling all over with sensation.

Spence wasn't the only one who needed to get laid. It had been a long—very long—dry spell for her. And now she was sweaty and moist and her pussy was wet and clenched with the need for orgasm. She reached between her legs to stroke herself, conjuring up images of a brown-haired devil with piercing blue eyes and a sexy smile.

She snatched her hand away and bolted upright in bed.

No. Oh, hell no. She wasn't going there again, wasn't going to stoke the fires of her fantasies and insert Spence in the starring role. That would only make things worse.

She rolled out of bed, turned on the light, and pulled on her capris and a breast-hugging workout top, then laced up her tennis shoes. If she was too pent up to sleep, then she'd go for a run. Outside, where she could work up a good, draining, breath-stealing sweat. The compound was secure, so she'd be fine outside. Grange had already told her she was free to roam outside any time of the day or night, as long as she stayed within the compound of the fenced acreage. And she'd already found the path that wound around and through the property.

No one was up and about when she went downstairs. They must have all either gone to bed or gone out. Good. The fewer questions she had to answer, the better. She grabbed a bottle of water and went outside, stretched a bit, then took off at a light pace, concentrating only on moving one foot in front of the other, digging her feet in and making distance count. The path was well lit so she was comfortable running alone. It wasn't like anyone was going to attempt to hop the high-tech security fencing around the property. Grange had state-of-the-art surveillance equipment to monitor the comings and goings of anyone nearing the compound. She was snug and secure there. She enjoyed the small amount of wind blowing through her hair, and swung her arms back and forth as she picked up speed.

She got lost in the run, her head clearing, her mind on nothing but forcing breath into her lungs. She'd worked up a good sweat and hoped by the time she made the run around the compound she'd be exhausted enough to sleep. Without thoughts, without fantasies, without thinking about Spence. She'd managed to empty her mind of everything, so when she spotted a light behind her, she had to tune in to the sound—the revving of a motorcycle engine. Refusing to stop, she kept on running at her designated pace until the bike came up beside her.

Spence. He rode alongside her for a bit until she took the run down slow and easy, then finally stopped, breathing heavy. She uncapped the water bottle and took several long swallows, then turned to face him. He parked the bike and climbed off.

They were on the back side of the property along a row of thick trees and bushes.

"I saw you out here when I came through the gates."

Master of the obvious, wasn't he? "Uh-huh."

"What the hell are you doing?"

"Uh, running?"

"It's almost two in the morning, Shadoe."

"Yeah." She took another gulp of water and blew out a slow breath, feeling her heart rate start to get back to normal. She was hot and sweaty, but at least there was a breeze to help cool her off.

Spence leaned against the bike and folded his arms. "So?"

"So what?"

"What are you doing out here?"

"Working off some tension. I couldn't sleep."

"Same as me, then."

She snorted. "Sort of. Only I didn't work it out with sex."

His lips lifted in a smile that made her weak in the knees. "Sex is better than running."

Did he have to remind her of where he'd been and what he'd been doing? "Yeah, you're right. It is. Maybe I should have grabbed one of the guys in the house and fucked him tonight. Would have saved me a middle-of-the-night run."

His smile died, replaced instead by a savage frown. "Don't."

"Don't what?"

"Don't mess with the Wild Riders. They're not nice guys."

He had a lot of nerve dictating to her. "I'm not looking for a nice guy."

He pushed off the bike and came toward her, bearing down on her in a slow, direct, and oh-so-imposing way like a man on a mission. Did he expect her to back up? He wasn't the worst that had been thrown at her, and she wasn't going to move. When he stopped, he towered over her, and she took in a deep breath—inhaling leather, and a musky scent that signaled pure male. Her female senses went haywire and her nipples hardened. She wanted to grab hold of his leather jacket and latch on to his mouth like she was starving for a taste of him.

Maybe she was.

"That's perfect, then," he said in answer to her earlier statement. "Because I'm not a nice guy."

She knew exactly what he was going to do and she had only an instant to stop him.

She didn't want to. So when he jerked her against him and planted his lips on hers, she melted against him. This was no easy kiss. His mouth was hot and hungry, his hands holding tight against her back and her hip, his fingers flexing and demanding.

Her entire body exploded in passion and hunger. She was enveloped with a wanton need she'd never experienced with such ferocity. She lifted her leg and wrapped it around him, centering her sex against his hard, throbbing cock. It made her ache, made her wet, made her want to tear off his leathers and drop down to her knees to engulf him in her mouth.

She wanted it all in this instant. He had too many clothes on, the barrier of his jacket, his jeans, his chaps, all serving to frustrate her because she couldn't get to his skin. But oh, his mouth, now *that* she had full access to, and he was a master at kissing a woman until her toes curled, until she was mindless and melting and wet and quivering. She even whimpered when he sucked her tongue. Her nipples tightened and she clutched the lapels of his jacket, dragging herself closer to him.

She couldn't breathe. Her heart pounded; her legs felt like they weren't going to hold her up any longer.

But then Spence grasped her wrists and gently pushed her away, breaking that sweet contact of his mouth against hers.

Momentarily dazed, all she could do was stare at him while her mind stayed in the sensual fog he'd weaved around her.

He climbed back on his bike and she had to fight to get her breathing and her pulse and her goddamned libido under control.

Then it hit her. Of course. He didn't want her. He'd already been out screwing someone tonight. He was probably exhausted.

Taking the defensive, she picked up her water bottle where she'd carelessly tossed it in the grass, unscrewed the lid, and took a long swallow, coating her dry throat. Then she put the lid back on, never once taking her gaze from his.

"I can understand you being unable to get it up twice in one night," she said.

His lips curled, then he laughed. "I don't owe you an explanation, but I wasn't with a woman tonight."

Her brow quirked. "I didn't realize you played for the other side."

He snorted. "Not what I meant. First, I didn't fuck anyone tonight. I went to the bar and played a few rounds of pool. And second, I can get it up and keep it up all night long, over and over again."

There went that melty sensation again, weakening her knees. She forced herself to stand solid and not waver, but the visuals of him doing exactly that were overwhelming.

"But I'm not about to toss you down on the weeds in the middle of the road and fuck you here."

Why the hell not? At this moment she wouldn't mind that one bit.

"And another thing—you'd better think about what you really want, because I'm not a relationship kind of guy, and I think that's the kind of man you really need."

He fired up the bike and rode way, leaving her alone on the path.

Her legs were shaking, remnants of the brief passion they shared still drilling through her nervous system, which was quickly being replaced by anger.

She turned around and started a slow jog back to the house.

How the hell did he know what she needed or wanted?

Even she didn't know the answer to that, but the last thing she wanted or needed was a relationship. Not at this point in her life, in her career.

And especially not with someone like Spence.

SIX

THEY WERE HEADING TO NEW ORLEANS. SHADOE'S THINGS WERE
packed, but they weren't traveling with her, they were going in a
car with AJ and Pax. She would be riding on Spence's bike.

She sure was experiencing a lot of new adventures on this assignment. But that was what she wanted, wasn't it? Though the idea
of being pressed up against Spence for nearly a day's ride wasn't
exactly a thrilling idea, she knew she had to keep her cover intact.
And her persona heading in was going to be stripper aka biker
chick, with Spence as her lover/bodyguard. Grange, Spence, and
Shadoe had spent the morning going over last-minute details, getting their covers completely set up, including the documentation
for their fake IDs. It was only then that she found out Spence was
not only acting as her bodyguard, but also her boyfriend. Grange
said it would allow Spence to stay close to her without arousing
suspicion, and keep everyone else away from her.

She didn't mind that; it was the "keeping Spence close" part she wasn't too keen about. She had enough to worry about without dredging up reminders of what had happened the night before, the way his mouth had felt on hers, the taut strength of his body when he'd held her, the hard ridge of his erection as he'd pulled her between his legs.

But she'd do what was necessary for the job, even if it meant sliding her thighs along Spence's and crushing her breasts to his back while they cruised along the highway.

She sighed and zipped up her boots, pulled the legs of her jeans down, and grabbed her jacket, then stepped into the bathroom to do a quick braid of her hair so it wouldn't blow all over the place in the wind. Then she headed downstairs to meet Spence. He was waiting at the elevator, talking with Grange.

He sure looked fine in black leather, his chaps cinched tight around his jean-clad ass, the leather hugging his thighs and legs. He wore a white T-shirt that only accented his tan and his blue eyes. She sucked in a breath and walked up to him and Grange.

"You ready, finally?"

Ignoring his attempt at insult, she nodded. "Yes."

Grange turned to face both of them. "AJ and Pax are already on their way and they'll meet you there. Stay in touch."

Spence pushed the button on the elevator that would take them outside to the garage. They rode down silently, and Spence led her to the stall where his bike was located. He took the bag with her few things she'd packed for the ride, then he climbed on.

Okay, admittedly, she was excited. She'd ridden a bit here and there, but never an entire day trip, and not in a long time. She loved motorcycles, loved the feel of the open road, the wind in her face, and the freedom associated with biking.

Despite Spence's surly attitude, she was going to look upon this as an adventure. Even if she had to ignore the rider in front of her. She climbed on behind him, situated herself, and leaned against the backrest. He fired up the engine and she felt a thrill at the hum and vibration of all that power underneath her. She couldn't hold back her grin as they pulled out of the garage and started down the road, though at a slow pace.

She really got a rush once they hit the highway, and Spence let out the throttle. She leaned back, the wind rushing by her, Spence moving in and out of the congestion of traffic with ease. It was incredibly freeing and as soon as they left Dallas city limits and cruised their way toward New Orleans, she was in total relaxation mode. Riding was a slice of heaven, and Spence seemed completely at home on the bike. Sitting behind him meant she could study him without him watching her, so she looked her fill. On a Harley, he fit well, like he and the bike were in sync. His ability to master the machine gave her confidence to relax and enjoy the ride.

They stopped for lunch in Alexandria, Louisiana, a bit more than halfway to New Orleans. Shadoe was eager to get off the bike by then. Though she'd had a great ride, it had been too long. She wasn't used to it, and her butt was sore.

Unfortunately, Spence said he didn't want to linger, just stop long enough to grab a bite, refuel the bike, and move back onto the road.

Yeah, right. She stretched out lunch as long as she could. She ordered a salad along with her meal, then perused the dessert menu, which caused Spence to shoot a glare across the table.

He could glare as much as he wanted. She was resting her butt.

She knew she couldn't put off the inevitable forever, though, and she passed on dessert, finished her drink, and used the bathroom. Then it was back on the road again. The break had helped though, so by the time they pulled into New Orleans she was okay.

A little numb from the waist down, but she was excited to see the city, especially the infamous French Quarter and Bourbon Street.

Where they were hopefully going to see some action and bring down a criminal.

Spence pulled into the driveway and she got off, eager to stretch her sore muscles. "Why don't you go get us checked in while I park the bike?" he suggested.

"Fine with me," she said, refusing to allow him to see her limp through the doorway into the lobby. But damn, her butt was screaming in pain.

She ran into AJ and Pax in the lobby, who stopped only long enough to tell her that her and Spencer's luggage was being stored at the desk, then scooted out the door, saying they were headed to a nearby bar. Well, good for them. She could use a drink, too. She went to the front desk and checked in, turned in the receipt AJ gave her for their bags, and they told her they'd bring the bags up to her room.

The hotel was nice. Comfortable, very French, ornate, but not ostentatious. She liked the wrought-iron everywhere, especially on the balcony in the room.

She loved the balcony, which looked down right over Bourbon Street. It would be a perfect spot to view all the partying going on every night. The lush greenery hanging from the overhead pots and woven throughout the railings gave a ton of privacy. One could do just about anything she wanted to in the dark on this balcony and not be seen.

Not that she'd be doing much of anything here, other than peering down at the people below. But if she were to do something, this would be a hot and sexy place to do it, a secluded balcony, her and her man engaged in some steamy sex up against the brick wall under the cover of darkness . . .

Ooh la la!

Of course she didn't have a man in her life, and she was on an assignment, so her fantasy fizzled into the ether. With a heavy sigh she walked through the French doors and closed them, turned down the AC to cool the air in the room, and the bellman arrived with her things, so she unpacked and put everything away.

She thought about taking a shower, but stretched her back, then yawned. The bed was glorious and looked tempting, so she stretched out across it, realizing she was utterly exhausted. When Spence came up she'd figure out a plan of action with him. She just needed to close her eyes for a minute. Or two.

SPENCE HADN'T INTENDED TO PULL UP A CHAIR AND JUST WATCH Shadoe sleep.

But he also hadn't expected to find her passed out facedown on the bed when he came in, either.

She had a really nice ass. It wasn't his fault that was the first thing he noticed. The jeans molded to her sweetly rounded cheeks perfectly, and her butt was stuck up there for him to ogle.

He'd run into AJ and Pax after he parked the bike, so he spent a few minutes talking to them, then got the room number from the front desk and came up here to find Sleeping Beauty out cold on one of the beds. She still had her boots on. He wanted to slip them off.

Hell, he wanted to slip off a lot of her clothes.

His dick twitched just thinking about last night on the running path. He hadn't intended to touch her, or kiss her. Getting involved with a mark as part of a case was one thing. Anything to get the job done.

He didn't need to fuck Shadoe to get this job done. He needed to *act* as her lover, not *be* one. Big difference. He preferred keeping his distance if sex complicated things.

In this instance, sex would definitely complicate things. Shadoe had *complex* written all over her. She was from a world he couldn't begin to fathom. She had a rich military daddy with connections high up in the government. One word from her and he'd be toast. He'd worked too damn hard to get where he was with the Wild Riders to risk losing it just because he got a hard-on over a woman.

There were plenty of other women he could get a hard-on over. Women not connected with a mission. Women he didn't have to work with. Women who were safe and uncomplicated.

He liked those kinds of women. Party, fuck, no strings, move on. Just his type.

So why wasn't he out finding one of those women right now, instead of sitting on an uncomfortable desk chair in this room, his feet propped up on the end of the bed, watching Shadoe sleep?

He should be bored.

He wasn't. While she slept, he could watch her. She had an innocent, unguarded expression that softened the frown lines on her face. Her nose was small, her lips full but not too full—kissable, perfect. Pink and plump. He'd enjoyed kissing those lips last night.

Her skin was lightly tanned, but not too much that it looked fake. More like she spent time outside—running, probably. She had a great body that no doubt came from intense workouts due to her job. She was firm, but not skinny. He hated girls that were so thin their ribs poked out. Every time he saw one of those types of girls he wanted to grab her and stuff a cheeseburger down her throat. Shadoe actually ate. He liked that about her. She had an appetite, knew how to fuel her body. Which no doubt gave her the womanly curves that made his dick hard.

He shifted uncomfortably and adjusted his cock, which, despite his good intentions about finding any other woman but this one, wasn't listening. Her hair had half fallen out of her ponytail, wisps of sable curls caressing her cheek. He itched to sweep them away and kiss the exposed part of her neck, then draw her tank top aside and spend some time getting to know her well-sculpted shoulder more intimately.

She had a nice back, too.

Shit. What was he doing taking inventory?

He was saved from any more excruciating realization of his own idiocy when she moaned and stretched. She rolled over onto her back and arched it as she raised her arms over her head, which pushed her breasts upward.

He fought the groan, and cursed his throbbing cock.

She lowered her arms and laid her hands over her stomach, then turned to face him, blinking sleepy eyes at him. She smiled.

"Sorry. I seem to have passed out."

"Yeah, you did."

"How long was I asleep?"

"About an hour."

She yawned and sat up, then pulled the ponytail holder from her hair, using her hand to shake out the curls until they spilled over her shoulders. When she gave him a sideways glance, he sucked in a breath.

Her half-lidded, sleepy gaze, her hair falling over her shoulders and framing her face, were so damn sexy it was like a gut punch. From innocence asleep to sex vixen in two point two seconds flat.

Yeah, he did need to get laid. Because his thoughts about his partner were heading in dangerous directions. He couldn't afford the distraction. His job was to hunt the rogue agent, and protect his partner.

He couldn't protect her if he was fucking her.

He pushed away from the bed and stood, dragging his fingers through his hair. "We should go to the club tonight, make an appearance so you can meet everyone and we can get the layout of the place."

She slid off the bed. "Great idea. I'll go take a shower and get ready. And I'm starving."

He nodded. "We can eat before we go."

Anything to get out of the confines of this box that contained a bed and a beautiful woman.

Whose idea was it to share a room anyway? It wasn't like anyone would check up on them to verify the story they were lovers. Damn Grange for being a stickler for cover accuracy. This was his fault.

At least the room had two queen-sized beds. Though Spence would have rather had a king to fit his large frame. His feet would probably hang off the bed.

He shook his head at that, realizing he'd slept in a lot of worse places than this fancy hotel with its too-small bed. He was getting spoiled in his old age.

He walked onto the balcony while he waited for Shadoe to take her shower.

Nice. Secluded, offering up privacy but with a voyeuristic angle. He liked that. You could do some fun things on this balcony.

If a guy was here to do fun things.

Which he wasn't.

He heard the bathroom door open and turned to see Shadoe stepping out, followed by a wave of steam. She had a towel wrapped around her body.

He turned away and looked down over Bourbon Street instead, making a mental note to buy beer to toss into the mini fridge in the room. He could use a cold brew right now to lubricate his dry throat.

Or maybe a cold shower. Yeah, probably a better idea.

He waited for her to finish up in there, then grabbed clean clothes, slipped into the bathroom, and turned on the shower, trying not to think about the fact that Shadoe had just been in here. He cleaned up and got out of there in a hurry, then dried off and put on his jeans. The bathroom was stifling, so he opened the door and walked out.

Shadoe was at the small vanity putting on makeup. Her hair hung in damp, curling tendrils behind her back. He wanted to pick up one of the trailing curls and play with it, but instead walked past her to grab his shirt. She turned halfway to watch him.

He felt her gaze on his back and smiled.

"You have a tattoo," she said.

"Yeah." He lifted his arms to pull the shirt over his head.

"No, wait. I want to see it."

In seconds, he felt warm hands skimming over the spot where the eagle had been tattooed. Her fingers arced over the outstretched wings.

He remembered the day he got the tattoo. He'd been told by Grange that he was going on his first assignment.

He'd made it. All that hard work, all his attitude finally shed— most of his attitude, anyway. He'd felt like he was free of his past.

"Why an eagle, and why flying like this?" she asked.

"Freedom."

His life could have gone in so many different directions, none of them good. That day, he'd felt free. He had his entire life ahead of him, he was soaring, and it all looked like blue sky to him. The eagle had seemed perfect.

"It's beautiful." She still had her hands on him.

He wasn't going to complain about that.

"Thanks."

"Do you have any more tattoos?"

He finally turned around to face her. "No. Not yet. Do you?"

She grinned. "None. Yet."

He cocked a brow. "Dying to get one, are you?"

"Actually, I'd love to. But I never know what kind of assignment I'll have, and a tattoo might not be the best thing to show on an undercover case."

"Put one where no one can see it." He pulled his shirt on.

"Hmmm, now there's an idea."

"And what would you get?"

"I haven't thought about it." She went back to the vanity and picked up a makeup brush.

He studied her, cocking his head to the side to look over her body.

She finally turned her gaze to his. "What?"

"Just trying to figure out what tattoo would fit you."

She laughed. "You don't know me well enough to answer that."

"You need a rose, but not a red one. It wouldn't look right on your skin. Peach, maybe. Or even some sort of white flower. But you're tough, too, so you'd need something hard to go along with that. Barbed wire, or a gun, maybe even a sword. Or a skull. A tattoo that says you're a woman all right—soft and sweet-smelling—but tread light, or you could get your head blown off."

She raised both brows. "Wow. Is that how you see me?"

He sat on the bed to slide on his boots. "That's how I see you."

"Huh."

That was all she said. Her gaze lingered for a few minutes, before she turned back to the mirror to finish her makeup, then took clothes in the bathroom and got dressed.

Which was good, because he needed to shut the hell up before he inserted his entire booted foot into his mouth.

Designing tattoos for her now? Next he'd be writing poetry. Or singing love songs.

Christ.

Pretty pathetic for someone who planned on keeping his distance from his partner.

She wasn't helping when she came out of the bathroom in a tight black leather miniskirt, black halter top, and thigh-high black boots with a stiletto heel. A thin silver chain wound around her neck, the end dangling between her breasts and disappearing into the low vee of the halter. She wore her hair loose, the curls falling around her shoulders and back. She wore more makeup than she usually did, her lips glossed up in pink, highlighting the mouth he'd kissed last night.

Making him remember. Making him want.

His cock woke up in a hurry. He knew he stared, but he couldn't help it. Especially remembering the way she looked when he first met her. The difference was incredible. From buttoned up, plain and severe, to full-on sexy bombshell.

But that's the persona she was supposed to portray—the sultry stripper—the kind of woman who could walk into a club and capture every man's attention.

Dressed like that, looking like she did, she was definitely going to command attention. He grabbed his gun and slid it into the back waistband of his pants, then pulled on his jacket to cover it.

Shadoe noticed his actions and nodded, bending down to lift her skirt up.

He arched a brow, glad for the show. Her legs were bare, her thighs the most mouthwatering things he'd ever seen. She lifted the skirt a couple inches. Strapped to her hip was a sheath with a slender blade. She smoothed her skirt down and shot him a smile. "I'm packing, too."

Was she ever.

"That's fine for tonight, but when you're up on the stage getting naked it's going to be kind of hard to conceal a weapon."

She rolled her eyes. "Well, duh. I know that. Just tell me if you can see it."

He looked at her with a critical eye. The skirt was tight, but it was leather so it didn't cling to her body like another fabric might. "Unless you let someone dance with you and feel you up, I think you'll be fine."

"No one will get close to me. I have a bodyguard." She waggled her eyebrows. "Besides, as my lover, you wouldn't let another guy touch me, now would you?"

"Not a chance in hell that's gonna happen."

Her lips lifted in a satisfied smile.

"Let's go. The club is a few blocks from here, so we'll ride. Think you can hike that skirt up enough to straddle the bike?"

"I can manage just fine."

He'd try not to think about all the skin she would show along the way.

They went downstairs and he brought the bike around, craning his head to watch as she held on to his shoulders, stepped on the peg, and swung her leg around the back, then settled on.

Sweet. Sexy. She wrapped her arms around him and nestled her breasts against his back. "All for show, of course."

"Of course." He gave the throttle a goose, letting the noise of the pipes vibrate through them both. She grinned, and he took off.

The ride was short, and Spence ached for a chance to really cut loose and take a ride out on the country. He wanted to see the bayou. He'd bet Shadoe would enjoy that, too.

But they weren't there to have fun and see the sights. They had a job to do.

He parked the bike in front of the Wild Rose and Shadoe climbed off. There were a couple dozen guys hanging around out front, and all of them zeroed in on her as soon as she stepped up on the curb. Hungry gazes followed her into the club, especially when Spence made sure to state loud enough that "Desi," their new headliner, had just arrived.

Since not just any stripper could walk into a club and be a headliner, Maria and Grange had provided the background for Desi as the upcoming newest thing on the circuit. With Maria's connections and Grange providing ID and fake background, Desi the headliner was born.

Several of the loiterers outside followed behind Spence. He'd just bet they were thinking that Desi would be dancing tonight.

Sorry, guys. You'll just have to come back tomorrow.

Though that thought didn't make him happy, either.

Why he should care if she stripped in front of these guys, he didn't know.

He didn't care whom she took her clothes off for. Hopefully it would be a packed club. The more people who jammed in here, the easier it would be to blend in and do their jobs. Shadoe was there to focus attention on her. She needed to embed herself as a feature stripper, so that every man there would want to spend time with her, to talk with her, to pay to have a moment, a half hour, an hour or more with her.

And maybe, if they were lucky, their rogue agent would show up and want some of "Desi's" time, too.

In a perfect world, anyway.

After a brief stop at the cage where Spence announced who they were, they were waved through with a smile and the bouncer said he'd notify the manager that Desi had arrived. Shadoe smiled and walked through.

The club was smoky dark, except on the square stage where the pole was lit up and a mostly naked dancer snaked her way around the cool metal before making her way to the edge of the stage to shake her stuff in front of eager, dollar-waving men. To

the left of the stage and built up several steps was a deejay choosing and playing the tunes. Rockin'-hard hip-hop music blasted
through the speakers set up all over the place. The thumping bass
entered through his feet and vibrated every part of his body.

Seats and built-in tables lined all three corners of the long
stage; various tables were set up beyond that. There were four privacy areas in the back of the club where lap dances were con-
ducted, mini stages for private parties complete with poles, and at
the back of the club a long bar that was filled to capacity with men
and women.

He followed along behind Shadoe, who seemed to have no
problem getting into character as she strutted in like she owned
the place, her hips swaying in an exaggerated manner. She stopped
at the end of the long bar and leaned over to say something to the
bartender, who tilted his head back and laughed, then nodded.

While she talked, Spence admired her legs and the hint of her
ass cheeks peeking out from under her very short skirt. A minute
later Shadoe had a short glass in her hands.

"Jack Daniels on the rocks," she said, tilting the glass back and
taking a sip.

He took the glass from her hand and shot the rest of the con-
tents down in one swallow, sliding the empty glass across the bar
and holding up two fingers to the bartender, who nodded. He
turned back to Shadoe, who arched a brow.

"Like your whiskey hard?" he asked.

She laid her palms on his chest and gleamed a wicked smile.
"Just like my men, baby."

She was in character, all right. Dangerous character. He would
have to remember the woman teasing him with her soft, warm
hands was Desi, not Shadoe. Which meant he'd have to pull her in
close and tease her back, not push her away.

This was a game, not reality. And when they walked out of the club, the game ended.

He'd also have to tell that to his dick, and keep reminding his dick, until it started paying attention, because right now Shadoe had a hip notched against his crotch, one breast pressed up against his chest, and her hands all over him, taking possession, making sure everyone looking in their direction knew that he belonged to her.

So he'd damn well make it clear from the start that she belonged to him.

He thrust his hand in her hair, jerked her back, enough to surprise her.

Her mouth fell open—exactly his intent. He took her mouth in a primal kiss. Fast, with intent, his tongue sliced in and licked along hers. He heard her moan, knew it wasn't an act, and his cock roared to life in a furious frenzy of heat, passion, and hunger.

He knew it was too much, that all he'd needed to do was wrap an arm around her and glare at every man in the place, and that would have been enough to set their relationship.

So maybe he'd wanted to stamp his mark on her for her benefit, too. She'd started this game.

He was going to finish it, and finish it his way.

seven

WHOA. SPENCE'S KISS WAS HOT. HIS TONGUE PROBED, RAVAGED, with every velvet stroke making it clear to Shadoe that he was the one in control.

She would have thought she'd balk at this public display of his possession of her. Instead, she melted into him, wanted more. A lot more. She was wet, hot, and her legs trembled.

She was going to have a hard time separating the act from reality. Then again, had she really been putting on a show for all the guys in the club, or had she been fishing for a reaction from Spence? She'd wanted him to pay attention.

He was paying attention now, wasn't he? But in a sexual way. Sure, he lusted after her—that much was obvious, from his hands on her ass to the hard cock pushing against her thigh.

She lusted after him, too. Her panties were wet and her nipples stood out like hard, painful points.

But that wasn't why she was here, and it wasn't why he was here, either.

She supposed they'd both better figure out a way to work through this thick sexual tension that seemed to linger between them, or neither of them was going to be clearheaded enough to get the job done.

She gently pressed against his chest and he pulled back, his eyes dark as a storm, and just as angry.

He brushed her hair off her face and leaned in, his tongue sliding along her earlobe as he whispered against it. "Be careful how you play this game, *Desi*," he said, emphasizing her stage name. "Be sure you know what you want before you start tussling with the big boys."

The big boys. Didn't he just sound like all the men at the academy, and like her father? Like she couldn't handle a little heat?

He didn't know her at all, didn't know what she'd had to endure her entire life. She loved nothing more than a challenge, and he'd just laid down the gauntlet.

She pushed at him, tilted her head back and laughed, then spun on her heel, grabbing one of the drinks the bartender had slid to the end of the bar. She downed that in one swallow, then picked up Spence's whiskey and shot his, too, sliding it back across the bar at the bartender. She turned her head toward Spence. "I'll have another." Then she walked away, focusing her attention on men who were definitely interested in "Desi."

But she also had a job to do. While she meandered along and said hello to people, she scanned the club, looking at faces to see if there were any she recognized. No one came up as familiar, but she memorized them all anyway so she could learn to spot regulars. It would be easier then to pick new ones out of the crowd.

A tall, good-looking guy in his early thirties came toward her from the back of the club. Dressed in jeans and a black polo shirt with the Wild Rose name emblazoned across the left pocket, he smiled and stopped in front of her.

"Are you Desi?"

"I am."

"I'm Brandon Black, club owner. Great to have you headlining with us."

She shook his hand. "I'm looking forward to it. It's a nice club."

"We get a lot of business here and our crowd loves headliners. Being in the Quarter doesn't hurt, either. We're filled to capacity every night, the action starts pretty late, and there's usually a line out the door waiting to get in."

"Sex sells, doesn't it?"

"It does here, *cher*. There are more than a few strip clubs in the French Quarter. I think we're one of the best. You've come to the right place."

"Vixen said it was the premier hot spot in New Orleans."

Brandon grinned. "She's a rocking hot act. We love having her here. I'm happy she recommended us."

"Well, I'm happy to be here for the next week."

"We can go over your schedule tomorrow when you come in. Typically you'll do two shows—one about eleven and then again at one in the morning. Work for you?"

"Perfect."

"Let's go into my office and go over your contract, talk payment terms, and the house-versus-dancer split."

Shadoe followed him through the doorway into a spacious office, conscious of Spence right on her heels. He closed the door behind him.

"This is my bodyguard, Spence," she said as she settled into the chair Brandon pulled out for her.

Brandon nodded and Spence took up position against the wall, nodding back to Brandon.

"You packing?" Brandon asked.

"Always," Spence answered, folding his arms across his chest.

"You have a permit for it, I assume."

"I do."

"Don't pull it unless you need to use it. I doubt it'll be necessary."

Spence's lips curled in a menacing smile. "I'll be the judge of what's necessary. My job is to protect Desi. I usually don't need a gun to do that."

"No, I imagine you don't." Brandon looked to Desi. "Some of our headliners like to come in and cause a ruckus, mostly to call attention to themselves. I like to get things straight when a new act comes in. I run a clean club, no brawls. We serve alcohol and lots of it, but we expect our patrons to treat the ladies with respect. If things get out of hand, my bouncers take it outside immediately. We protect our dancers, and anyone who causes trouble is history."

"Good. Spence won't be a problem at all, will you, baby?"

Spence arched a brow, but said nothing in response. Shadoe knew she was pushing her limits with her teasing, but frankly she enjoyed having the upper hand at the moment.

She finished up her paperwork and conversation with Brandon, and went back out to mingle with the crowd. As soon as she stepped outside, the deejay stopped the music.

"Hey, everyone. Our newest headliner has paid us a visit tonight. She'll be premiering tomorrow night with her new act that promises to be hot, hot, hot! Give a round of applause and go say hello to Desi!"

The spotlight hit her. Brandon moved away and even Spence backed up a step, though not far.

She was on, and it was time to perform. She put on a bright

smile, cocked her hip to the side, and waved. The crowd applauded and whistled, then the spotlight dimmed.

Brandon came up behind her and pressed his hand to her back. "Why don't you go make the rounds, drum up some advance excitement for your show tomorrow night?"

"Sure." What she really wanted to do was grill everyone in there, including Brandon, find out who were regulars so she could get a feel for who to watch. But that wouldn't work. A stripper wouldn't ask the manager about those things. She was on her own, which meant she was going to have to work the men in the place. Get close to them, get to know them, and start remembering faces, which fortunately for her was easy.

The rogue agent wouldn't be able to slip in unnoticed. As soon as she saw him, she'd know. Which meant she'd have to start spending a lot of time at the Wild Rose.

She sauntered over to one of the large tables filled with men, doing her best to exude confidence. They were already turned her way and watched her approach with gleaming expectation. One got up and gave her his seat. Another bought her a drink. She was sociable, but didn't get physically close to them. She laughed, encouraged them to buy more drinks, but nursed her own. Maria had taught her how to play the game. Make money for the club, be sexy, talkative, show some skin. She could do that, even though flirting didn't come naturally to her.

But somehow, knowing Spence loitered just behind her made it easier. Nothing was going to happen to her. He'd protect her.

Not that she needed protection. She could take care of herself without his help. And she'd better remember that, because at that moment one of the guys sitting next to her slid his hand in her hair and stroked the back of her neck. She turned to him and offered a teasing smile.

What she really wanted to do was turn over his chair and shove her boot in his throat.

Before she could move away and reclaim her personal space, Spence grabbed the guy's wrist and slammed it down on the table. He leaned around Shadoe, his expression calm but his voice laced with venom.

"Look all you want. Don't ever touch her again or I'll lay you flat, whip out my switchblade, and with one cut feed you your balls. Got it?"

The guy, no lightweight himself, broke out in a sweat. He nodded. Spence let go of his wrist and moved back to his position behind Shadoe.

She had to fight back the smirk. Okay, so she could have taken care of that on her own, but she supposed laying down an elbow to the throat would have cost her the cover she'd created. And that wouldn't do at all. So as much as it galled her to play the part of the pretty, brainless female, she'd endure it while she was Desi.

They stayed a couple hours and Shadoe tried to visit with all the guys. She was friendly, stopped at a few tables to chat, then she and Spence left. Throughout it all he'd hardly said anything. She supposed he wanted to portray the persona of the strong, silent bodyguard. Whatever. After that scene where he pulled the guy's hand away, no one else touched her. He'd done his job; she'd done hers. But he sure seemed to be in a foul state of mind.

And they said women were moody? Ha.

Spence took them back to the hotel, but instead of pulling into the parking garage, he drove up in front of the hotel, but left the engine running.

"What are you doing?" she asked.

"I need a ride so I'm letting you off here."

"I'll go with you."

He hesitated. "I need to let off some steam, Shadoe."

What did that mean? "I could use a ride, too. It sounds like fun."

He looked over his shoulder and down at her skirt. "You're hardly dressed for a ride."

"It's warm out. I'll be fine." When he didn't move, she tapped his back. "Go."

With a muttered curse that she heard all too clearly, he revved up the engine and peeled away from the curb. He drove out of the French Quarter, out of the city itself, through the night.

Shadoe nestled her back against the padded sissy bar and enjoyed the warm breeze blowing in her face, and the view of the broad expanse of Spence's back, letting her mind wander.

She should be thinking about the case, or about preparing for her debut at the Wild Rose tomorrow night. Instead, she thought about how hot Spence looked sitting on his Harley, his muscled body showcased well in tight shirt and jeans. She thought about leaning forward and placing her hands on his hips, then his thighs, about how far her fingers could wander toward his cock.

She thought about a lot of things, none having to do with the case and all having to do with Spence. Her body flushed with heat, her nipples tightened, and her pussy quivered. Straddling a revved-up vibrator wasn't hurting her libido any, either.

She was so focused on fantasizing about Spence that when she turned to the scenery again, she was surprised to find he had exited the main highway. They were on a small two-lane road, with bayou on either side. The nearly full moon cast a glow over the murky water, lending it a spooky quality. Myriad branches stuck up amidst the moss-covered creeks and ponds that lay silent as a blanket of liquid silver. Shadoe was afraid to breathe as they rode by, certain that the roaring sound of the bike would put a ripple in the otherwise undisturbed surface of the water. Of course, nothing shattered the eerie calm, not even the motorcycle flying down the narrow road.

She had no idea where they were, and didn't really care, since she assumed Spence knew how to get back to the hotel. She thought about asking him where they were going, but figured since he was in such a surly mood, he'd probably give her a smartass answer, so she stayed in her own good mood and didn't bother talking to him.

He finally pulled down a narrow single-lane road, lit only by the single headlight on the bike. Shadoe leaned forward and wrapped her arms around Spence, feeling a shade unsteady on the gravel road. When he finally pulled to a stop and turned off the engine in front of a lake, she breathed a sigh of relief and climbed off.

Shadoe took a few steps and looked around, inhaling the smells of earth and dark water and the mossy trees that hung over them like a sheltering canopy.

"This is lovely." The bank coming up from the lake sloped, so she sat and pulled off her boots and stood again, letting her toes sink into the cool grass.

"Might be snakes."

She arched a brow. "Then I guess you'll just have to suck the venom out if one bites me." She knew he wouldn't bring her to an area where snakes crawled around.

Would he?

He smiled, his white teeth gleaming in the dark. "Suck, huh?"

He had to latch on to that one word, didn't he?

"So what are we doing out here?"

He shrugged. "I needed a ride to clear my head."

"What's bugging you?"

"Nothing."

"You just said—"

"I know what I said. Just leave it."

She rolled her eyes. And they said women were hard to fathom. "You've been cranky all night. What's your problem?"

"I like to come here to think," he said, ignoring her question. He walked toward the edge of the lake and stared out over it.

She followed, curious to know what was on his mind. She was curious about a lot of things, actually.

"You've been here before?"

He nodded. "Lots of times. It was a slice of life I wished I had, but knew I never would."

Then it dawned on her. "You're from around here."

"Yeah."

She knew he had a Southern lilt to his voice, but she hadn't been able to place it. His drawl was deep and husky—and oh so sexy—but she hadn't detected any Cajun influence in his voice.

"How long have you been gone?"

"Since I was eighteen—so, about twelve years or so."

"Do you miss home?"

Despite the darkness, she caught his frown. "I would never really call this place home."

"What do you mean?"

"It was a roof over my head, but I stayed away as much as I could."

"Why?"

She knew she was prying, but she figured if he didn't want to talk about his past, he'd say so.

It took him a minute or so before he spoke again. When he did, he turned his head to her. "Sometimes it's easier to stay away."

"I don't understand."

His lips lifted. "No, you wouldn't. I'll bet your daddy loves you, treats you like a princess."

She snorted. "I may not have grown up on the streets, Spence, but my life wasn't all about tea parties and frilly dresses."

"Uh-huh." He turned and looked out over the water again.

And just like that, he'd labeled her. Rich girl, privileged, couldn't possibly understand the pain he'd endured, the suffering of his childhood.

"You don't know me."

"Daughter of a military father. Your mother dumped and ran when you were young. No siblings. You went to private school. Other than a lousy mother, seems to me you had it all."

Now it was her turn to stare across the lake, to remember the loneliness, the isolation. The expectations, the feeling that she could never measure up. How many times had she heard it? Felt it. Knew she was a failure no matter what she did.

At least Spence had been born male. He was leaps and bounds ahead of her as far as her father was concerned. She had been damned because of her sex from the day she was born.

"You don't know me at all, Spence. But there's nothing I can say to convince you I'm not who you think I am, so you just go ahead and keep thinking I'm the spoiled rich girl if it makes you feel better about being the misunderstood boy from the wrong side of the tracks."

He looked over at her and frowned.

"I'll be at the bike when you're done taking your poor, pitiful walk down memory lane."

She turned and started her walk through the thick grass. Spence's fingers around her wrist stopped her halfway up the slope. She turned to face him. He looked angry. At what? At her, or something else? Someone else?

"You don't know me, either."

She cocked a brow. "Don't I? I've run up against your kind all my life. Guys who think I owe them something because of this supposed life of privilege I led. You judge me based on my father and my address, but it's you who doesn't know me. You don't know anything about my life because you're too wrapped up in feeling sorry for yourself."

"Then tell me."

"Tell you what?"

"About your life. What was so bad about it?"

Did he really think she was going to believe he cared? "I don't think so." She tried to jerk away from him, but he held firm.

"I'm serious, Shadoe. Tell me."

He sank to the grass and pulled her down with him. Since he had a pretty firm hold on her arm, she had no choice but to sit.

And then he straightened out his legs, shifted his hands behind him, leaned his weight on them, and turned his head to give her his attention.

Disconcerting, to say the least, having a gorgeous man with deep blue eyes stare at you like that. She stretched out her legs and kicked off her boots.

"Okay, tell me what was so bad about your life."

She shook her head. "I'm not interested in spilling my guts to someone who doesn't give a shit."

His lips curled. "How do you know I don't give a shit until you try me?"

"Is this how you avoid talking about yourself?"

"What do you mean?"

"You turn the topic to the other person, make it about them so the heat is off you."

Now he grinned. "Maybe. But we're not talking about me right now. You're the one all worked up over your upbringing, not me. So tell me about it."

Shadoe disagreed. She figured Spence was pretty worked up about a lot of things, primarily about being back home. "I'll talk about me if you talk about yourself when I'm finished."

He shook his head. "Doesn't work that way."

"Then I'm not going to play."

"Too bad. I think you want to talk to someone about what's bugging you."

She laughed. "There's nothing bothering me."

"Right. You've had a stick up your ass from the minute I met you."

She lifted her chin, refusing to take the bait. "And you're carrying more than a couple bags of chips on those shoulders."

Now he smiled. "Nah, that's just my natural charm, darlin'."

"You're full of shit."

"Maybe that's what's on my shoulders instead of chips." He pushed off his hands, lifted both arms, and sniffed. "No, no shit there."

Unable to resist, Shadoe laughed. All the men she knew were so serious. She never knew any that could so easily make fun of themselves, and look so damn sexy while they did it. "You are something else."

"That's what they tell me."

Yeah, he was definitely full of it. And evasive as hell, too. He had a great way of changing the subject. "Grange knows you're from here, doesn't he?"

"Yeah."

"Despite the bullshit, it's obviously painful for you to come back here. So why would he do that to you?"

"We're not pussies, Shadoe. We all have to face our demons head-on. Grange knows that better than anyone. We tackled the past a long time ago. It's done."

"Is it?"

"For me it is."

She looked out at the water, the serenity so compelling she could get lost in it, forget why she was here and what brought her to this point in her life. The way she drove herself, the way she'd competed with men since she was a child. And all because of her father. She often wondered if she was in this job because it was what she loved and wanted to do with her life, or because she had some driving need to prove to him that she could do it, that she could be as good as any man.

"If you don't get it out into the open, it'll eat away at you."

She snapped her gaze to Spence's. "Get what out?"

"The anger inside. It'll distract you. You need to get rid of it."

"I'm not angry."

His lips lifted. "Yeah, you are. Is it Daddy or just men in general?"

She snorted. "Put your textbook away, Professor. I already went through psych eval at the academy. I passed."

"I'm sure you did. But you're still pissed off, and it'll affect you on the job. You need to be able to trust your partner."

"You mean you can't trust me unless you know everything about me."

"Yes."

"Then it should work both ways, shouldn't it?"

He didn't have a snappy comeback to that. Good. Did he think she was stupid? Why did he want to know about her past anyway? The last thing most guys were interested in was listening to a woman drone on about her woes.

He couldn't help her. Correction—she didn't need any help. There was nothing wrong with her.

"I'm ready to go back." She grabbed her boots and lifted her foot to slide the first one on.

"My dad was a drunk, my mom not much better than him," Spence started.

Shadoe laid the boot down on the grass.

"Money was spent on booze for both of them, which meant my little brother and I went hungry. A lot. So if Trevor and I

wanted to eat, it was up to me to find food. Most of the time
Mom and Dad would come home from work, open up the bottles
of beer and whiskey, and they'd be dead drunk and passed out by
nine."

"They didn't feed you?"

"No."

"How old were you?"

"I was twelve or so. Trevor was nine."

A stab of pain knifed through Shadoe's middle. What kind of
parents neglected their children that way? "Did you have any
other family? Anyone you could go to?"

He shook his head. "We lived out on the bayou. People keep to
themselves and don't get into anyone's business."

"What about school? The principal or counselor?"

He turned his gaze to her. "Did you think I was going to tell
anyone? They'd take us away, split up Trevor and me. I couldn't let
that happen. At least at home we were together."

She wanted to fold him in her arms and hug him, but knew a
man like Spence would see that as her thinking he was weak. She
thought him anything but. How could he survive a childhood
like that? "How did you eat?"

"I started stealing money from my parents' wallets. Just a bit
here and there, not enough that they'd notice. Or so I thought."

"They noticed."

"Eventually. You don't take a dollar's worth of booze money
from a drunk and have them not notice," he replied with a grim
smile. "My old man figured it out, then my mom mentioned she
thought her wallet was short, too. All hell broke loose after that
and I paid the price."

Her eyes widened. "He beat you?"

Spence shrugged. "That was nothing new. By that age I was
pretty used to it, so I could handle it."

A child so used to beatings he shrugged them off at age twelve. Shadoe was horrified. "How bad was it?"

"He didn't break anything that time. Just a few bruises and a cut lip. I survived."

"Jesus, Spence. Why didn't you—"

"Because of Trevor." The look on his face was fierce. Angry. "It was my job to protect him, to take care of him. Because they sure as hell weren't."

She fought back tears at the thought of a twelve-year-old boy—a child himself—forced to become caregiver to his little brother. She was appalled and angry on his behalf. "What happened then?"

"I got smarter. No stealing from the drunk parents. I figured out another way."

"Which was?"

"I stole from everyone else."

His grin spoke of pride. "Who?"

"Other classmates. Neighbors. Merchants in the small town we lived in. Anywhere and everywhere I could. Money, food, whatever it took to feed my brother and me."

How could he not be angry—still carry that anger with him? She would. "Your parents should have been arrested."

"Trevor and I survived. It's the only thing that mattered."

"How long did this go on?"

He shifted, turning on his side and leaning his head against his hand. "The years went by; my parents lost their jobs. You can't drink like they did and hold down a job. My dad eventually took off and Mom went on welfare. I hated that. Everyone knew it. I took shit for it."

"From your friends."

He let out a short laugh. "Friends don't laugh at you when you're down. I had no friends. Just Trevor. He and I were tight."

"Did he steal, too?"

His brows winged. "Hell no. I wouldn't let him, though he knew what I was doing. I didn't want to ruin him. I wanted him straight. I had high hopes for him to make something of himself despite the shithole we grew up in. He was smart, ya know? Fucking awesome grades in school. Teachers loved him. By the time he was sixteen I knew he would go on to college. He had the stuff to get scholarships. I had to keep him on the right track, make sure that happened."

She didn't like the direction the conversation was headed.

"What did you do?"

"I got him the hell out of that house that always smelled like booze and failure. Set him up with foster parents. A really nice couple who had a son Trevor's age and had always wanted more kids but couldn't have them. They were always nice to us, fed us whenever we were over there. They contacted Social Services, petitioned the court, got Mom's parental rights taken away."

"How did you manage that?"

His devilish smile said everything. "I went around the system. I'd played it for years so I knew the ins and outs. It didn't take a rocket scientist to walk into that filth that was our house and realize it was a shit environment for a kid."

"What about you?"

"I was nineteen by then, and in trouble. I hightailed it out of there long before it all went down. I wanted to steer clear to pave the road for everything to go right for Trevor."

"You abandoned him?" As soon as the words left her mouth, she regretted saying them. His sharp frown made her feel two inches tall.

"I did what was best for my brother. I was a thief, a lowlife, and he was already way too close to me. I saw the writing on the wall. If I didn't get out of there, I was going to taint him."

She didn't believe that, but she kept her mouth shut this time.

"I'd already had too many close calls with the law and I was skirting the edge. I had to go underground, and I wasn't going to leave Trevor alone with a useless, drunk, out-of-her-mind mother who wouldn't take care of him. So I . . . made arrangements."

"How did Trevor take it?"

Spence shrugged. "I don't know. I guess he got over it. Last I heard he was in medical school." His wistful smile made her heart ache.

"He's going to be a doctor?"

"Yeah. Pretty cool, huh?"

"It's amazing. You did a wonderful thing for your brother."

He shrugged. "He was destined for good things anyway. I just shoved him in the right direction."

"You saved his life, his future. He survived because of you. He became what he is today because of what you did for him, because of the sacrifices you made for him."

Shadoe had been wrong about Spence. What he must have endured all those years. The suffering he went through. He was right. Between her life and his, there was no comparison. She was ashamed for feeling like she'd had it bad. He'd lived a childhood of hell, without love and warmth. Except for his brother.

"Why don't you look him up now?"

He shook his head. "No point in that. We cut our ties. He has his life and I have mine."

"But look what you've done with yours. You have an amazing life—"

He shot her a glare. "That I can't tell him about. You know that."

She nodded, understood, hated that he couldn't share his success with his brother, show him what he'd become. For all Trevor knew, Spence could be in prison. Or dead.

That annoyed her. But it wasn't her place to object, or frankly, to even care. She wasn't involved with him other than as his partner on this case.

The problem was she did care. More than she should. She felt his pain, even though he tried hard to mask it under shrugs and grins and nonchalance. She reached over and laid her hand on his arm, offering the only support she could.

"I'm sorry."

"Don't do that."

His tone was harsh.

"Why not?"

"I don't need your pity."

"You think I pity you?" She laughed. "I don't pity you at all, Spence. I admire you."

He looked appalled. "For what?"

"For what you've done with your life, for the sacrifices you've made. The amazing strength to endure what you did. Most guys growing up like you did wouldn't have done what you did for your brother. Many would have ended up just like your parents."

"That was the last thing I wanted."

"Obviously. Which is why I admire you. You set a good example for your brother."

He snorted. "Yeah. Lying, cheating, and stealing are great examples."

"You did what you had to do since you had no other resources. I'm sure he understood that you did all those things because you loved him."

"I'm no hero, Shadoe. Don't think of me that way."

She smiled, refusing to let him denigrate himself. "You're not a bad guy either."

"You still don't know me at all."

"I know more about you now than I did an hour ago."

"I'm not a nice guy."

He stood and she did, too, bending down to grab her boots.

"I think you're a really nice guy." She didn't care that he didn't think so. She needed him to hear it, to understand it. He probably never heard it often enough.

"I'm really not a nice guy, Shadoe," he said again.

She was about to argue, but she didn't expect the lightning quick move he made, sweeping one arm under her, using the other to jerk her against him. Shocked, she dropped her boots and gasped.

She had only a fraction of a second to see the need, the anger flash in his sharp blue eyes before he bent down and slashed his mouth over hers. She didn't have time to ponder why he was doing this. Her mind went utterly blank and she forgot everything but the feel of him against her, the taste of his mouth, and the full blast of awakening inside her body.

EIGHT

SPENCE'S KISS WAS ANGRY. IN THE BACK OF HER PASSION-muddled mind, Shadoe recognized that he wasn't kissing her because of any sudden urge to make out. He wanted to punish her. He was striking out at her, trying to prove to her that he was anything but a nice guy.

She didn't care, because his kiss was mind melting, toe curling, and everything she'd always wanted out of a kiss. To be swept off her feet, rendered senseless by a man who knew exactly what he was doing, who knew his way around a woman's body.

The way he touched her—not tentative in the least, but bold, with no hesitation, grabbing her ass to haul her up against his rock-hard erection—was anything but nice. Did he think she was going to push him away because he was rough with her? Anything but. Her nipples tightened at the fierceness of his passion, the hungry need evidenced by the way he dug his fingers into her arm, swept his hand along her ribs to lift her shirt so he could feel her bare skin. And all the while his lips moved over hers in this driving, claiming way, his tongue a velvet torture device that made her weak in the knees. Her pussy wept with joy at the way he devoured her.

She wanted more, and let him know by clutching his arms and drawing closer to him, moaning against his lips, rocking her hips against him. He answered by growling, and, oh man, did that excite her. She'd never been with a man who was so amazingly animalistic like Spence. Hell, she'd never been with a man who was so much like a man. So primal, even in the way he smelled—earthy, sexy, potent. She wanted to strip him down right there, push him onto the grassy slope and fuck him hard.

Instead, he pulled away from her and dropped to his knees, using his hands to stroke her hips, her thighs.

She held her breath as he stopped there, his fingers teasing the hem of her skirt before sliding up inside. He began to lift her skirt, inch by slow, torturous inch. Every touch of his fingers against her legs made her pussy swell, her clit quiver in anticipation.

"Spread your legs for me, Shadoe," he said, keeping his gaze focused on her legs—between her legs.

She parted her legs, and he continued the slow rise of her skirt, raising it over her hips to reveal her black thong panties. He removed her hidden sheath and knife and laid them on the ground next to him, then leaned forward, spread his fingers wide over her ass cheeks and buried his face into the vee of her crotch.

"Oh, God," she whispered. Her knees went weak and she laid her hand on the top of his head. His breath was hot against her sex, making her wonder if she'd be able to keep standing if he was going to continue doing this to her.

"You smell good. Like a hot summer and wildflowers." He

pulled her panties aside and licked along the curve of her thigh. Her legs buckled and Spence reached up to hold her hand. She whimpered as his tongue trailed along the outside of her pussy lips, teasing, tantalizing, promising . . .

"These panties are in my way, Shadoe." He didn't ask for permission, he wasn't gentle, just gave a hard tug and they were gone, shredded and tossed aside, and she was bare. Spence tilted his head back, and she'd like to say it was a smile he gave her with the slight tilt of his lips, but that devilish gleam in his eyes didn't really go with a smile. It was more of a threat—a "prepare yourself for this" kind of warning. Because then he leaned in and his mouth was on her sex, covering her clit, his tongue licking along her folds. Hot, wet, devastating. She moaned and quivered uncontrollably as he dominated her pussy. She bucked against his lips, but she had nowhere to go. He cupped her buttocks, held tight to her, licked her with the long, measured strokes of his soft tongue, lapping her up like a quickly melting ice-cream cone. She was dying from the sweet, hot pleasure, seared from the inside out, unable to stop the flood of sensation that hurtled at her at uncontrollable speed.

Spence was relentless, his mouth everywhere, exploring, dipping, licking, and sucking. He bit the inside of her thigh, and the painful pleasure rocketed her. He licked her from one end to the other, and she wanted to cry out and beg for more. When he took hold of her clit and sucked, she wanted to scream.

And then she did, because her orgasm rushed at her out of nowhere, blindsiding her with forceful heat and swirling sensation. She rocked against Spence's mouth, craving contact with his tongue as she rode out the crest of the wave, then crashed over again, surprised that her climax went on seemingly forever. It had been such a long time since she'd been with a man, the drought had ended in a torrential downpour. When she was spent, when the contractions inside her had died down to tiny, pleasurable pulses, she looked down at Spence, embarrassed to see his head tilted back, a watchful expression on his face.

Her cheeks flamed hot. She'd never had a man watch her come before. All her experiences with sex previously had been rather . . . benign and uneventful. Certainly nothing like this, and never in public. And never with a man so incredibly . . . male.

She didn't know what to say, or what to do. She'd always been in bed with other guys.

Spence stood, licked his lips, that same expression on his face as he loomed over her.

"You are so goddamn gorgeous when you come," he said, drawing her against him. "You make my dick hard." He grasped her wrist and placed it on his erection. She shuddered at the feel of his shaft pulsing against the palm of her hand. Her lips parted with her panting excitement when he held on to her wrist and rubbed her hand back and forth across the steely ridge of his cock. "I want to fuck you, Shadoe."

"Yes." All embarrassment fled at the rough demand in his words, the promise of the actions to follow.

He dropped down to the ground, pulling her on top of him. He laced his fingers through her hair and held on while his mouth found hers in another kiss that devastated her senses. How was she supposed to think straight when he kept plundering her into mindless oblivion? Did it even matter, when all she wanted to concentrate on was the feel of his lips against hers and his hard cock pressed between her legs?

She gave no more thought at all other than to her senses. The way he smelled, the feel of his hard body against hers, the way he looked at her when she lifted up to catch her breath. For someone who seemed so light and easy and filled with humor, he could sure get intense at times—especially now, when his eyes turned a stormy blue, and he frowned at her like he was angry. But she knew it wasn't really anger that fueled him; it was passion, the same driving need that compelled her to rock against him, the need to feel his cock rub against her pussy.

He grabbed her hips and rolled her over so that he was on top of her now, the hard ridge of his erection angled right on her sweet spot. She gasped.

"Like it there?"

"Yes," she managed, though she was panting pretty heavily now. Damn him, if he kept moving against her clit with his cock that way, she was going to come again. "Spence, please."

"Tell me what you want."

"Fuck me. Hurry, I'm going to come again."

He arched a brow. "Are you?"

Instead of giving her what she wanted, he rolled to the side and palmed her sex, dipping his fingers into her wet pussy and spreading her juices all over her clit. She tightened, and when he swept his hard, hot hand all over her sex, she splintered, holding tight to his wrist to keep him right there while she rocked against him, crying out as the sweetest pleasure imaginable sizzled through her.

She felt wasted. Sweetly, perfectly wasted. But still, his hand lingered on her pussy, his gaze never wavering from her face. She bit down on her lower lip as he began to move his fingers around her clit, teasing her pussy lips. When he slid one finger inside her, she gasped.

"Wet," he said. "Hot."

He entered her with another finger, and she let out a low moan, the fire she thought was banked now growing again, gathering momentum.

"I'm going to make you come again, Shadoe. And this time I'll be inside you when you do."

She'd never been overly sexual. Yes, she enjoyed sex. She liked getting off when she was with a man. But never . . . never . . . three times in such a short period of time.

"I don't know if—"

"You will. Look how fast you got off those two times. I'll make you come again."

He was so sure of himself, of his ability to get her there. She believed him. God, did she ever believe him. The way his fingers moved inside her, made her believe. He was magic, seemed to know exactly how to touch her, with his palm pressing down over her clit at the same time he finger fucked her with deep, measured strokes. Her pussy tightened around his fingers as he dragged a response out of her she thought was impossible. She lifted against him, craving more.

"I want to get you naked and lick you all over," he whispered against her ear, with each word sliding his fingers deep inside her, only to pull them out ever so slowly. "But not out here, not in the grass. I want to be able to see you bathed in the light, to take my time. And my dick is rock hard and I want to bury it balls deep inside you until I come hard. You ready for that?"

"Yes. Fuck me." By the time he pulled away from her she was shaking. He settled between her outstretched legs and got on his knees, pulled a condom packet from his pocket, and unzipped his pants, drawing his jeans down just enough to pull out his cock.

Damn, it was beautiful. The head was wide, a deep, angry purple, his shaft steely thick just like the rest of him. She wanted to touch it, to slide her fingers and her mouth all over it, but instead he slid the condom over his cock and settled between her legs.

"We'll play later."

She was counting on it. She spread her legs wider and lifted while he placed the head of his cock at the entrance to her pussy, slid one hand under her butt, and eased inside her.

Shadoe tilted her head back and absorbed the sensation of Spence filling her, the way her pussy squeezed his shaft as he drove all the way in, the way she pulsed around him in welcome. He fit her perfectly. Hot and hard and oh, God, he was an expert at fucking, going slow at first, letting her feel every glorious inch of his shaft, then driving in hard, quick thrusts that made her delirious with pleasure.

And his hands—the man had incredible hands, and he used them to touch her everywhere. She wasn't even naked, yet he lifted up her shirt to skim his hand over her breasts.

"When I get your clothes off I'm going to suck your nipples." He tweaked the bud, flicked it with his finger. She felt that all the way to her clit, and it made her pussy clench around his cock.

"Ah, Shadoe, your pussy squeezes me." He rocked against her, grasping her hip in a tight grip, his fingers digging into her soft flesh. He instantly let go.

"Don't."

"Can't bruise you. You're on tomorrow night."

Dammit. She wanted him to take her hard, to leave marks on her, to make her his. She couldn't explain this primal need; she only knew she wanted it, had to have it. She lifted against him, wrapped her legs around him. "Touch me, Spence. Be rough. I don't bruise easy."

With a low growl he took her mouth, sliding his tongue in to wrap around hers. He kissed her deeply, tucking his arm around her and using his hand to arch her upward. And then he began to dig hard, driving his shaft against her with deep, rhythmic strokes.

The sensations were so intense she couldn't hold back, didn't want to hold back. She raked her nails along his upper arms as she shook with uncontrollable spasms and splintered around him, her pussy gripping him in intense, quick bursts as she came.

"Ah, Christ," he murmured against her lips, then she felt his own control shred, reveled in it as he pumped hard and fast, then shuddered, sliding his mouth down her neck to bite against her shoulder while he rocked out a loud, intense orgasm of his own.

She held him, smoothing her hand along his arms, wishing they were both naked so she could feel his sweat-soaked skin against her own, but loving this anyway as he came apart and held her in his strong embrace.

It took a while before she became aware of the wet grass underneath her. Spence rolled her over on top of him and swept his hands over her back, smoothed her skirt down over her naked butt. He looked at her like she was a stranger, his brows winged in a deep frown.

Not exactly the kind of expression you want on a man's face after he's made love to you.

"What?"

"Nothing," he said, holding on to her as he sat them up, then helping her stand. He cleaned himself up and zipped his pants. "We should get back. It's a long ride."

Interesting. Did he have regrets about this? She didn't. It had been . . . amazing. But she felt his withdrawal; it was more than physical. There was an emotional wall between them that hadn't been there a few minutes ago.

"Spence."

He picked up her boots, handed them to her, a smile on his face replacing the frown from earlier. "Fucking is fun, Shadoe. Don't make it more than that."

She slid into her boots, refusing to be irked by his careless dismissal of what had happened between them. "I wasn't going to."

She should have known better, should have realized that a man like Spence didn't look at a woman as anything more than an object to fuck. He wasn't in it for the emotional or the sharing, just the physical pleasure.

Well, just fine. That wasn't going to happen again.

"Ready?" he asked.

She gave a short nod, not trusting her own emotions enough to even speak to him right now.

They climbed on the bike and headed back to the hotel. Shadoe couldn't wait to get back to the room, to take a shower and wash the night away. How stupid could she be?

Though as she sat on the bike and the wind cleared her head, she realized Spence *had* shared a lot with her tonight. He'd shared his past, his history, his pain. And he'd probably not shared that with a lot of people before.

Maybe he hadn't wanted to, but it had slipped out. And maybe that's what had irritated him. Did he think she'd feel sorry for him now that she knew? Or that she'd pity him?

She didn't know what to think, or what to do about Spence. Figuring out what went on in a man's mind was nearly impossible. But she'd admittedly felt something for him tonight, and it wasn't pity.

She wasn't the type to give up easily. But getting involved with a mission partner spelled disaster. They both needed clear heads and focus for this mission. She had to concentrate on finding the rogue agent, and get through this whole stripper act. Wasn't that enough to handle without getting involved with her partner?

Yet Spence intrigued her. There were both hard and soft sides to him that begged further exploration.

Damn, this was a mess and a half, wasn't it?

She had some thinking to do.

nine

SPENCE RAN HIS FINGERS THROUGH HIS HAIR AND PACED THE
hotel room, feeling more and more like he walked a cage. Sharing
this space with Shadoe was going to be torture, especially after
what had happened between them last night.

He spit out a curse and pushed through the double doors leading outside to the balcony, hoping the morning air would clear his
head. No such luck. It was sticky hot outside already and he knew
he'd find no clarity there.

What the hell had he been thinking? Other than Grange and
the other Wild Riders, he'd never told anyone about his past. The
only reason the other guys knew about it was because Grange in-
sisted they all talk about what had happened to them—he hadn't
had a choice but to comply if he wanted to stay in the group. And
that talk had been a long time ago, when they were all still kids.

Old wounds Grange had made them open up, talk over, and then never discuss again.

So why now, and why with Shadoe, a woman he barely knew? He'd wanted her to talk about herself. His intent was to find out about her, gain some insight. Instead, he still didn't know jack about her or her relationship with her father. But she knew everything about him, since for some reason he'd started talking and couldn't seem to shut his mouth.

Goddammit. He hadn't thought about Trevor in years, had tried to bury that part of his life, his past, all the ugliness. His focus was on looking ahead, never behind.

Maybe it was because they'd ended up back here where he'd grown up, and that had dredged up the memories. Hell if he knew. He wasn't the type to psychoanalyze, to think about the whys of things. He lived in the now, never in the then. You couldn't go back and change what had happened; you could only live your life going forward, so there was never any sense in taking a walk back into the past.

He sure had last night though, hadn't he? And Shadoe had listened, asked questions, never found fault with what he'd done. She thought of him as some kind of goddamned hero.

He snorted. He was no hero. Trevor was the hero.

His gut tightened at the thought of his brother. He wondered where Trevor was now. Was he successful? He'd always wanted to know, but never allowed himself to find out. What would be the point? He wouldn't contact him . . . couldn't. He'd wanted the past dead and buried, wanted to cut out that part of his life and forget it had ever existed.

Until he'd unearthed it last night, shared it with Shadoe. That had made it real again. Raw.

He looked over the balcony railing at the street cleaners below, systematically washing away the remnants of last night's revelry from Bourbon Street. He wished he could do the same thing.

He dragged his hand through the short clips of his hair. God, he was so fucking stupid. The whole night had been like that. Shadoe had gotten under his skin from the first night he'd met her, and that never happened with women.

Women were fun. They smelled good, he enjoyed fucking them and spending time with them, but that's where it ended. He didn't do relationships. He didn't do the whole talk-and-get-to-know-you kind of thing. He partied with them and had sex with them. He purposefully chose the kind of women who wouldn't get attached.

Shadoe wasn't that kind of woman. Even worse, she was his partner on this case.

So what the hell had he been thinking pouncing on her like an animal in heat last night? To shut her up about thinking he was some kind of hero? Or had he done it for some other reason?

He didn't even want to ponder what he felt. He didn't do feelings any more than he did relationships. He wasn't the kind of guy to dissect that shit. He liked women, he fucked them, then he moved on. Any sense of a woman wanting more than that and he was history.

Fortunately, when they got back to the room last night, Shadoe was in no more of a mood to talk than he was. She went right into the bathroom, took a shower, and climbed into bed without a word. He did the same. It worked out perfectly. He was afraid she'd want to talk about what had happened between them.

She hadn't.

She was probably pissed at him because he blew her off right after he fucked her. Too bad. She'd have to get used to it, because that's who he was.

Not that he was going to have sex with her again. That had been a huge mistake and wasn't going to be repeated. It was time to concentrate on their job and not on each other.

But man, she'd been sweet last night. Hot, sexy, she fit him perfectly and matched his passion and needs.

His cock twitched at the memory of her coming apart for him time after time. She was a mix of innocence and seductress in one beautiful package. And he hadn't gotten her naked, hadn't been able to touch her skin and taste her all over. He'd wager he'd be able to taste the sweetness in her.

He cursed his growing erection and his wayward thoughts, refusing to go down that road. It wasn't going to happen again.

"Good morning."

He half turned to see her standing in the doorway wearing a pair of soft gray shorts and a cotton tank top. Her hair was mussed from sleep, her cheeks rosy, and her eyes barely open.

She couldn't be any sexier than if she were standing there stark naked.

She made his dick hard and his balls quiver. He wanted to scoop her up and take her back to bed and fuck her for about five hours until he stopped thinking about her.

Instead, he turned away. "Mornin'."

She moved out onto the balcony alongside him and laid her hands on the railing. She didn't say anything for a few minutes, which gave him time to gaze at her out of the corner of his eyes. The light morning wind blew her hair across her cheek. She didn't bother to pull it away. He wanted to. Then he wanted to kiss that soft spot on her neck. And the wind kept lifting the short tank top, giving him a peek at her flat stomach. He wanted to kiss that, too.

He also wanted to groan and run away so he wouldn't have to stand next to her, inhale the scent of her soap and shampoo. Want her.

This was stupid. There were all kinds of women out there he could have without much effort, women who could easily help him take his mind off Shadoe. She was nothing special.

"I'm sorry I pried into your personal life last night," she said, her voice barely above a whisper. "I had no right and it made you uncomfortable. I won't do it again."

She had made a half turn, her hip now leaning against the railing so she faced him. He had no choice but to do the same, otherwise he'd look like a coward.

"No big deal. Don't worry about it."

Her lips lifted. "You can ask me anything you want about my past, my childhood, my father, and I'll answer it. I figure I owe you that much."

Yeah, since he'd spilled his guts to her last night. "I don't need to know anything about your personal life."

Her half-smile died. "But last night you said—"

"Yeah, well, last night was last night. Today we need to work on the mission, and start focusing on that."

"Don't we need to get to know each other so we can work well together?"

He slanted a wry grin in her direction. "Darlin', I don't need to know you at all to work with you. I've already seen you naked shaking your tits up on the stage. What more do I need?"

He pushed off the balcony and walked through the doors into the room, feeling ten times the asshole for what he'd just said. But if she hated him for it, good. It would make things easier.

On him, anyway.

He heard the balcony doors shut and Shadoe went into the bathroom. He kept his back to her, deciding the less time he spent looking at her, the better. She came out a short while later dressed in capri pants and a skimpy tank top. Her hair was pulled back in a ponytail and she wore no makeup.

"So what's the plan for the day?" she asked, her persona all business now.

"I thought we'd grab some breakfast and play tourist today."

She arched a brow. "This is hardly a vacation."

"Yeah, I know that. But we also know where the drug deals have gone down, so I want to do some strolling down at the riverfront."

She nodded. "Ah. Now I understand."

"Pretty woman like you should be able to start a conversation with lots of guys. And if nothing else, you can hand out your business cards and say you're there to drum up potential customers for your show tonight."

She grinned. "Perfect. After all, I am a new headliner and I want to draw a crowd. So we'll have a good reason to be out and about mingling where the men are just in case we're asked. You're smart."

"Nah. I just give good bullshit."

She laughed, so she must have gotten over his insult. Not that it mattered whether she did or not. He didn't care what she thought of him. Many women thought he was an asshole.

They were usually right.

"I need to head down to the club after breakfast and before we go sightseeing. I have rehearsal."

"How long will that take?"

"About an hour or so. I want to get a feel for their walkway and stage. I want to practice my act and work with the deejay on music."

"Fine. We'll head there after we eat, and then to the docks after."

"What about Pax and AJ?"

"They have their own assignments, but they'll be at the club tonight. I don't want anyone to see us with them. As far as anyone's concerned, they're just customers. You can mingle with them at the club, but no more than you would any other guy there."

"Okay."

SHADOE TRIED TO KEEP HER HEAD INVOLVED IN THE BUSINESS OF her job. Easier that way and less emotional. She and Spence went downstairs and had breakfast at the hotel's restaurant. Shadoe had already arranged to have the hotel send all her gear to the club, so they rode over there. The club wouldn't open until four in the afternoon, so she knocked on the door. It was opened by an older man with a balding head of silvery hair.

"I'm Desi, the headliner," she said.

He nodded and pushed the door all the way open for her and Spence to enter, then pulled it shut and locked it behind them.

Without the lights on, the club looked different. There really wasn't much to it in the daytime, without the bouncing light and blaring music. The tables were empty; the place was clean and practically bare. The walls were dark, the carpet a deep, rich burgundy. There were a few girls on stage dancing and pulling off their clothes, but they didn't look like pros. The music was low enough that she could hear herself think. She caught sight of Brandon seated at the front of the stage. She headed in his direction.

"Hey," he said with a smile. "Glad to see you."

"I'm here to rehearse and get the layout of the stage, if that's okay."

He nodded. "I'm auditioning a few new girls for midweek replacement. Give me about fifteen and I'll be finished up here."

"No problem. It'll take me that long to get ready."

Brandon pointed down a hallway on the left. "Changing room is through that door. Ariele is in since she wanted to work on a new act. She'll help you find a locker for your things. The hotel delivered them about an hour ago."

"Great. Thanks." She turned to find Spence, but he was already seated at the bar, looking appropriately stoic, mean, and bored, which she wasn't sure was an act or not. She didn't hang around long enough to find out, but instead pushed through the door leading to the dressing area.

A beautiful petite brunette was in there. She turned around and lifted her lips in a smile. Her face could stop traffic. Heart-shaped, with full, pouty lips and a generous smile, a tiny nose and big blue eyes. She couldn't be more than twenty-one or twenty-two at the most, and was dressed in very short boy shorts and a tiny bra that barely covered her nipples. Her hair hung midway down her back and was shiny and perfectly straight, unlike Shadoe's unruly, untamable curls.

"Are you Desi?" she asked in a very strong Southern accent.

"Yes, I am. You must be Ariele." Shadoe went over and held out her hand.

"Oh, honey. Here in the South we hug." Ariele wrapped her arms around Shadoe and gave her a tight squeeze. "And aren't you just so pretty. Welcome to the Wild Rose."

"Thanks. Brandon said you'd show me a locker I could use."

"Oh, sure." Ariele led her to the back of the room where a row of lockers stood, then opened one. "You'll want to get a lock for yours. Most of us can be trusted not to get into your stuff, but there are a few who'll dig into your things."

"I brought a lock with me, thanks." Shadoe started unpacking her bag.

"So what's your theme, Desi?"

"Leather and bikes."

"Oh, that's hot. The guys here will go crazy."

"I hope so. I'm nervous."

"Don't be. The crowd's friendly and guys always have plenty of money to throw around. The bouncers take good care of us and make sure no one gets out of hand. If you know how to shake your stuff, you'll rake it in. Besides, you're a headliner. They always make the best money."

Once Shadoe finished unpacking her costumes, she turned to Ariele. "Well, I'm a new headliner, so I'm still just a touch nervous about it, but yes, it's very exciting. How long have you been here at the Wild Rose?"

"Three years. I started when I was eighteen, right out of high school. I hope to make headliner within the next year. I've been taking dance lessons and worked my way up from starting on days and afternoons to nights and weekends, where you make much better money."

Shadoe smiled. "Sounds like you've been working hard and you're doing all the right things. And you certainly have the looks and body for this line of work."

Ariele's face brightened. "Do you really think so? Thanks. That means a lot coming from someone like you."

Shadoe had no idea if Ariele would make a great stripper or not, or even if she could dance well. But the girl was friendly and talkative, and if she'd been here for three years, she undoubtedly knew everyone, which meant she was the perfect person to get to know well.

"I'd love it if you'd take a look at my act and give me pointers."

Shadoe swallowed. Oh, God. Like she could offer advice to a seasoned pro like Ariele? She'd have to fake her way through it. "Sure, I'd be happy to. Why don't you go on first? I was going to rehearse my act before I go on tonight, but watching you will help me get a feel for the layout of the stage."

"Great idea. I'll see if Brandon's finished with his auditions, then I'll queue up my music. You can watch from out front and tell me what you think."

Ariele bounded through the doors like a bubbly, excited teenager. Shadoe shook her head and wandered back through to the club and took a seat next to Brandon, who was scribbling notes on a pad of paper.

"Find anyone good?"

He looked over at her. "A few possibles. I thought you were going to rehearse."

"Ariele conned me into taking a look at her act and offering pointers."

He grinned. "She's enthusiastic and motivated. One of my best dancers."

"Is she?"

"Yeah. She's reliable, has her head on straight, and doesn't drink up my profits, and she has goals."

"She said she wants to be a headliner."

"She might just get there. Let me know what you think."

Great. Another person who thought she knew what she was doing.

Ariele's music started up. Something funky and modern. A current hip-hop musician, the lyrics were easy to catch and talked about a woman and lovemaking and getting a girl's clothes off. Appropriate for stripping.

Ariele came out onto the stage and it didn't take her long to grab the pole and do a few twirls. Shadoe was impressed. It took some good upper-arm strength to hold on to that thing and slide around. She even hung on it upside down before moving away and doing her striptease.

She took her clothes off too fast, but once she did she had an incredible body. It was no wonder she was moving up the ladder so quickly. She had a nice, tight, well-toned body, perfect breasts, and a great ass. Not an ounce of fat on her. And she smiled all the time like she really loved what she was doing, unlike some of the girls Shadoe had watched dance, who looked like they were bored while they did their routines. She was sure a lot of guys couldn't care less about a girl's expression, but Shadoe figured it couldn't hurt to at least act like you enjoyed your job.

When Ariele was finished, Shadoe rose and went up on the stage to talk to her.

"Well, what do you think?"

"I think you're gorgeous. You obviously take good care of your body."

Ariele nodded. "I'm a vegetarian. I exercise all the time, take dance lessons and yoga. I don't smoke or drink and I inhale water by the gallon."

Shadoe grinned. "It shows. You have beautiful skin."

"Thank you. How about my dancing?"

"I like your act a lot. You could slow down a bit, tease the guys. You take it off too quickly."

"They teach us to do that. They want us to get naked as soon as possible."

"I know. But even fifteen seconds longer drives the suspense up. You want to make them crave you. By the time you're down to your G-string you want them drooling and laying their tongues on the stage for you to step on with your stilettos. You'll get more money out of them that way. Always leave them wanting more. Trust me, you're worth the wait."

Ariele's eyes twinkled. "That's great advice. Thank you so much."

Shadoe received another tight hug from Ariele, and then it was time for her rehearsal. She steadfastly ignored Spence, who she felt staring at her. Tough. She'd had more than enough insult from him last night. She was doing her job and that job meant acting like a headliner stripper, not casting glances at her bodyguard every few seconds.

She gave her music to the deejay, informed Brandon she just wanted to work on her moves and would forgo the stripping until tonight. Brandon said he didn't care what she did; the stage was hers. He had to go to his office to work on the liquor inventory so he could put in an order for the week.

After he left, she went up onto the stage and waited for her music to come on. This stage had less length than the one in Dallas, but was wider, so she adjusted her act to accommodate it. She also found that no one paid any attention to her while she practiced. Ariele watched her for a few minutes, but then her phone rang so she ran off to the back room. The only one seemingly with his eye on her was Spence, and he frowned the entire time. She doubted that had anything to do with her act.

Once again, he seemed to be in a bad mood, and that seemed to be directed at her. Or maybe he was always like that. She didn't really know, nor, she decided, did she care. Last night she'd made a crucial mistake by having sex with her partner.

Sex meant involvement. It meant emotions, which clouded her judgment.

It wouldn't happen again.

ten

WHILE SHADOE DID HER THING AT THE CLUB, SPENCE HAD plenty of time to think and plot how they were going to handle things down at the riverfront. He'd already studied the shipyard—it was secure and they couldn't just walk in there, but they could loiter nearby, get a feel for the area, how much freedom people had to come and go. In the meantime, Shadoe could start learning faces, see if any of them turned up as regulars at the Wild Rose.

She finished up her gig, said her good-byes, and came up to him. He pushed off the barstool and without a word they left the club.

She was as quiet as he was, the tension thick between them again. He'd thought maybe they'd worked through it, that they could put last night behind them.

Maybe they couldn't, because something sure hung between

them right now. They were going to have to push through that wall, though, because they had a job to do.

"Ready to do some sightseeing?"

She nodded and they climbed on the bike, pulled away from the club, and drove down to the riverfront. Spence found a place to park and they walked toward the river, trying to blend in like the hundreds of tourists strolling along the sidewalks there. He took it slow, deliberately trying to give Shadoe time to look at faces, though all they could see right now were tourists. It took them awhile to veer off toward the docks, where the shipyards were located, and when they did, he picked up her hand and entwined his fingers with hers.

Her gaze shot to his.

"We have to appear like we're a couple just strolling along and having a good time, maybe even not paying attention to our surroundings, but each other. Try to act like you enjoy my company."

Her brows dipped below her sunglasses. "I will if you will." She squeezed his hand, and it wasn't a gentle squeeze either. He smirked at her.

"Now honey, let's not fight. We're supposed to be lovers."

"Keep it up and I'll give you a love bite you won't ever forget."

He laughed as they walked down the street. "Will it be near my dick?"

Shadoe snorted and pushed her body into his but, like him, watched the activity going on at the shipyards. They hugged as they walked, appeared to be gazing at each other, but Spence kept his focus on the docks, and so did Shadoe. When he wasn't watching, she was, and then it was his turn.

"See anyone who was at the club last night?" he asked when they stopped at the corner.

"Not yet. Let's cross to the other side so I can get a closer look around." She grabbed his hand and pulled him across the street.

He jerked her to a stop when she would have run over to the shops, pulling her against him. She tilted her head back.

"Not so fast, darlin'. Let's plan this out before you go rushing in there."

"Okay." She moved her sunglasses up on top of her head so he could see her eyes.

Those eyes mesmerized him, like warm whiskey surrounded by dark lashes. She tilted her head to the side and blinked. The way she stared at him, so direct, like she could see inside him—like she wanted him—he felt the tug in his balls. Her tongue snaked out and licked across her bottom lip. Did she have any idea what that conjured up in his mind? Her mouth on his dick.

She was in his arms, her body soft and yet firm. He knew as an agent she was required to be physical, so she was in great shape, yet she had the lush curves of a woman. He liked feeling her, still would like to see her naked, all the way naked so he could explore her with his hands and his mouth. She wasn't pulling away. And his dick continued to harden, his imagination gone haywire now.

"What are you doing?" She frowned as she obviously recognized his growing erection cocked against her hip.

"I'm getting hard thinking about you."

"Well . . . stop that."

"Then quit looking at me like you want to eat me."

Her eyes widened. "I wasn't looking at you like . . ." She stepped away. "Whatever. You're full of shit, Spencer."

He grabbed her around the hips and pulled her against him again. "Uh-uh. You're not supposed to fight with me. We're lovers, remember."

She spoke through gritted teeth. "I was not looking at you like that."

Teasing her was easier and way more fun than thinking about how hot she was. Less trouble that way, too. "You want me. Face it. I'm irresistible."

"You're full of yourself. Let's go."

"Kiss me first."

She rolled her eyes. "How about I knee you in the groin instead?"

"Will you kiss it after?"

He saw the tug of a smile at the corners of her lips. "I'll bet you get a lot of women into bed with your charm."

"It works on occasion."

She shook her head. "Can we move on now?"

"I guess, since I'm not likely to get any out on the street corner."

"Not from me, you aren't. But if you'd like, I could help you hunt down a hooker."

"Funny." He took her hand and they strolled along the docks. Considering how she was dressed, she got plenty of attention from the dockworkers, which worked out to their advantage. Of course since she was with him the men weren't as obvious as they would be if she were alone or walking with a group of other women, but she was pretty enough to gather some gawkers.

Her sable hair shone like spun silk in the sunlight, the slight breeze blowing her hair back as they walked along. She had long, tanned legs that showed off well in her capris, and the scoop neck of the tank top allowed a generous amount of cleavage. Enticing without being obvious, she'd dressed the part of innocent seductress perfectly. The dockhands were all but drooling as they leaned over the railing of the ships.

"You have a fan club."

"I do?"

"Yeah. Give them a smile."

She turned her head in the direction of the guys looking at her, and lifted her lips in a shy grin. Then she broke off from him and moved through the open gates and toward the closest ship. Several guys were loitering near the gangplank. Spence stayed a few steps behind her, enough to offer protection but not to crowd her.

"Hey, guys," she said, reaching into her bag to pull out her card. "I open tonight at the Wild Rose. I don't know what you all do in your off time, but if you have a free few hours, come see me."

As soon as she started handing out business cards, a crowd began to gather, especially when Spence stood there with his arms folded in front of him and didn't interfere.

Suddenly Shadoe became very popular. Hopefully she was scanning and memorizing faces. She seemed to be doing a fine job talking them up, laughing, and asking them to come spend their money at the Wild Rose.

You'd think these guys hadn't been around a woman in years the way they hung all over her. Shadoe handled it well, though. When they got too close, she'd lay a palm on their shoulder and tell them to back off, then motion her head toward Spence as a warning.

The guys all seemed friendly and good-natured, not out to cause any trouble. He had his gun tucked into his pocket just in case anyone wanted to take it a step too far. He didn't think anyone was that stupid, especially since they were on the job.

After about fifteen minutes of chatting them up, she waved good-bye and came back toward him. They moved off down the street and the crowd of guys went back to work.

"We should see several of them tonight, or at least sometime this week," she said. "And now I have a lot more faces to place with the dockyard."

"No one struck you as familiar?"

She shook her head. "Not yet, but our guy wouldn't be working the docks anyway."

"Still, this is where the shipments come in. It's not just the agent we need to be concerned about. There's a connection to the club, too. Packaging and distribution, maybe, but no one's been able to pinpoint who or what yet."

"I know. That's why the more faces I learn, the sooner we'll be able to piece the puzzle together."

They headed down the street, passing the rows of ships. Shadoe grabbed his arm, her nails digging in. She spun around and pulled him in the opposite direction.

"What is it?"

"There's a guy talking to someone over there. I recognize him from the club."

Spence looked over at all the dockworkers. There, standing outside the office, were two guys. "The ones near the supervisor's shack?"

"I guess so. A small building right by the gate."

"That's it. Which guy?"

She kept her gaze averted. "Tall, thin, kind of sandy-colored hair that he wears long. He's got on jeans and a white muscle shirt."

"Got him." Spence didn't recognize him. "Who is he?"

"I don't know. He works at the Wild Rose, though."

"In what capacity?"

"Don't know that either. I didn't have time last night to figure out what everyone did. I do recall him wearing a Wild Rose T-shirt though."

Spence nodded. "We'll have to keep our eye on him."

"What's he doing?"

"Right now, nothing. Just leaning against the doorway talking to some guy holding a clipboard. The conversation looks light and friendly, so they could be just buddies."

"Or it could be something more."

"Let's get out of here before he sees us. I don't want to make him suspicious of us, because I want to keep an eye on him at the club."

Shadoe nodded and they backed up until they found a side street, then headed to where Spence had parked the bike. He pulled his keys from his pocket and turned to her.

"Do you ever reach a maximum of things you can remember?"

She shrugged. "Not so far. I memorized every word of every textbook in college and at the academy, and that was quite a bit. I don't think you have to worry about me being unable to store all the faces. I can still remember every face I've ever seen from childhood."

"That's an incredible gift."

"Sometimes a burden. There are times you want to be able to forget things, and you can't."

He knew all about the need to forget the past. He could well imagine there were things she remembered that she didn't want to. "Having a photographic memory would suck."

She laughed. "Sometimes it does. Other times, like for this job, it can come in handy."

They stopped for lunch, then went back to the hotel. Spence got in touch with Grange and gave him a report. Shadoe spent the next few hours pacing the room. When she got tired of being inside, she went onto the balcony and walked its length, then came back in and paced some more.

He picked up on her tension, as well as her glances at the clock on the nightstand every few minutes.

What was she nervous about? Her performance at the club tonight?

Probably. He sure as hell wouldn't want to strip in front of hundreds of people. Dallas was one thing. The Wild Rose was a popular club and this was summer tourist season. The place would be packed. Plus, AJ and Pax would be there, too. In addition, she'd have to keep her eyes open in order to sight the rogue. That was a hell of a lot of shit to deal with for someone who was new to the job.

He couldn't blame her for being on edge, wished there was something he could do to ease her tension, but he knew all about being edgy on a mission.

Sometimes an undercover role was fun to play, and other times it was nothing more than a giant pain in the ass. In Shadoe's case, he could well imagine she didn't consider what she had to do to be fun. Even a seasoned agent would probably go dry-mouthed at the thought of shedding her clothes for the job.

He'd dated a lot of strippers. You either had to be in it because you loved it or because you loved the money, and either way you didn't give a shit about parading around naked. It wasn't the kind of job for a woman who'd spent her life sheltered in private schools. He gave Shadoe credit for even taking this assignment. Talk about stepping outside your comfort zone. She was way outside it on this job.

Maybe he'd get her drunk. That would relax her, but it might affect her performance, too, dammit. He'd just have to come up with something else, because at the rate she was pacing they were going to have to replace the carpet in the room before they checked out.

"Uh, why don't you try a hot bath?"

She stopped, turned to him. "What?"

"You're tense."

"No, I'm not."

"You've been walking a hole in the floor for the past four hours."

She scanned the length of the carpet, then turned back to him. "No, I haven't."

Oblivious, too. "Okay. How about dinner?"

She palmed her stomach. "Oh. Ugh. That doesn't even sound good."

That's what he figured. "I'll go get you some ginger ale or something to settle your stomach."

"Would you, really? That would be great. I need to take a shower and start getting ready."

Now it was his turn to glance at the clock. It was nearly eight. Yeah, they should head that way. "Well, I'm hungry and I'm going to grab a burger while I'm downstairs. You go get ready. I'll bring you something to drink."

"Thanks."

He went down to the restaurant and ordered food for himself and a drink and some fruit and cheese for Shadoe. Maybe she wouldn't eat much, but she could at least pick at the food. He knew if she went without eating anything, she'd probably get sick. When he opened the door to the room, she stood there by her bed with a towel wrapped around her naked body. The smell of her filled the room—shampoo, soap, everything that was female about her.

He laid the food down on the table and unscrewed the top on the bottle of ginger ale. She came over and looked down at the food. "All this for you?"

"No. Just the burger and fries. I brought you some fruit and cheese. Try to eat something. You won't make a good headliner if you pass out while dancing, and we're going to be there late tonight."

She took a sip of the ginger ale and used her fork to spear a slice of cheese. "Yes, Mom," she said with a smirk.

"Make fun all you want, but you're eating, aren't you?"

She sat at the table and not only ate the fruit and cheese, she also snatched a few of his fries. He grinned at her back while he ate his burger.

Now, at least, she might survive the night. One less thing he'd have to worry about.

Not that he was worried about her or anything. He just had to make sure she didn't drop the ball on the assignment. That was his only concern.

He sure enjoyed watching her in that towel. She had pretty shoulders. Well toned, and her towel had started to slide down her back, revealing a smooth expanse of skin that he'd love to explore with his fingertips. Or his mouth.

As if she'd felt him studying her, Shadoe cast a look at him over her shoulder, tossing curls of damp hair behind her back.

Their gazes locked and held. Spence knew he should turn away, but there were her eyes again. Something about the way she looked at him drew him, held him. He saw warmth there, and desire, things he'd had far too little of in his life, things he'd never thought he'd missed, or wanted.

Until now.

Her mouth opened and she ran her tongue over her bottom lip. Such a sweet invitation. He leaned in, knowing he shouldn't, grasped her chin with his thumb and forefinger, brushing his lips against hers, just to take a taste.

Her lips trembled and she sighed, then she placed her palm against his chest and pushed away. "I need to go get ready."

Her eyes were glassy, her nipples hard and visible against the thin towel.

She knew and he knew that if they started this, it would take a while to finish. His cock had hardened fast and he was damned uncomfortable as he watched her walk away and close the bathroom door.

So much for keeping things professional between them. One look at her and he was hard and had forgotten all about his resolve. Yeah, he was great about his convictions, wasn't he? Good thing she'd stopped. He wouldn't have.

He cleaned up the food and waited for Shadoe to come out of the bathroom. She did, in jeans and a tank top, her makeup on and her hair curled.

"Nice outfit."

She looked as if he'd just accused her of murder instead of complimented her. "This isn't my costume."

"Didn't think it was, though you could strip in that and no one would care."

She shook her head. "It gets better."

"I imagine it does. Can't wait to see it."

"Yeah. I'll bet. You ready?"

Spence should know better than to try to compliment a woman. He should have just kept his mouth shut.

She sat stiff as a column of steel behind him on the bike, her thighs rigid against his as they rode to the club. After he parked and they got off, her expression was just as stiff as the rest of her.

"You could try smiling." He reached for her hand but she jerked it away. She was going to self-combust if he didn't get a shot of tequila in her.

"I am smiling."

"No, babe, you're not. You're stiff as a board, too." He laid his hand on the small of her back. "Relax. You're not on for a couple hours."

She inhaled and blew it out, then walked inside, nodded at the guys at the front, and let Spence lead her toward the bar. Spence ordered two tequila shots and offered one to her. She shook her head. "I don't want to drink tonight."

"This will just take the edge off. You're so tight right now you won't be able to bend. A shot or two won't affect you."

She accepted the glass and downed it in one swallow. She turned and hitched herself up onto a barstool, then leaned back to watch the dancer, cocking her head to the side as if studying her moves.

"You're better than she is," he said, leaning close to whisper in her ear.

She snorted and turned to him. "She's a pro."

"You're still better." He liked being able to talk to her this way. Kept him close enough to her that he could smell her shampoo. God, he was pathetic. Or maybe just horny. If he kept her distracted, maybe she'd relax and stop thinking about whatever made her so tense.

"See anyone you recognize from today?"

"No."

"What about the guy you saw here last night? The one who works here?"

She scanned the club. "He's not here. Maybe he's off tonight."

"He might be coming in later, too. And none of the guys you talked to on the docks are here?"

She shook her head. "Not yet, but they know I'm not on until eleven. Maybe they'll come in later. Or not at all. I hope we pack in a good crowd tonight. I'd hate to fail at this."

"You're not going to fail. It's barely past nine. Strip clubs don't start hopping until after ten. Quit worrying."

"Easy for you to say. You're not the headliner. If I get fired after the first night, our cover is blown."

She really was going off the deep end. He was going to have to lighten her up or she'd depress the customers, which wouldn't be a good kickoff night for the new headliner.

Pax and AJ walked in, caught sight of Spence, and made sure to grab a table on the other side of the club. Shadoe's muscles tensed even further once she caught sight of them strolling past.

He slid his hand under her hair and massaged her neck. She seized up at first, but the more he rubbed, the more her shoulders relaxed. She kept her focus on the dancers, and he continued to gently work the muscles of her neck.

Her hair fell over his arm like a silk waterfall. Touching her made his dick hard. Hell, everything about her made his dick hard. He gave up on the thought of keeping this impersonal. Being next to her, drawing in her scent, and touching her were going to give him an erection and there wasn't much he could do about it. Since the bodyguard-and-boyfriend cover allowed him to touch her, he could get hard and no one would think anything of it. It worked for their assignment and hey, it was a bonus for him.

Though the hard-on was damned uncomfortable, and being turned on made his mind wander. Like thinking about bending her over the barstool, pulling down her jeans, and thrusting into her until he came. Or laying her on her back across one of the tables and licking her sweet pussy until she had a wild orgasm, then fucking her until they both came.

None of those thoughts helped tamp down his raging libido. He needed to start paying attention to what was going on around him. He searched the club. It was crowded already, so he scanned faces. He might not have a photographic memory like Shadoe, but he had a good recall for people he'd just met the night before. Brandon, the owner, was nowhere in sight—probably in his office if he was on the premises at all. He'd remembered the guys in the front when they'd walked in, so they were the same ones from last night. He hadn't caught sight of the bouncers yet. Only two dancers had been on so far, and they weren't repeaters from the night before.

He tunneled his fingers into Shadoe's scalp and gently rubbed there, then signaled the bartender two fingers. He slid across two more shots. Spence handed one to Shadoe.

"You keep feeding me drinks and rubbing my head like that and one of two things is going to happen."

He downed the shot and laid the glass on the bar. "Yeah? What two things?"

"I'm either going to fall asleep or have an orgasm."

He grinned and watched her shoot the tequila. "I vote for the orgasm."

She took a deep inhale, then let it out, shuddering. "I could use one. It would relax me more than the tequila, though the massage is helping a lot."

He leaned into her, laid his hand on her upper thigh, and squeezed. "I can make you come."

Her gaze shot to his. "Here? I don't think so."

"Where's your sense of adventure?"

She laughed and shook her head. "I have a great sense of adventure, but this is not the place."

She had no idea. Anyplace could be the right place, given a good imagination. He had a really good imagination.

"I need to get back there and get ready, meet the girls."

He nodded, already formulating a plan. "Okay."

She slid off the barstool and disappeared through the double doors leading into the dressing area.

He'd give her a half-hour. Then he was going to find her and take care of her.

After all, it was his job to make sure she was relaxed before she went on stage.

Or at least distracted enough that she wasn't tense.

He grinned and ordered another shot of tequila.

Backstage was a bustle of estrogen, noisy with lots of women talking, and mostly in various stages of undress. If Shadoe had any reservations about hanging out naked with other women, she was going to have to get over that phobia in a hurry. Fortunately, she'd gotten past that a long time ago in private school, where community showers were required, and she'd never been the modest type anyway.

Ariele was there, along with two dozen other women of various shapes, sizes, and colors. They were packed into the dressing area like sardines, reminding her again of college. But there was laughter and yelling and squealing as everyone caught up on gossip and some argued, while others chatted one-on-one in whatever corner they could find. Some of the girls even had their boyfriends in there. No one bothered to care about that. Others were on the phone chatting up a storm.

Some were friendly, like Elan, a petite mocha-skinned beauty with a quiet elegance and an incredible French accent. She had mesmerizing doe eyes and full lips that men no doubt fell in love with.

Spitfire was a perfect name for the fiery redhead with pale skin and huge breasts. A bundle of energy and nonstop talker, her green eyes flashed with life. She talked so fast Shadoe understood only half of what she said. She was incredibly exuberant and obviously the welcoming committee of the bunch.

Star was a cool raven-haired beauty with gray eyes that seemed to always assess. She didn't say much, wasn't exactly unfriendly, just wasn't overly social either. She nodded when Shadoe introduced herself. Shadoe noticed she didn't seem to be chatty with any of the other girls. She sat at her table putting on her makeup and kept to herself. Maybe she was shy; maybe it was just her personality. Could be something else, but people who weren't friendly weren't to be trusted, at least in Shadoe's opinion. She'd have to keep her eye on Star.

"So you're the new girl."

As Shadoe sat at her makeup table to do her face, she looked up into the eyes of a very tall, gorgeous blonde with big blue eyes and a knockout figure. "Yes, I'm Desi."

"I'm Cheri, and I'm the lead here. We'll see what kind of headliner you are."

"Quit being such a bitch, Cheri," Ariele said, moving over to stand next to Shadoe. "Can't you just welcome Desi?"

Cheri lifted her chin and glared at Ariele. "I just did, didn't I?"

Cheri walked away and Ariele flipped her off. "Cow." She turned to Shadoe. "Don't pay any attention to her. She thinks she's hot shit and has delusions of being a headliner." Ariele leaned in to whisper, "Which will never happen, because she has about as much sex appeal as stale bread. Wait till you catch her act."

A dancer with a chip on her shoulder, and she already hated Shadoe? Great. "Thanks for the heads-up."

Ariele patted her shoulder, then went off to get ready for her act. Shadoe was pretty much ready other than getting dressed, and she had an hour to kill before she went on. She could throw on a robe and hang out at the doorway to watch the other dancers, get a feel for their rhythm.

That might help relax her. If they could do it, she could, too.

She didn't know why she was so tense tonight. It wasn't the first night she'd stripped. She'd done it in Dallas to a large crowd and hadn't thought much of it at all.

Then again, maybe that's because back in Dallas she'd just

thrown herself on the stage without thinking about what she was doing.

She'd had plenty of time to think about it since, and she had the added pressure of the case now, of watching for the rogue agent. Plus, AJ and Pax were out there watching.

Which really should be no different from Spence seeing her strip, right?

Who was she kidding? It *was* different. Tonight, everything was. She grabbed a robe and tied the sash, then slid out the door and down the hall. The blaring music pounded in her temples and jacked up her already haywire nervous system. The hallway was pitch-dark and she had to feel the wall to make her way toward the light at the entrance to the doorway. She intended to linger there and peek at the dancers, hopefully gain some courage that way, but she crashed into something huge and immobile. It took her only a second to realize she'd run into a large, hard body, definitely male.

"Sorry," she said, trying to focus in the darkness on the face of whoever she'd run into.

"No need to be sorry."

"Spence. What are you doing back here?" She pivoted, certain someone was going to come rushing up to them and bust them, but she didn't know why she was so nervous. Some of the other girls had their boyfriends in the dressing room. Spence in the hallway was no big deal. After all, he was her bodyguard and her boyfriend—at least that's what everyone was supposed to believe. He had every right to be back here.

"Just came to check on you."

"I'm fine. Get back out there."

Instead, he pulled her against his chest. "Coming out to take a peek?"

"I was." She pulled the robe sash tighter around her.

"Then let's go take a look."

"I don't think—"

He didn't give her time to finish her sentence, but instead wrapped his arm around her middle and walked her toward the doors, then stepped back to the corner. There, she could watch the dancers but the corner was recessed so they were out of the swinging doorway.

"This is a good spot."

"I guess so." He hadn't let go of her. He was so big, his body pressed up against her. She felt him everywhere, and she was naked underneath her robe. His fingertips rested just under her left breast where he no doubt felt the rapid thumping of her heart.

"Relax, *Desi*," he whispered in her ear. "Just watch and let me take care of you."

Take care of her. What did he—

He moved his hand upward, sliding it inside her robe to cup her breast. Her breath caught and for only a fraction of a second she thought about darting away. But it was dark here and even the other girls wouldn't see them. They used a different door to enter and exit the stage.

Her lips parted as she fought for breath. The thought of being caught was both mortifying and tantalizing as Spence slid the pad of his thumb across her nipple. His breath, hot and tinged with the scent of tequila, sailed across her cheek. She felt the hard ridge of his cock as it grew more insistent against her hip.

"I've thought about you all day, and tonight," he whispered against her ear. "About leaning you over one of those barstools out there and fucking you from behind. Or laying you across the table and eating your pussy until you scream."

Her legs trembled as she picked up images of him doing those things to her. She wanted that, wanted him to take her in so many different ways. Her nipples tightened, tingled with need as he flicked one with his fingers, then rolled it, pinched it.

"Do you like to have your nipples sucked, Shadoe?"

"Yes."

"Soft and gentle, or harder?"

"Hard." She could barely speak. Her throat had gone dry, but between her legs, she was wet. So wet.

Spence parted her robe and slid his hand across her hip. She shuddered at the contact of his palm on her skin.

"Shhh, relax, baby. I'm going to make you come. I'm going to touch your pussy, pet your clit, and shove my fingers inside you until you come for me."

Oh, God. He really meant to do that, didn't he? "Spence, I . . . I have to . . ."

"You don't have to do anything but relax and let me take care of you."

He gripped her hip, pushed against her, let her feel his cock. She remembered last night, how it felt inside her, filling her, and oh, she wanted that again. She wanted *him* again, in so many different ways. But this . . . this was erotic, naughty. Anyone could come through those doors, including Brandon. What would he think? Would she be fired?

Her clit quivered. The thrill of the forbidden.

"Do it," she begged. "Make me come, Spence."

It wouldn't take long. She was already on the verge and he hadn't touched her there yet.

When he did, when he cupped her sex with his huge, calloused hand, she arched against him, rocking her pussy toward his hand.

"Yeah, that's what I like, Shadoe," he whispered, abandoning her stage name. She loved hearing him say her name, loved the way he slid his palm across her naked sex.

"I can smell you. When you go out there tonight, when you shake your pretty cunt in front of all those guys, they'll be able to smell it, too, and know you're mine. They're going to want you, to want to fuck you, but only I'm going to fuck you."

She reached up and twined her arm around the back of his head. "Yes. Only you."

He slid two fingers inside her and she rose on her tiptoes, needing more, needing him deeper.

"You are so wet, Shadoe. So hot and tight. I want my dick inside you."

"Spence." She wanted that, too.

"Later tonight I'm going to fuck you hard until I come."

She closed her eyes, oblivious now to anything but the pleasure he gave her, his fingers stroking her hard and fast toward an orgasm she craved more than the air she breathed. And when it hit, she shrieked, the sound muffled by the loud music beyond the doors. Her pussy gripped his fingers in a tight vise as she rode a blasting climax that left her shaking and disoriented.

It was Spence who withdrew, turned her around and pulled her robe together, then tilted her chin back and kissed her. "Now go get dressed and relax. And remember, you're mine to fuck later."

She shuddered at the powerful confidence in his voice, her mind awash in visuals of the two of them alone later.

She already wished it was later.

She nodded and walked on unsteady legs back to the dressing room, wondering if it showed on her face when she went through the doors.

No one paid any attention to her, fortunately. She cleaned up and fixed her hair and makeup, then grabbed a bottle of water and took a couple long swallows before letting out a very satisfied breath.

Wow. Spence was a genius. She wasn't only relaxed now, she was a quivering pile of Jell-O. Tension gone. She smiled and went to grab her costume, ready to take on her job as headliner.

eleven

BY THE TIME SPENCE FOUND A SPOT TO STAND NEAR THE STAGE, the club was jammed solid. He even recognized a few of the guys from the docks today.

Good. Shadoe would be happy to know her efforts hadn't been wasted.

And hopefully she was more relaxed now.

Though he was wound up tighter than a string on a bow after what went down in the darkened hall. Her scent still lingered on him and the way she shuddered and came apart was burned into his memory. He'd gotten his erection under control, but he'd had to do some serious thinking about math and fishing to get it there.

Now he was going to have to watch her strip.

This was going to be a test of his endurance.

He noticed AJ and Pax had moved to a table near the stage.

Assholes. Pax lifted his gaze and winked. Spence's arms were crossed and he lifted a middle finger. AJ grinned, then turned his attention to the girl currently dancing on the stage, a long-legged, dark-skinned beauty named Elan, if Spence remembered her name right. She had lush, slow moves that were meant to seduce.

All the girls had some kind of special talent, all were decent dancers, and Spence wasn't the least bit interested, which was rare for him. He tended to gravitate toward strippers. They tended to be just like him—not all that interested in permanent relationships, out for a good time, and no strings attached. His kind of woman.

Shadoe? Not that kind of woman at all. She was from a solid family—okay, maybe a broken home, but she had a stable father—military, even. Good schools, great job, a future ahead of her. She had goals and ambitions and none of those included stripping or fucking around with no strings attached.

So what was the attraction? Something about her seemed just a little bit lost. She reminded him of someone, but he couldn't put his finger on who. He just felt . . . close to her, a kinship. There was definitely an attraction. He wanted her, but then, he loved fucking women, so desiring her didn't surprise him.

The music had stopped after the last dancer, and the stage went dark. Men crowded all around, eager to see the headliner. He hoped Shadoe had stayed relaxed enough, because the front end of the club was wall-to-wall guys.

"Ladies and gentlemen, your attention please," the deejay announced. "From Dallas, Texas, let's give it up for Desi!"

The lights hit the stage opening just as the sound of revving motorcycle engines—loud and heavy on the throttle—shot through the speakers. Smoke poured from the floor and filled the stage. Her music queued up and *Desi* burst through the door.

Spence stopped breathing. She wore a floor-length black leather duster, buttoned at the top but the bottom flapped back as she walked. She had on those fuck-me thigh-high boots that made his throat go dry. When she got to the front of the stage, she jerked the coat open and threw it off, revealing a black leather bra and matching leather boy shorts that barely covered her assets. Both were decorated with silver studs just like a bike seat. When she turned around to shake her ass, emblazoned on the back of the shorts was the name *Desi* in silver studs across her butt. The lights shined right down on her perfectly rounded butt cheeks, which looked even better encased in tight black leather.

Goddamn. He didn't think he'd ever seen so many guys not yelling and catcalling. They were as stunned as he was. No one moved—except Shadoe. Her hips swung from side to side as she bent her knees and swayed down to the floor, touching her fingers there. She searched the crowd, seemingly making eye contact with everyone, but he knew she looked for him. She found him, smiled, winked, then threw her head back and laughed like she was having the time of her life. Then she raised up and shimmied around the stage in a frenetic dance, using every part of her body to move.

The club woke up, especially when Shadoe gave a high kick, leaped, and grabbed the pole, doing a double swing around it. They went wild.

She had them in the palm of her hand then, and she knew it. He caught her smirk, the gleam in her eye. She pulled off the bra, then the boy shorts, leaving her in only her black leather G-string. She shook her stuff, prancing around the stage like she owned it.

And for three minutes, Spence believed her to be the headliner she was. She was confident, in charge, and sexy as hell.

She rocked it. Money flew all over the stage, and when she finished, the floor was covered in bills. The bouncers had to keep guys from clamoring onto the stage after her, especially when she crawled over to them and cocked her hip toward them so they'd tuck money in her G-string.

She owned every man in the joint.

Hell, she'd owned *him* during that dance. And he wanted to tear apart every guy who thought he had a chance with her. Even AJ and Pax had been riveted, their mouths open as they watched Shadoe with lust in their eyes. He'd seen the way they looked at her. He knew those guys, knew their sexual needs. If they even thought for a second—

No way was *that* going to happen. Not with Shadoe. Not ever. Primal instinct had kicked in and he wanted to pull every man away from the stage and shout that the woman up there was his.

Fuck. What was wrong with him? He snapped his gaze back to Shadoe. Her gaze had found his again and he read the desire in her eyes, the slight smile meant only for him.

The song ended, the stage went black, and Spence realized his hands were clenched into fists.

Now who was tense? Beads of sweat trickled down his temple. He swept them away and went to the bar to get a beer, downing half of it in a couple swallows.

AJ sidled up to the bar next to him. It was crowded and noisy and no one paid attention to the two of them.

"Goddamn, that was hot," AJ said, taking the beer the bartender gave him before turning around to face the stage.

Spence didn't say anything. AJ arched a brow. "You screwing her yet? Because if not . . ."

"Fuck off."

AJ's lips lifted. "Guess you are. Too bad." He tilted the beer bottle to his lips and walked away.

Asshole. AJ and Pax could just go find another woman willing to play their game of threesome.

Spence whirled around at the sound of cheers and clapping. Shadoe had walked through the door . . . or rather, Desi had. She was dressed in a white minidress that cut high on her thighs and scooped in around her breasts in halter fashion, tight and low. She wore white stiletto heels, so she was definitely dressed the part.

He moved over to the doorway where she stood, crowded in by eager new fans. Two of the Wild Rose bodyguards had already taken position on either side of her to keep her from being rushed by the guys.

Spence muscled in, much to the irritation of the crowd. He elbowed more than a few of them in his efforts to get to her.

"Hey, that's my bodyguard," she said, motioning for them to let Spence through.

She smiled when he made his way to her side. He felt like ten times an idiot for not being backstage to accompany her out. It was time to remember his cover and stop thinking with his dick.

He took her chin between his fingers and tilted her face up to press a kiss to her lips. "Nice job," he murmured before he straightened.

"Thanks." Her smile widened, then she looped her arm in his and made her way through the throng.

"Give the lady some breathing space and she'll have time to visit with everyone," Spence said.

They backed away and the bouncers ahead of them cleared a path. One of them turned to her. "We've set up a table for you in the back. Looks like you're going to be busy for a while."

Shadoe pushed her hair away from her face. "Wow. It certainly seems that way, doesn't it? And thanks."

She took a seat at the long black table and it didn't take seconds for about six guys to sit down with her, their faces eager.

What? Did they expect her to strip at the table? Not fucking likely.

"How about a drink?" she finally asked.

At least she knew what to do.

They fell over themselves getting a drink for her. Spence rolled his eyes. The next hour went that way, while Spence took up position behind her, watching for anyone who got too close or thought they could put his hands on her. Typically his glare would put anyone off, but the few brave ones who pushed their luck got removed in a hurry.

Shadoe left after the first hour so she could take a break before her second show at one. He led her to the bar and she took a seat at the end spot.

"Feel okay?"

She grinned. "I feel great."

"You should. You're the star tonight."

Her lashes dipped before she tilted her head to look at him. "I don't know about that, but wow, it sure was way more than I expected."

"You did a great job. You were hot."

Her smile hit him right in the balls. "I'm glad you thought so."

"Everyone thought so."

"But I'm glad *you* thought so."

He lifted his hand to the back of her neck again. "Your tension seems to be gone."

Her body vibrated with her laugh. "Yes. You did a fine job taking care of that. Thanks."

"My pleasure."

She laid her palm against his cheek. "I'll see to your pleasure. Later."

His nostrils flared. He leaned into her. "You make my dick hard."

"I hope so."

Her second act was as good, if not better, than the first. Like the show in Dallas, she wore the leather with the fringe and drove the guys into an even higher-pitched frenzy.

There was no doubt about it—Desi was a hit.

"She's rockin' hot as hell," Brandon said to him after Shadoe finished up her second act.

"That she is."

"You are one lucky man."

"That I am."

"I'll bet you stay busy keeping all the guys away from her."

"Yes."

"You trust her?"

He snapped his gaze to Brandon's inquisitive face. "What does that mean?"

Brandon raised his hands. "Simple question. A lot of the girls get swelled heads from all the attention. The boyfriend thing rarely lasts."

"We've been together . . . awhile. We're doing just fine."

"Okay. Just checking."

"You looking for a date, Brandon? Because if it's with my woman, we're going to have a problem." He couldn't believe he was even having this conversation. Spence typically didn't give a shit how many guys a girl dated. He wasn't around one long enough to find out, or to care.

Even though this was his cover and nothing more, Brandon's suggestion and innuendo pissed him off.

"Not at all, man. Just making conversation, trying to get to know one of my dancers. I'm not interested in her, trust me." Brandon did a double-time backpedal, then made excuses to hurry off and head back to his office.

Good thing, because owner or no, Spence was seconds from connecting his fist to Brandon's face.

Which wouldn't do much good for the mission, would it? He had to keep this from getting personal, on a lot of fronts.

Once again, Shadoe came out, this time dressed in some hot green skirt and belly-baring top that clung tight to her curves. She took her table and let the guys come to her, and they did, in droves. Spence stood guard over her while she was gracious and friendly and kept them drinking, which would probably make Brandon really happy.

This part of it was fine, as long as the guys didn't touch.

Touching the girls was off-limits, especially a headliner. You could look, you could talk to them, but you couldn't touch. There were always some guys who thought those rules didn't apply to them, like the one sitting beside Shadoe right now. Slick, a little older, Spence pegged him right away as a regular, someone who knew all the girls, as well as all the employees at the club. He probably got granted "special favors," like opportunities to visit one-on-one with the headliners.

In fact, the guy nodded to one of the bouncers as soon as he took his seat next to Shadoe, and the bouncer nodded back and moved toward Spence. No doubt his intent was to distract Spence so the slick dude could put his moves on Shadoe.

Spence had been working the grift longer than anyone. He knew the game. But he let the bouncer move up next to him, just to see how he planned to play it.

"Your woman is popular."

Spence nodded. "She always has been, even before she became a headliner."

"Piss you off, having all these guys hang on her?"

"I know where she sleeps at night."

The bouncer turned to him. "I'm Lance."

"Spence." He didn't take his gaze off Shadoe.

"My wife dances here."

That got his attention. "Yeah? Who?"

"Cheri. Tall blonde."

"Oh yeah. Pretty."

Lance nodded. "She's lead dancer here."

"And how long have you two been together?"

"Five years. We've been at the Wild Rose for three."

"Work together all the time?"

"Hell yeah. I need to keep an eye on my investment."

His investment? Like his wife was property? What a dickhead.

Shadoe coughed and his gaze went immediately to her. He crouched down, certain he was going to have to pummel the asshole sitting next to her.

"What's up, babe?"

"Remind me later to tell you something," she whispered in his ear.

"You got it." To make a point, he gave her a deep kiss, lingering longer than necessary. When he pulled back, her eyes were glazed and she gave him a promising smile and sigh.

He straightened and Lance was still there.

"What was that all about?"

"Just keeping an eye on my investment," he said, tossing Lance's words back at him.

Whatever was going on between Lance and the guy sitting next to Shadoe, it never materialized. But maybe that's because Spence moved off to Shadoe's right and made eye contact with the guy. Unpleasant eye contact. Long enough and hard enough that the guy grew uncomfortable and left the table. Soon after that, Lance left, too.

By three in the morning he'd had all he could take of guys jockeying for position to be near Shadoe. She'd left the table and wandered around for a while, visiting with people at each of the tables and at the bar, but the crowds finally began to thin.

"Let's get out of here," he said.

She nodded. "I'm more than ready for that. Let me go change."

He was ready, too—to get Shadoe alone. Watching her parade

around in tight clothes, and then strip twice, had him hot, hard, and bothered as hell. By the time she came out the back door, he had the bike engine revving.

She cocked a brow and climbed on. "You in a hurry?"

"Yes. Get on."

She did, and he broke speed records getting back to the hotel.

She leaned in and wrapped her arms around him, her breasts pressing against his back.

"You *are* in a hurry, aren't you? You need something?"

When he didn't answer, she moved her hands down over his ribs. "I know what you need." She laid her hands on his thighs and squeezed. "I wish I could reach your cock from here."

He groaned and hit the throttle, rocketing them through the stoplight. Good thing the hotel was only a couple blocks away. He pulled into the parking garage, took her hand, and pulled her along back up to their room, not saying a word.

He couldn't speak, his throat as tight as his balls. He slid the key card into the door slot and held the door open for her. She walked in and he shut the door behind them, watching her as she dropped her bag, then sauntered out onto the balcony. She cast him a knowing look over her shoulder, a glimpse of a smile, then disappeared through the double doors.

He followed. She stood there bathed in the moonlight, visible for anyone to see.

"Out here?"

She nodded.

He wasn't going to ask twice. He walked farther out onto the balcony and grasped her wrist, pulled her into the darkness, then flipped her around, slammed her back into the wall, and put his mouth over hers.

She wrapped her arms around him. Her lips latched on to his with a hungry passion that matched his own, surprising him with its power. He expected her to be tired, to say no, to at least be surprised by his assault, not to equal his need.

But she did. She wrapped a leg around his hip and rocked her pelvis against him.

His cock was already hard, had been from the minute he'd tasted her mouth. Now it was a raging desire that couldn't be stopped. He stripped off her shirt, glad she hadn't worn a bra. He filled his hands with her breasts, then kneeled on the concrete floor and filled his mouth with her nipples. He'd wanted to taste them for as long as he'd known her, since that first day she'd stripped for him and revealed those tight nipples and perfect breasts. He flicked his tongue over one hard bud, then pulled it into his mouth and sucked. It felt like soft velvet, and she tasted like sweet cream, just like he knew the rest of her would. He couldn't wait to go down on her, needing her flavor against his tongue. He kissed his way down her ribs and her belly, jerking at the zipper of her jeans, fumbling it like he had back when he was a teenager and inexperienced. God, how old was he, anyway? And why were his hands shaking? This wasn't his first time. He should be suave about this, not in a hurry at all, but taking his time getting to know her body.

Yeah, right. He yanked her jeans down to her ankles, pulled her panties off, and covered her sex with his mouth.

She moaned, and her body jerked as his tongue found her clit. She tangled her fingers in his hair and grasped it in her fist, holding tight while he sucked the little bud, nibbled it with his teeth, licked her all over, and slid his tongue inside her creamy pussy.

"Jesus, Spence. That's just so . . . Oh, oh, I'm coming." She bucked against his face and shuddered, crying out with the force of her quick, rushing orgasm.

He really liked to hear and feel her come, to taste the juice rolling onto his tongue from her climax, to know that he brought her there so damn fast she couldn't hold back.

In the darkness, he heard her panting, felt the sheen of sweat on her thighs as he held on to her, continued to kiss her thighs, her hip bone, making his way back up her body.

He kissed her breasts again, loving the way they fit into his mouth, the way her nipples hardened when he sucked them, the way her heart beat erratically against his hand as he held on to her.

He met her mouth with his in a hungry kiss, ready to swoop her into his arms and carry her to bed. But when he pulled her away from the wall, she turned him around and pushed him against the cool brick.

"My turn," she said, her voice a dark, husky whisper. "Do you think I'm going to miss the opportunity to stay outside a little longer?"

"I think you're an exhibitionist."

Her lips tilted. "Maybe I am."

She didn't seem to mind being naked on the balcony. Maybe she wanted people to see them. His cock jerked against his pants. Yeah, he was in a hurry to be inside her. Whether it was on the balcony, in the bed, or on the floor, he didn't care.

She lifted his shirt off, her hands everywhere—across his shoulders, his neck, his chest—and all followed by her sweet, hot mouth. She kissed him with wild abandon, bit him, tasted him, licked at his nipples and sucked at them the way he'd suckled hers. He shuddered as the sensation shot straight to his cock, making it quiver in anticipation.

"Shadoe."

She ignored his warning plea, dropped to her knees the same way he had done. "I've wanted to do this." She opened the button of his jeans, and with damned slow movements drew the zipper down, her fingers brushing his erection and making him grit his teeth. She pulled his jeans over his hips and to the floor.

"I love a man who goes commando," she said, burying her face against his hip, biting him there, then licking along his hip bone, heading to his crotch. "God, you smell good." She licked his inner thigh, making his legs shake.

Spence was a strong guy, but Shadoe made him weak in the knees. No woman had ever made his legs shake before. But when she grasped his cock in her hand and stroked him, he palmed the wall for support. And when she swirled her thumb over the crest, he had to bite down on his lip to keep from moaning.

When she placed her lips over his cockhead and took him inside her mouth, he let out a groan, knowing he was at her mercy.

She slid his shaft along the wet heat of her tongue, using her hand to stroke and guide her movements, closing her lips over him to create a perfect suction. Farther and farther in, then out, she sucked and stroked him, and now he wished they were inside, bathed in light so he could watch her. Instead, all he could do was feel the soft glide of his dick along her tongue, the grip of her lips as she squeezed the crest before taking him deep again, all the way to the back of her throat.

Then she swallowed, and he wanted to drop to the floor and die right then. She had him literally by the balls. He was hers for the taking.

She tilted her head back, her mouth filled with his cock, her warm brown eyes dark with desire.

"Yeah, baby, suck me." He reached down and grabbed her hair, twisted it around his hand, and used it to guide her, to fuck her mouth with gentle thrusts.

She took everything he gave her, and then some, cupping his balls and massaging them until he knew he had no hope of holding back. He felt it churning deep inside him, ready to erupt like a boiling volcano.

When she hummed, it was a vibration in his balls and he couldn't hold it in any longer.

"I'm going to come in your mouth, Shadoe. You want that?"

She only pushed forward to take more of him, held on to his hips, and took away the last ounce of his control. The blast nearly launched him off his feet, sending shots of light behind his eyes as he erupted into her mouth. He pulled on her hair, holding her in place while he shot a stream of hot come into her willing throat. She dug her nails into him, which only added to the white-hot pleasure jettisoning from within him. He gave her all he had, until he was limp and sweaty and utterly astounded by this woman on her knees before him.

He bent down and lifted her, kissed her, tasting himself on her lips. That made him linger at her mouth, slide his tongue inside to lick at hers, intensifying the flavor. Despite what he'd just been through, his cock jumped at the taste of her, the mingling of her flavor and his in their mouths.

He was ready for more. Was she? He rolled his thumb over her nipple. It was hard.

"Did it excite you to suck me?"

"It made my pussy wet, Spence. Fuck me."

He didn't need to be told twice. He kicked off his boots and discarded his jeans, then scooped her into his arms and carried her into the bedroom.

SHADOE'S ENTIRE BODY VIBRATED. BEING HELD BY SPENCE AS HE carried her to the bed was thrilling. Making him come, having his cock in her mouth, and being in control like that was something she'd never experienced—had never wanted to before. But with Spence, oh, how she'd wanted to.

Ever since she'd taken the stage tonight for the first time, had seen his heated gaze when she'd made eye contact with him, she'd known he wanted her. But it was more than that. It was the way he looked at her, burning a hole through her skin with his eyes, possessing her as his gaze raked over her.

Spence was one gorgeous man. As soon as they'd stepped in the club, the other girls had zeroed in on him, looked him up and down in feminine appreciation. She knew the feeling, and it had only increased when she stood on stage tonight and met his eyes.

What an incredible, empowering feeling had come over her at that moment. To be desired by a man like Spence was amazing. She didn't understand it, couldn't explain it, but damn had she ever been turned on. And it had lasted throughout the night. Her giddiness had nothing to do with wowing the crowd. She couldn't care less about that. She'd done well on stage because she'd played to Spence and him alone. No one else had existed for her.

Just like no other man existed for her right now, except the one who held her, his powerful arms bulging with muscle. So strong, so capable of such violence, and yet he laid her so tenderly on the bed, and followed her down there to lay a kiss on her that left her without breath, without words.

She didn't need words. Neither of them did. Not when they had hands and mouths and their bodies to speak with. He stripped off her boots and jeans—she giggled at how they hung from her ankles—and spread her legs, placing his fingers around her ankles to hold her in place.

"Do you think I'm going to try to escape?" she asked, propping herself up on her elbows.

"I just want to look at you."

He'd turned on the bedside lamp. Soft, filtered light filled the room. Not enough to be glaring, but enough so they could see each other. Right now he looked straight on at her sex. It made her quiver.

"I love the way you taste, Shadoe." He crawled between her legs and took a long, slow lick of her pussy.

She watched him, mesmerized by his tongue. "I love the way you lick me."

"I like making you come."

She was rather embarrassed by that. "For some reason, you make it easy. It's not always that way."

He cocked a brow. "Really."

"Really."

Then his lips lifted. "Good."

Men and their egos.

Now that they'd both had an orgasm, the sense of urgency had worn off—somewhat, anyway. But this was also the first time she'd gotten to see him naked. And oh, man, was he something.

"Stand up by the bed," she said.

"What?"

"I want to look at you."

He laughed, but complied.

His body was massive, all lean muscle, no fat. Wide shoulders, narrow waist, strong thighs, and a really impressive cock. A cock that apparently liked being looked at, because it hardened while she watched. She lifted her gaze to his.

"That's interesting."

"I was hoping you'd think so." His cock rose, then bobbed up and down.

She laughed and scrambled off the bed to walk around him, laying her hand over the tattoo on his shoulder blade. She kissed the eagle and the word *Freedom*, then laid her head on his back and wrapped her arms around him.

"Shadoe."

"Yeah."

"What are you doing?"

"Holding you."

"Why?"

What a question. "Because you feel good."

"Oh."

He turned around and she tilted her head back to look at him. His eyes were mesmerizing. So hard, so blue, so sexy. The man was just one huge ball of intensity.

And right now, he was all hers.

"You going to stand there and ogle me all night, woman, or are we gonna fuck?"

And the way he talked to her—no bullshit—always saying what was on his mind. Even that turned her on. "I think we're going to fuck."

"Good." He pushed her on the bed, reached down, grabbed a condom from his jeans, and crawled after her. "I need to be inside you. My dick is hard and has been all night, ever since you pranced out onto the stage."

She lay on her back and placed her feet flat on the bed, raised her knees, teasing him by spreading her legs. "I think you were hard before I 'pranced' onto the stage."

He rested his hands on her knees. "You're right. Making you come gets me hard. Did you like that?"

Remembering the way he got her off in the darkened hallway made her juices flow, her clit quiver. "You know I did."

"I'll do that for you every night before your show."

"God, Spence. You make me wet."

"Wet is good." He dropped down between her legs and slid inside her with one thrust.

Shadoe gasped, then arched against him, meeting his thrust with a desperate need to feel him buried deeper. He cupped one hand underneath her and lifted her, driving her clit against his shaft, splintering her as he rode her with relentless power.

He sought to dominate, to control. She'd never been one to give up power in the bedroom. With Spence, though, it didn't matter. He mastered her and she didn't question it. She needed it, craved it.

She gave up everything but the sensations, the way he moved inside her, dragging his cock against her most sensitive spots, knowing exactly where to touch her, to kiss her, to bring out the most pleasure from her body. He'd pull out halfway, then slide back in, hitting her G-spot at the same time his shaft rubbed her clit.

No man knew her body this well, how she'd react, where the areas were to drive her crazy. Spence did. She looked at him, watched the way he seemed to concentrate on the points that drove her to the brink. He focused on her, on what she needed.

Astounding.

It didn't take her long at all to find a climax again, shattering like fragile glass, her body pulsing like the hard beat at a nightclub. But Spence wouldn't let her come down from that high, instead continuing to fuck her, this time harder, faster. He picked up his own rhythm and took her there again, digging his fingers into the soft flesh of her buttocks as he pushed himself deep.

"Spence."

"Yeah, baby, I know."

He did know. He kissed her with depth, tightened his hold, and ground against her. She felt him everywhere and came again, cried out his name as she fell and this time took him along for the ride.

She felt like she was on a softly floating cloud, barely registering anything in the realm of reality. Spence pulled out and left the bed only for a moment, then gathered her against him and wrapped his arm around her, kissed the back of her neck, his warm breath against her hair.

She couldn't remember ever feeling so content as she drifted off to sleep.

TWELVE

SPENCE SAT IN A CHAIR AND NURSED A CUP OF COFFEE, watching Shadoe sleep. Her hair had fallen over her eyes. The sheet covered only the lower half of her body, giving him a great view of her naked back. Her arms were raised so he had a nice peek at the side of one breast.

He leaned back in the chair and wished he were a painter or a great photographer. He'd like to have that picture preserved forever.

Christ, now he was waxing poetic. Hardly his style, but this was what she'd reduced him to—watching her sleep and musing about her face and body. If the guys could see him now, they'd laugh.

He'd known Shadoe only a few days, and in that time something had happened to him. Something kind of profound.

He felt something for her. She was his match sexually—wild and untamed and game for anything, with no reservations. Her passions were boundless. He liked that in a woman. She had no ulterior motives, wasn't clingy, just seemed to enjoy having sex with him. What man wouldn't love that about a woman?

But she'd made no claims on him, hadn't asked him what was going to happen between them in the future. Last night after they'd had sex, she curled up next to him and passed right out, hadn't needed words or anything between them.

She was just like a man, except she was all woman.

He was starting to think he'd miss her when this case was over, and he didn't like thinking that way. He liked going separate ways with a woman after the fun and games had ended. He didn't want to think about "after," and what that meant. He didn't do relationships.

Relationships led to ties, ties led to marriage, and marriage led to bringing kids into the world. Having kids meant responsibility, taking care of someone other than yourself. His parents had failed miserably at that. Spence had done a good job at being a free spirit his entire life. He intended to keep it that way, not run the risk of fucking up some kids' lives like his parents had done.

"You look deep in thought, and how long have you been staring at me?"

He hadn't even realized Shadoe was awake. "A while."

"It's creepy. Or maybe really nice." She pushed her hair out of her face and sat up, mindless of her breasts out for his view as she shoved a pillow against the headboard to lean on. She inhaled. "And is that coffee?"

"Yeah. I got one for you. It's probably still hot." He passed her one of the containers.

"You satisfy all my cravings. Thank you."

He smiled at that, and watched her take a deep drink of the dark liquid, then lick her bottom lip. His cock twitched, and he resisted the groan. It seemed everything she did—even the simple act of drinking coffee—made his dick hard.

"How long have you been up?"

"An hour or so."

She looked over at the clock on the nightstand. "Oh, God, it's almost eleven already."

"You keep late hours as a stripper."

She snorted. "Yeah, right. This whole gig is going to throw off my schedule. I'm an early riser. I jog before dawn every day."

"Not while you're on this case."

She lifted her shoulders and rolled her head from side to side. "So what's on the agenda for today?"

"Last night you wanted me to remind you to tell me something."

"Oh, yeah. That bouncer who stood by you talking while I was sitting at the table?"

"Yeah?"

"That was the guy I saw on the docks yesterday."

"Lance?"

"I guess so."

"Interesting. He's also married to Cheri, who he said is the lead dancer there."

Shadoe wrinkled her nose. "She's a bitch and a half."

He laughed. "Some of them are."

"I don't think she was very happy that I came in to steal her thunder."

"I saw her dance. You have nothing to worry about."

"Well, thanks for that. But tell me about Lance."

"He wanted to distract me, I think, so one of the customers could put the moves on you."

"Yeah, I had a couple like that. I took care of them before

they got out of hand or before you had to step in to break their arm."

"Too bad. I might have enjoyed that." He didn't like anyone touching her. Dammit, he didn't like that it bothered him, either.

"Next time I'll give you a heads-up, then."

"I think we should keep our eyes on Lance."

She laid the coffee cup on the nightstand. "You think he might be involved somehow in the drug dealings?"

"I don't know. Something about Lance bugged me."

"Well, I know Cheri bugged me, but it could be just her personality. I can work on the girls, try and get to know them better, see what I can find out. The dancers usually know exactly what's going on inside a club."

"Okay. Brandon asked me about you last night, too."

"He did? What did he say?"

"He asked about you and me, about our relationship. I think he wanted to know how tight we were, if there might be room for him."

She arched a brow. "Are you serious?"

"Yeah. Some guys aren't so possessive of their ladies."

"That's . . . interesting." She couldn't keep the worry out of her voice.

"Don't worry about it. I don't share what's mine."

She tilted her head to the side and studied him. "Good to know. Since I'm not interested in being shared. It's really an incestuous group in that industry, isn't it?"

"It can be. Some are very loyal. Most aren't. It might make our jobs easier if they all have loose lips."

"Would it make our jobs easier if *we* weren't so tight?"

He took a long swallow of coffee. "What do you mean?"

"What if we weren't so close to each other, but . . . branched out a bit. Do you think that would allow us to gather information more easily?"

"You mean act as if we're open to the idea of seeing other people."

"Yes."

He had to force himself to remember this was a case. They weren't really a couple. He had no claim on Shadoe. She could fuck every guy at the Wild Rose if she wanted to in order to gain information, even if the thought of it made his gut twist.

"What do you think we'll gain by doing that?"

She shrugged. "I don't know. It was just a suggestion."

"I'll consider it." *When hell freezes over.*

"Okay."

He stood. "I'm going to take a shower. Then we can get something to eat."

Shadoe watched Spence close the bathroom door. She picked up the coffee and took a few sips, pondering their conversation, which had both confused and enlightened her.

Waking up and finding Spence sitting beside the bed staring at her had made her feel warm, cared for. Actually, it had turned her on. He'd been studying her. She'd opened her eyes and peeked at him through the veil of her hair covering her face. He'd been lost in thought, his gaze focused on her face.

He could have thought anywhere. On the balcony, at the desk, even downstairs in the lounge. Instead, he'd sat beside the bed to look at her. A woman would have to be crazy not to be flattered by that. Her first thought had been to drag him back into bed with her for a repeat of last night.

Until he'd launched right into mission mode. Too bad. But she'd gone there with him, and then she'd made the suggestion about pulling off the act of being available to others, and she'd noticed the storm flare up in his eyes.

Spence was jealous. She allowed a small smile of triumph over that. She couldn't recall ever having a guy jealous over her. This was a first and she'd decided to revel in it for a few minutes. Oh, he'd done a fine job of trying to cover it up, but she was a woman and a woman could read a jealousy signal from miles away. He didn't turn down the idea because he thought it was a bad one—he'd turned it down because he didn't like the thought of her playing with another guy.

Maybe they were only together for the duration of this mission, but while they were together, he wanted it to be just the two of them. And that meant no touching by other guys.

Her smile widened. She couldn't help it—it felt good to be desired. And protected, even though she didn't need to be. She was a trained field agent and could take care of herself, but this wasn't at all like he was trying to keep her safe. He was trying to keep her to himself, which was something entirely different.

Something she liked. Something that made her stomach tumble and gave her a warm feeling all over.

She wasn't sure she knew what to do with these growing feelings for a man who obviously didn't know what to do with them either. He was clearly in denial over how he felt about her. She honestly wasn't sure how she felt, either.

The sex, of course, was phenomenal. She wouldn't mind continuing that. But she also knew herself. She wasn't indiscriminate about sexual relationships. She wasn't a party girl who went out and had sex with random guys without getting involved.

Involved being the operative word. And that's what scared her. The same thing probably scared Spence, too.

Though it shouldn't, since they couldn't really get involved. When this assignment was over, she was going back to D.C. to resume her career, to get her next assignment, which would take her heaven only knew where in the world. And Spence? He would go back to Dallas, to Wild Riders' headquarters, and get his next assignment from General Lee, which would lead him somewhere around the country, too.

They'd never see each other again. They worked for two different branches of the government, and lived in two different states when they weren't working. Neither one of them had careers that were set up for relationships, so even though they'd enjoyed their time together, Shadoe knew they both realized this was nothing more than an affair—something finite. It would end.

The problem was, she didn't know how to have an affair. Maybe Spence was better at it than she was, knew how to handle it without getting involved. She'd dated a bit here and there in college, had a few sexual flings over the years, but nothing that would qualify as a relationship. She'd had goals and ambitions, and falling in love would have gotten in the way.

Spence didn't seem the falling-in-love type.

What a pair they made. Maybe that's why they got along so well together. It would be easy enough for her to stop dreaming about a happily-ever-after with Spence when she knew up-front there wasn't going to be one.

Not that she'd been thinking along those lines, of course.

She took her shower after Spence came out, passing him without a word. She pondered that while she showered, musing that in the light of day they seemed so . . . separate. Like actual partners on this mission, while at night they were more like lovers.

No wonder she was confused as hell. After her shower she did her hair and makeup and got dressed and went in search of Spence, who was sitting outside on the balcony. She took a seat next to him, blowing out a breath at the wicked heat and humidity that already made her feel like she needed another shower. The sun burned bright and hot overhead, not a cloud in the sky and no breeze to provide any cooling relief. Today was going to be blistering.

"Agenda?" she asked when he didn't say anything.

"Nothing, really. Not until we hit the club tonight. Maybe we'll go in early and mingle with the bouncers and the dancers, see what we can dig out of them."

She nodded. "Time for me to get friendly."

He slanted his gaze her way, looking utterly sexy wearing dark sunglasses. "With the girls, you mean."

She propped her feet up on the balcony railing. "You're kind of possessive with your women, aren't you?"

He turned his head to stare out over the balcony. "Don't know what you're talking about."

"You made it clear you don't want me fraternizing with other men. Are you always like this with women you fuck?"

He paused for a few seconds before answering. "No."

Honesty. Interesting. "Then why are you like that with me?"

"Because you're different than most women I fuck."

"How?"

"I don't know. Just . . . different."

She tried to keep her smile at bay, but couldn't. "I see."

"What do you think you see?"

"Nothing. Are you as confused about our relationship as I am, Spence?"

"We don't have a relationship, Shadoe. We're having sex. It's great sex. We're mission partners. When the mission is over, the partnership and the sex will end."

She wouldn't be hurt by that unemotional statement, because she knew he was trying to convince himself as much as her. "That's what I keep telling myself. So why does it feel like more than that?"

"Maybe it does to you."

"And maybe it does to you, too." She stood. "I'm hungry. Let's go grab something to eat."

She left him on the balcony, refusing to turn around to see if he'd follow. If he didn't, she intended to eat downstairs at the restaurant. She didn't care. She was hungry and she wasn't going to wait around to see what kind of mood he was in.

By the time she opened the door to the room, he was on her heels to close it behind them both. She marched to the elevator and jammed the button.

"You're in kind of a snit this morning."

The doors whooshed open. She stepped inside and jammed the *Lobby* button. "I'm not in a snit."

"Yeah, you are. What's bugging you?"

She stared straight ahead. "You are."

"Why's that?"

"I don't know." Yes, she did.

"As far as I know I haven't done anything—yet this morning—to piss you off."

She turned to him. "Denial, Spence. This whole thing between you and me is just as confusing for me as it is for you. I know we don't have a future together."

The doors opened and two couples stood there.

"I know it's just sex between us."

She turned to the couples gaping at her. "Wait for the next one. I'm talking here."

They stared, wide-eyed, while Shadoe leaned in and pressed the button to close the elevator doors. She tilted her head up to Spence, who had started smiling. When she glared, he held up his hands in surrender.

"You're on a roll. I'm not about to stop you."

"Yes, there's sex between us. But there's more. I know it and you know it."

"Like what?"

She inhaled, let it out. "I don't know. And that's what makes me crazy. We're so alike, you and I, even though you deny it."

"We're nothing alike."

The doors opened at the lobby. Glad for the fresh air and the space, she walked out and turned to him. "You know, you're absolutely right. We are nothing alike. Because I see the truth where you can't." She walked away.

He grabbed her arm. "Where are you going?"

"I need to be alone."

"No."

"Don't tell me no. You're not my keeper."

He leaned in. "No, but I am your partner."

"Which doesn't mean that I can't go enjoy a meal by myself. Give me some space, Spence. I need some time to myself."

She jerked her arm away and walked out the front doors of the lobby, turned right, and headed up the street, not really knowing where she was going. But it was the French Quarter and restaurants were abundant. Within three blocks, she'd found a little café where she treated herself to a latte and a beignet, which she ate and drank inside the air-conditioned shop at one of the tables by the window. She enjoyed the bustle of tourists walking by as well as the time alone with her own thoughts.

She'd certainly had a classy temper tantrum back at the hotel, hadn't she? And for what purpose? Because Spence didn't see things the same way she did?

That shouldn't come as a surprise to her, because he was right. They weren't alike. They didn't see the world in the same way. They didn't come from the same background. The way she thought about their relationship may be entirely different from the way he thought about it. Which didn't make her right and him wrong.

She was getting too emotional, too wrapped up in thoughts of Spence the man instead of Spence the partner.

That would have to stop.

This was her first mission. She'd have to concentrate on acting more like an agent, and less like a . . . woman.

Exactly the type of thing her father would accuse her of. That she was weak, emotional, that she couldn't possibly hold up to the stresses and strains of a government job like a man could.

Bullshit.

She *could* do it, could separate her emotions from the job. The first thing that would have to go would be the sex. Too bad, because she'd really started to enjoy that part, figured it wasn't harming anyone, wasn't hurting the case, and in fact probably enhanced it. After all, she and Spence were supposed to be lovers. What better way to build on their cover than to actually act like lovers?

But she obviously wasn't going to be able to fuck someone she worked with and keep emotion out of the equation, so the sex was going to have to go out the window in favor of concentrating on her job. The last thing she wanted was to bomb her first assignment and ruin her career, all because she thought with her pussy and her emotions instead of her head.

And if she got any more wrapped up in Spence, that's exactly what might happen.

Firmly resolved to make changes in her relationship with Spence, she finished up the last of her latte and went outside. The rev of a motorcycle engine behind her caught her attention. She turned and saw Spence parked on the corner.

She walked over to him. "Did you follow me?"

"Of course I did. I had to find you after I went to get my bike, but I drove around for a while until I saw you in the window."

This whole resolve thing would be a lot easier if he wasn't always around. And sitting on the bike looking sexy as hell.

"You gonna stand there and stare at me like that, or are you gonna climb on?"

With a sigh, she got on the back of the bike. Spence throttled up and rode them out of the French Quarter, headed out of the downtown area, away from the tall buildings, and across the bridge. The cool air from Lake Pontchartrain provided blissful—if only temporary—relief from the oppressive heat. He took them up north around the lake and into the woods—deep into the woods, where families lived in white trailers nestled alongside one another like refugees.

She knew what they were—survivors of Hurricane Katrina—people who'd lost their homes and everything else. They stayed and were waiting to rebuild. Some waited a very long time.

Spence pulled down a dirt road where broken trees littered the landscape. He turned off the bike, and Shadoe climbed off to take a look around. Nothing along the landscape but trees that looked like they'd been haphazardly scooped up by a giant bulldozer and shoved miles along the dirt, shredding the terrain along the way.

"Why are we here?" she asked, turning to see Spence standing on top of a mound.

"You want to know why we have nothing in common? This is why."

"I don't understand."

"I grew up here."

She whirled around, searching for a house. "Where?"

"Right where you're standing. This used to be a mobile home park. We rented one of those dinky ones. A one-bedroom. Trevor and I slept in the living room on a sofa bed."

She couldn't imagine. "Where is the park now?"

"It got swept away with the flood. Everything's gone."

Her stomach dropped. "How do you know?"

"I came back and worked here for a while afterward. To help

out." He wasn't even looking at her now. "I had to do something. This was my home. Now it's just dirt."

It wasn't just dirt. There were memories that couldn't be washed away. She couldn't even fathom losing your home, everything that had once been your childhood. All those memories, gone in an instant.

She moved to him and laid her hand on his shoulder. He jerked away and pivoted to face her.

"I'm trying to make you understand, Shadoe. This was my life. Dirt as my backyard. No paved sidewalks. Not even my own room. Dogs barking. Crime everywhere. No big yellow school bus. No smiling parents. Nothing like what you had."

Her stomach clutched in pain for the child who had been denied love and tenderness. Despite what he thought . . . she knew. And it was time she shared her side with him.

She found a fallen tree trunk and sat on it. "I had a beautiful home on two acres. I didn't need the big yellow school bus because Daddy always drove me to school. He didn't trust anyone else to do it, and my mother was always off doing . . . something else that she thought more important. When Daddy was on duty or for some reason couldn't take me, Mother had one of the servants take care of me.

"Because Daddy was a high-ranking military officer, security was always an issue. It wasn't like I could play out on the street with other kids. We lived in an isolated area. Our property had fences—tall fences that I couldn't see out of. Only the best for my father, you know. Mother hated it. She wanted to live in the city. She was from New York, a socialite. She'd moved to D.C. after she and my dad married, thinking he'd get out of the military and make a career in law or politics, not realizing that the military was my father's choice of career.

"She thought she could change him. But he came from a strong

military background, one forged by his great-grandfather and followed by his father and his brothers. My mother, though strong-
willed herself, didn't stand a chance in changing a Grayson."

Spence had sat on the dirt in front of her. "And you ended up
in the middle of it all."

She shrugged. "It was fine when I was at school. I managed to
make a few friends."

"Yeah, I know how that is. It only got ugly when you went
home."

"If he made her stay home, she drank. And when she drank,
they argued. He didn't want her to drink. Actually, there were a
lot of things he didn't want her to do." She raised her gaze to his.
"My father had a lot of rules."

"For you, too, I'll bet."

She allowed a smile. "I broke his cardinal rule the day I was
born. I wasn't male. His brothers all had male children. He had a
girl child. And, oh, how they tortured him about that. He never
lived that down. I was his biggest failure and because they never
let *him* forget it, he never let *me* forget it."

Spence picked up her hand. "Most men would be thrilled to
have a daughter."

She laughed. "Marshall Grayson isn't most men. He was always outstanding in everything he did. And he got everything he
wanted."

"Except a son."

She nodded. "He blamed my mother for that, too."

"Uh, doesn't he understand how biology and genetics works?"

"It didn't matter. He wanted to try again for a son, but for
some reason my mother never got pregnant. Personally, I think
she hated him and couldn't bear the thought of having another
child with him. My guess is she took birth control pills and didn't
tell him. I wasn't an easy pregnancy, and of course I ruined her

figure, or so she told me over and over again. She said she'd never want to go through that again."

Spence rubbed her hand with his thumb. "Nice thing to say to a child."

She shrugged. "They never said nice things. I don't really think they were aware what they said, or that words could hurt."

"But they still hurt, didn't they?"

She looked down at the ground. "Yeah, they did. You allow them to hurt you for a while, until you steel yourself against the words they hurl at you so they don't have power over you any longer."

"Why did she leave?"

Her gaze snapped to his. "How do you know that?"

He had the decency to dip his gaze. "I peeked at your file. Figured you had read mine so I wanted to know who I was going to be working with."

She sighed. "Thief."

He grinned. "Well, yeah."

Then she laughed, unable to help herself.

"Go on. Tell me more."

"Things got ugly right after my twelfth birthday. The arguments were growing worse; my mother took more and more trips away. I remember hearing them screaming at each other one night, so I crept out of my room and hid at the top of the stairs. My father said if she was going to be gone all the time, she might as well be gone permanently. Mother said that suited her just fine, but he wasn't going to saddle her with me, because she wanted a fresh start—without a kid as baggage. She was still young, still beautiful, and she could start over again."

"Jesus, Shadoe." Spence got up, moved to the tree trunk, and put his arm around her.

She wanted to shake him off, but she craved the comfort. She hadn't dredged up the ugliness of her past in a long time, had tried to bury it under ambition and school and determination to be the best at whatever she did. She rarely indulged in the pain, and when she did, she was always surprised to find it still as raw as ever. She had hoped time would heal.

It never did.

She leaned into him, unashamed at needing this—at needing him—even if it was only temporary.

"What did your dad say?" he asked.

"He told her to pack up her bags and get out. He'd give her a settlement, but that was all she'd get. She didn't need the money, anyway. Her family had all the money she needed. All she wanted was her freedom. She didn't need anything. Not my dad. Not the life she'd built with him."

It was still hard to say the words. "Not me."

Shit. The tears came despite her refusal to ever shed a tear over the bitch who'd given birth to her, the woman who may have given her life but who had never really wanted her.

Spence folded her into his arms and caressed her hair, whispering against her ear. "It's okay, babe. Let it go."

She clutched his shirt, buried her face against his chest, and sobbed. She cried for what seemed like forever, pouring out the pain she'd held in her heart since she was twelve years old, wondering why the mother she loved had never loved her back.

She didn't have answers then; she didn't now. She never would.

"Sometimes there are no answers," Spence said, seemingly in answer to her unspoken thoughts. "Sometimes people are just really fucked-up, self-absorbed assholes, and their kids pay the price for it."

Shuddering, she sniffed and raised her head, knowing she must look a mess. "Some people shouldn't be allowed to breed."

He smiled. "Amen to that, darlin'." He swiped his thumb under her eyes. "I hate that they hurt you."

"I hate that they hurt you, too."

He shrugged. "I'm a big tough guy. I can take it."

"I'm a big tough girl. So can I. But at one time we were both just kids. And the people who were supposed to love us didn't take care of us like they should." She pushed back from him a bit so she could gather her balance, emotionally. "That's what I've been trying to tell you, Spence. You might have this image of me as the princess in the ivory tower. And granted, I had a roof over my head and a hot meal for dinner every night. I had clothes to wear and a good education, so there's no comparison as far as what you had to endure versus where I came from."

He started to say something, but she stopped him. "Let me finish first, please. What I think makes us alike is the hurt. The raw pain of not being loved when we needed it. Of feeling that maybe we failed somehow, that we didn't deserve it."

She stood and began to pace, needing to get her thoughts in order before she messed this up. "When you opened up to me and told me your story about your childhood, it really hurt me. And the reason it hurt me was because I knew how it felt. No, I didn't know how it felt to go hungry, or to have to resort to running the streets and stealing in order to survive, but I know how it feels to be thought of as less than worthy of love. You may think a lot of things about me, Spence, but you can't take that away from me. I wasn't loved."

He studied her for a few seconds, then stood and went over to her, laying his hands on her shoulders. "It's nothing to wear like a badge of honor, Shadoe."

"We survived it, didn't we? Look where we are in our lives. Look at the careers we have."

"True enough. We're both survivors. We could have each ended up just like those who made us."

"But we haven't, have we?"

"No, darlin'. We haven't."

"We're alike in a lot of ways. And I hate when you push me away and try to go all solitary-man-on-the-mountain on me."

He cocked a brow. "Excuse me?"

"You heard me. You think you're the only one who's ever felt the way you feel. Well, you're not. I hurt, too. I feel lonely, too."

"So what are you trying to say, Shadoe?"

She wrapped her arms around herself, knowing she was losing sight of the big picture, that her emotions were getting the best of her again. "I don't know, exactly. Only that I'm tired of feeling lonely. That I think with you I've found someone who could really understand where I've been and what I feel, and you want to be all tough guy and pretend not to give a shit. And that pisses me off.

"The problem is, you do give a shit. I know you do."

He reached for her face, cupped her cheek. "I can't give you what you need. I'm not that kind of guy."

She shuddered out a sigh. "That's a knee-jerk reaction. I'm not asking for forever, Spence. You and I have futures elsewhere when this case is over. We both know that. But while we're together, couldn't we really be . . . together? Wouldn't it be nice to just have a moment in time where we could both be a little less lonely?"

His eyes were so filled with pain, the pain she felt, too.

Come on, Spence. Just this one time, give in.

"Don't think about it, don't analyze it, and don't put a future stamp on it, because there isn't one. It's just right now, for these couple weeks or however long we have. We're kindred. We understand each other. Let's share each other while we have that time together."

He looked at her, and for the first time, she saw understanding in his eyes.

Then he nodded. "Yeah. You're right. Let's do that." He pulled her into his arms and laid his mouth on hers, brushing his lips across hers in a kiss so tender the tears sprang fresh in her eyes.

This was the moment she wanted. It was all she wanted.

The loneliness evaporated in an instant, just as it always did when Spence held her in his arms.

THIRTEEN

IT HAD BEEN A LOT OF YEARS SINCE SPENCE HAD ALLOWED himself to feel anything emotional. It was always safer to stay closed off. No one could hurt you that way. He'd learned that valuable lesson a long time ago.

But hearing Shadoe's story about her parents—her lunatic bitch of a mother who thought partying and society and her image were more important than raising her own child, and her regimented, idiotic father who thought the gender of one's child actually mattered—it's a wonder Shadoe had ended up as well-adjusted as she seemed to be. She was educated, vibrant, exciting, and any man would be damn lucky to have her in his life.

She could have been really messed up by her childhood. Instead, she'd turned it around and decided to make herself worthwhile, not dependent upon needing a parent's love or approval—though he figured she indirectly sought her father's approval by the line of work she'd chosen. But he wasn't going to get into that with her now.

Not when he held her and her body felt good against his, not when he stood in this place that reminded him of hell, and she felt and smelled like heaven. Not when everything sweet about her could help erase everything horrible about his past.

He inhaled her scent, obliterating the smell of dirt and destruction around him. No one was within miles of this place—no one came here anymore. They were completely alone.

He let his hand drift down her back and deepened the kiss. His intent in dragging her into his arms hadn't been sexual—not initially anyway. He'd only wanted to comfort her. But as usual, getting within close proximity of Shadoe, breathing her in, made him want to be inside her.

She moaned against his lips, her hands roamed over his shoulders and down his arms, reaching for his fingers. Her grip was strong, her intention clear.

She wanted this as much as he did, this joining they both often seemed so desperate for.

He pulled away. "You sure? Here?"

She nodded. "Yes. Now."

She was right—they were alike in a lot of ways, especially the need for sex without caring where they were or who might see them. He really liked that about her.

"Hang on."

He had a blanket in the bag on his bike. He grabbed it and spread it out on the small patch of grass in the shade, then lay down on it. "Come here."

She came down on top of him and he brushed her hair away from her face, brought her mouth to his, and tasted her, slid his tongue inside to capture and tangle with hers. He hooked his leg over hers, drew her body closer, as close to his as they could get fully clothed.

He wasn't going to be able to fully undress her out here, even though he doubted anyone else was around. But he could feel her, touch her, make love to her out here in this place where he could replace dismal memories with one that would always make him smile.

Shadoe lifted her head and graced him with the curling of her lips—that smile that always managed to calm the storm inside him. She was right. He was going to have to stop fighting their relationship and do as she suggested—just enjoy it while they had it, because they both knew it wasn't going to last.

He didn't want to hurt her. Enough people had done that to her already. But as long as she went into this relationship with her eyes wide-open, then it would be okay.

He smoothed his hands down the sides of her body, lingering over each of her curves. She laid her forehead on his shoulder and slid upward, gripped his shoulders and raised up to sit on him. That put her pussy right in contact with his hard, pulsing dick.

She shook her hair behind her back and smiled down at him, digging her nails into his chest. She sucked her bottom lip between her teeth and cast him a smoldering, sexy look that told him his kitten was in the mood for some rough play.

He gripped her hips, squeezed. She rocked against him.

"Tell me what you want," he said.

"Get up."

He did, moving off the blanket. Shadoe stood, too, turned around to face him, reaching for the zipper of her jeans. She drew the zipper down, then tugged the jeans over her hips, doing a slow turnaround so her back faced him as she drew the jeans over her perfectly rounded ass.

Then she dropped to her knees and bent forward on her hands, throwing him a look and a grin over her shoulder.

Oh, yeah. Oh, hell yeah. He got down on his knees behind her.

"I like the way you think, darlin'," he said, grasping the globes of her ass to rub his hands over them.

"I thought you might. Now hurry up and fuck me."

He jerked his zipper down and put a condom on, positioned himself against her, then slid inside her with an easy thrust. He closed his eyes for a second, felt her body grip his cock as she pulsed around him, welcomed him. He sucked in a breath at the sweet pleasure of being inside her.

He leaned forward, reached around to cup her sex, felt how wet she was.

"You like doing it outside?"

"I like you fucking me. I don't care where it is."

He pulled back, powered in deep, felt her walls grip him in a tight glove. "I'll keep that in mind. I might just decide to fuck you whenever and wherever."

"Whenever," she said, hissing when he thrust hard again. "Wherever."

He moved his hand over her hip, down the fullness of her ass cheek, and gave it a short, hard swat. She tensed, then tilted her head back and moaned, her pussy contracting around his cock.

"Damn, Spence."

"Like that?"

"Yes."

He knew she would. Somehow, he'd known she'd crave a bit of the unusual. He loved that about her. He smoothed the red spot he'd created, then moved his hand to a different spot and gave her ass another hard swat, the sound echoing off the empty woods. So did her loud cry. She bucked back against him, taking in more of his shaft. Wetness spilled against his thighs.

His woman craved more. Now he wished they were alone, in a place where he could have her naked, where he could really explore what there could be between them. But he'd make do. He grabbed her ponytail and held tight, giving it a slight tug to jerk her head back, then used his other hand to give her ass cheek another quick spank. She continued to cry out, but it was from pleasure. He knew the difference, would never intentionally hurt her, but wanted to drive her crazy.

From the wild way she rocked back against him, the way she tilted her head back, the sounds she made, the way her juices flowed over them both, he'd say he succeeded.

Hell, her reactions drove him crazy, too. His cock felt like throbbing steel; his balls quivered with the need to burst. But still, he rode her, giving her deep, long thrusts, pulling back when he sensed she was close to the edge.

Not yet, baby. Not for a while yet. He wanted her ragged and damn near unable to breathe before she went over. He wanted them both dangling off the cliff.

Shadoe clutched the blanket, curling her fingers into fists. "Spence."

That one word had been spoken in a low, guttural tone, her breath torn from her in a rasp. He knew what she wanted. He partially withdrew and gave her short, quick pulses, enough to tease, but not enough to let her come. "Not yet."

She growled at him. He smiled, reached for her ponytail again and tugged, this time harder.

"Goddammit, Spence." She pushed against him, taking his cock in between her tight pussy lips.

"Fuck." He let go of her hair and grabbed her hips, drove deep, pressing hard against her. "Is this what you want?" He withdrew, and began to pump against her with hard, fast strokes.

"Yes. Oh, God, yes. That's it." She came apart then, arched her back, and dropped her upper body to the ground, lifting her butt in the air. That gave him even more room to go deeper, and he did, driving as much of his cock inside her that he could, feeling her walls clench around him with the waves of her orgasm. She trembled around him and he let go, wrapped his arms around her and rocked against her as his orgasm exploded, nearly knocking him to the ground as wave after wave of intense hot pleasure rocketed through him until he was empty.

Spent, he grabbed Shadoe around the waist and rolled them both to the blanket onto their sides. It took several panting breaths for him to even attempt to breathe, let alone talk.

He drew her sweat-damped hair away from her face. "You okay?"

"Mmm."

"What does that mean?"

"It means I might be dead. Don't talk to me right now. I need a nap."

He snorted. "There are probably bugs all over the ground."

"I don't care. I'll share the blanket with a snake. I'm exhausted."

"Let's go back to the hotel. I'll run you a hot bath. Then you can take a nap."

"Oh sure. Tease me."

"It's a promise. I'll even wash your back."

"Now this I've got to see. You're on."

They straightened up and Shadoe folded the blanket to put away on the bike.

Spence surveyed the broken-down area that he used to call the nightmare of his home.

Somehow, it no longer held the bad memories it used to.

Shadoe came up to him and laced her fingers with his. He turned to her. "Thanks."

She tilted her head to the side and quirked a brow. "For what?"

"For banishing a few demons for me."

She smiled and pressed a soft kiss to his lips. "I've always wanted to be someone's knight in shining armor. Thank *you* for that." She pivoted and headed toward the bike.

Spence shook his head. She really was an amazing woman.

It made him wish he was a *forever* kind of guy.

But he knew better.

They headed back to the hotel and, true to his word, the first thing he did was run a bath for Shadoe. He even put in those smelly bath salt things women seemed to like that made the water purple and soft. He liked that it made her smell good. Actually, he liked anything that required her to be naked. She slid into the tub and he sat on the edge like the good servant he'd promised her he'd be, washcloth in hand.

"Are you really intending to scrub my back?" She cast him a dubious look.

He dipped the cloth into the water. "I said I was going to, didn't I?"

"I think you should get in here with me."

"Smelling like lavender isn't my thing."

"What if you smelling like lavender turns me on?"

He laughed. "Then I'd say there's something wrong with you."

She snorted. "Okay, maybe you can take a shower afterward. I'll probably need to do the same, since I'm sure there's dirt and twigs and God only knows else in my hair. So get in here with me and wash my back, slave."

He liked playing with her. She relaxed him, and he was rarely relaxed. He stripped off his clothes and climbed into the tub with her. It was one of those oversized whirlpools, with the flowing waterfall faucet in the center. He pulled Shadoe in front of him and grabbed the cloth. She'd put her hair up with a clip, so tiny little curls escaped along the back of her neck. He wanted to kiss them.

"You're not washing."

"Sorry." He rubbed the cloth along her smooth skin, kissing everywhere the cloth had been.

"Mmm, this is nice. I could get used to having a manservant."

"Don't get used to it. I don't service women."

She half turned to face him, giving him a tempting view of one breast and nipple. "Is that right? Seems to me you've been doing a fine job servicing me lately."

"Is that what you think I've been doing?"

"Well . . . I feel pretty well serviced."

"Maybe you should service me for a change."

Like a quick-moving storm, her eyes changed in an instant. From playfulness to dark desire, they went from light brown to smoldering whiskey. There was such temptation in her eyes. Spence lost himself there every time he looked at them.

"You want me to service you."

"Yes."

She turned fully around to face him. "Tell me what you want."

Now that was tempting, though the question was easy. What did every man want? "Suck me."

Her smile transformed her face from temptress to sexy angel. "I'd love to. Sit on the edge of the tub."

He grabbed the edge of the tub and hauled himself onto the ledge.

She inched across the water and laid her hands on his knees. "Now spread 'em for me."

He did. Wide.

She stared straight ahead at his cock and balls. She didn't even need to touch him. Just her looking at him like that got him hard. And she kept her gaze there, watched him get that way, which made him even harder.

"You're beautiful down here." She smoothed her hands from his knees along his inner thighs, her hands like wet silk, water trickling off her fingertips. "Every inch of you a man." She moved her hands inward, slid her thumb over the sac containing his balls, then swam in farther between his legs so her shoulders were cradled between his thighs.

She laid her head on one thigh, and lifted her hand, letting water drip over the top of his cock, seeming to be entranced by the stream cascading over his shaft. She watched until there was nothing but droplets, then circled him with her hand, stroking him from base to tip, covering his cock with the satiny water and her slender hand. He leaned farther back and arched into her hand, loving the softness, so unlike his hard, calloused hand. She touched him differently than he touched himself, almost reverently, as if she was afraid she'd hurt him.

"I won't break, Shadoe. Squeeze it, touch it any way you want to."

She did, gripping him harder as she stroked him, moving slowly at first, then rising up on her knees. Water sluiced off her shoulders, her arms, her breasts, making her look like a goddess rising from the sea.

He wasn't the type of guy who saw poetry in a woman's body, but goddamn if Shadoe didn't put him in that frame of mind. And when her lips parted and her tongue snaked out to lick along the crest of his cock, his mind emptied of everything but the sight of her pink tongue and how hot it felt on his cockhead, and how he wanted to come right then, to see it burst over her tongue, inside her mouth.

He shuddered, and her gaze met his. She closed her lips over the head, and he felt her tongue swirling over him as she sucked him into the deep recesses of her velvety mouth. He held the back of her head while she engulfed him, her hand coming up to circle his shaft, the other to cradle his balls and squeeze him gently.

He wanted to erupt, to scream out in pleasured agony. But he wanted to fuck her again. He wanted to do everything to her, with her, right now. He was torn.

She pulled back, releasing his cock from her mouth with a loud pop. "Do it. Come for me, Spence. Let me feel it."

Without waiting for him to answer, she gripped him in her hand again, touching him with hard, measured strokes.

"Christ." He had no voice left, not when she closed her lips over him again, that hot, wet heat surrounding him, sucking him into a vortex of indescribable sensation and taking all his resolve with it. She released her hand, gazed into his eyes, and took him deep into her throat. That's when he lost it and let go with a guttural cry. He held on to her head as he gave her everything he had, unable to even breathe as the orgasm ripped from every nerve ending in his body and left him shattered and drained.

Shadoe laid her head on his thigh again, stroked his other leg, a contented smile on her face. When Spence finally had his sanity back, he decided payback was only fair.

She might look the serene goddess right now, but he intended to rip away her sanity next.

"Thank you, darlin'." He pulled her out of the water and against him and gave her a lingering kiss. When he drew away, her eyes were glazed over and her lips were plump from his kiss. She licked them.

"You're welcome." She started to sink back into the water, but he held her firm.

"We're not finished yet, Shadoe."

"We're not?"

He shook his head. "Stand up."

He pulled her against him. Now it was his turn to slide into the water. He rested his head against the side of the tub.

"Straddle my shoulders, babe."

She widened her stance and placed her legs in between his arms and his the side of his chest, placing her pussy in the perfect spot.

He looked up and grinned at her.

"Oh" was all she said, then her lips curved.

He said nothing, just grasped her butt cheeks and pulled her closer to his hungry mouth, placing it over her sex.

She smelled like the lavender bath water, her bare skin silky and wet. It made it so easy to glide his tongue over her naked skin, to taste her sweet cream as it flowed from her. She tilted her pelvis out, held on to the wall for support, and closed her eyes, letting out a small gasp as he licked around her clit.

Oh, man, she had a pretty pussy, and when she stood like this he could really see it clearly, could play with all of her with his mouth and his fingers. He slid his tongue inside her, used his thumb to swirl over her clit and around her pussy lips, and just generally enjoyed playing with her. He wanted to see what she liked, where it felt good for her, watching her reactions as he licked and sucked her.

Shadoe liked pretty much everything, but she really enjoyed it when he sucked her clit and tucked two fingers inside her to fuck her. Her whole body went rigid, her eyes opened, and she tilted her head down at him to watch.

He really liked it when she watched him, her golden brown eyes focused on what he did, encouraging him with her visual signals.

He licked the length of her, and her lips parted. She began to pant and he gave her laps with his tongue around her clit.

"God, Spence, that's going to make me come."

He gripped her ass and dug his fingers in, bringing her sex closer to his mouth, burying his face in her sweet fragrance and pressing his tongue hard against her clit. She shuddered out his name and held on to his hair, jerking and pulsing as she came until she sank into the water and crashed against him.

She soared upward, cradled his face between her hands, and pressed her lips to his in a wild, untamed kiss, before she pulled away and rested her head against his shoulders.

They lay like that for a long while, until the water got cold and Shadoe started to shiver. Only then did he pull her out of the tub and they took a quick shower together. They dried off and fell into bed together. Shadoe passed out almost immediately.

She needed the nap. He enjoyed just holding her, stroking her back and her hair, listening to the soft sounds of her breath.

Yeah, she was right. There was nothing wrong with this togetherness thing, as long as he never lost sight of the fact that it wasn't going to last.

Love and relationships never did.

But this was the first time in his life that he almost wished it could.

THE WILD ROSE WAS PACKED AGAIN. SHADOE HAD ALREADY gone on once, and like last night, she was surrounded by admirers. Tonight she decided she'd wander around and meet people instead of being stuck at a table. That would give her a chance to mix and mingle and see faces.

There were repeaters from last night, several of the dockworkers she'd seen the day before, and even some new ones. Lots of tourists, too. Brandon told her there were always new faces coming into the club every night, and that was the tourist trade coming in. Some came back, some frequented other clubs, some might come infrequently. He told her you could never set a schedule or determine regulars at a club in the French Quarter, which made her photographic memory even more critical on this mission. And for the first time ever, she felt it would be a useful tool. No way could someone memorize faces night after night and hope they could spot the rogue agent out of thousands of faces studied in the agency's data banks.

She would, though. She'd nab this bastard selling out to the Colombians.

She saw Pax and AJ sitting at one of the center tables—a great spot to do a little viewing of their own. Though she wasn't sure if they were really on the job or just ogling the dancers. She went up to their table and bent down to wrap her arms around them.

"How's it going, guys?"

AJ tilted his head up and graced her with the kind of smile that would turn any woman's knees to jelly, his stormy gray eyes filled with trouble. "Hey, baby. You looked hot tonight, as usual."

"You sure did, honey. Hard for a guy to concentrate on anything but watching you," Pax said, his lips tilted in a sexy smile. Between the two of these guys, a woman didn't stand a chance. Pax's face was model worthy, all chiseled cheekbones and strong jaw, and just perfect, kissable lips.

She laughed. "I'll bet you say that to all the girls."

"We usually do," AJ said with a wink.

"So, anything happening tonight?"

Pax shook his head. "Just a lot of pretty naked ladies and guys who want to get into their G-strings."

"Guys like you?"

"Always," AJ said, tipping his beer her way. "But we've got an inside line we're working."

Shadoe arched a brow. "Do you? And what might that be?"

"Hey. Are you trying to pick up my guys?"

Shadoe straightened and saw Ariele coming to a stop at the table to rest a hip against AJ's chair. AJ slid an arm around her waist.

"Me? Not at all. Just stopping to say hello. So, these two are yours, huh?"

Ariele laughed. "Well, they are a handful, but they sure know how to show a girl a good time."

Both? At once? *Oh, my.* Shadoe's gaze flitted between AJ and Pax, who grinned back at her. "That sounds like fun."

Ariele's eyes sparkled with desire. "It is, Desi. You should try it sometime."

She thought about Spence. One guy . . . or at least one particular guy . . . was more than enough for her. "I'll give that some thought. Time for me to make the rounds. The three of you have fun."

Pax pulled out the chair between AJ and him and patted it for Ariele to sit. "We intend to."

The threesome had already tuned her out before she even walked away. She shook her head and started to move on when she felt an arm slide around her waist. She stilled, then tilted her head to find Spence there. She smiled up at him.

"Where have you been hiding?"

"Talking up Lance a bit." He led her to the corner of the bar where they had some privacy and ordered them a couple of drinks.

"Find out anything?"

"Not really. I wasn't hitting him up for information, more just to get friendly with him, see if he'd eventually open up."

"If he's anything like his wife, I wouldn't count on it." Shadoe's gaze drifted to Cheri, who had just taken the stage dressed all in white, sprouting white boots and angel wings.

"No surprise what her theme is."

"Yeah." Shadoe wrinkled her nose as she watched Cheri glide

across the stage. Technically, she was a very good dancer, with great flexibility and awesome moves. It was easy to see why she was the lead. But she lacked something several of the other dancers had in droves—passion and a love for what she did. It was clear that Cheri's heart wasn't in stripping. She was out to get rich or become famous, or maybe use this as a springboard to something else. But she didn't give herself to her audience, didn't make eye contact with the guys. In fact, she looked . . . bored, walking around on the stage like she expected to be worshipped.

Of course she had a killer body and she used it to her advantage, and all the guys seemed to love it, so maybe to them—and to the Wild Rose—it didn't matter. But Shadoe saw right through Cheri to the greedy opportunist she was.

She turned to Spence. "What do you think?"

He shrugged. "She sucks. Ariele and Elan are better. They play to their audience."

She nodded. "Exactly what I was thinking."

He leaned in to flick his tongue against her earlobe. She shivered. "But you're the best, darlin'."

She laughed. "You're biased because you get to fuck me."

"Maybe. I still think you make contact with your audience. Guys like that."

She beamed at his praise. "Thank you."

After Cheri wrapped up, she said, "I had an interesting conversation with AJ and Pax."

"About what?"

"I think they're both fucking Ariele."

His lips lifted. "Probably. That's what they do."

"What's what they do?"

"They share women."

"Really?"

"Yeah. It started a long time ago. They just kind of fell into it.

194 JACI BURTON

They've been best friends since they came to the Wild Riders. They do everything together, always have. That just naturally extended to women.

"So . . . um . . . why?"

He shrugged. "Guys don't really talk all that much about sex. That's just how they do it. I guess they like it that way."

"That's interesting."

He laughed. "Why? You interested?"

"Me? Oh, hell no. I have my hands full enough with you."

"Good." He pulled her against him and kissed her, his mouth hot and demanding. When he drew away, she was out of breath.

"I can't get enough of you," she whispered. "You make me forget my job."

"Is that a bad thing?"

She caressed his cheek, loving the scrape of beard bristle against her palm. "I don't know. I'm supposed to mingle with the customers."

"Screw the customers. You've mingled enough for a while. You can hang here with me until you go on again. Make them hungry for you."

"You just want to make them jealous."

His gaze was wicked. "Maybe."

He turned her around and pulled her back against his chest, then wrapped his arms around her so they could watch the other dancers. Her gaze gravitated to Ariele and Pax and AJ. Pax had his hand in her hair. AJ had his hand in her lap, both of them leaned in close whispering to her. And Ariele seemed to revel in the attention from two men.

Yummy. Not really Shadoe's reality, but she could well imagine the fantasy—how incredibly enticing and erotic that could be.

Ariele finally pushed back from her chair, kissing both of them before she moved on to the next table. After she left, Shadoe let her gaze drift around the club, watching the other dancers mingle with the crowds. Cheri—minus Lance—came out of the doorway and was greeted with a large crowd of admirers. She had a haughty look about her, almost queenly, as if she expected the adulation. She let her "entourage" follow her around, but never really engaged them. Ugh.

Star was on the stage doing her thing. She was a good dancer, but like Cheri, never seemed to engage her audience.

Elan was back in the lap dance area—a private room off to the side, barely visible through the curtained-off area. She had a guy enraptured at the moment by lying on his lap, her head on his knees while her legs split in a vee, doing a very revealing dance.

And Spitfire had a group of guys totally enthralled at one of the tables while she chatted nonstop in her usual effervescent way.

Other dancers mingled with men at the tables or danced at the side poles set up throughout the place, little mini shows meant to keep everyone entertained no matter where in the club they sat.

It was then, while Shadoe watched one of the dancers twirling the pole in the dark corner at the back of the club, that she spotted a familiar face. At first she thought it was someone she'd seen the night before, but it wasn't. The face was familiar. A jog of recognition hit her immediately.

"I'll be back in a minute." She pulled away from Spence's grasp and took a walk toward the back of the club, trying to appear nonchalant, stopping to smile and chat with customers along her way. She got a drink from the bartender and made her way through the crowd, staying hidden so the man wouldn't catch sight of her.

She leaned against one of the thick black poles so she could watch. She needed to get a better view of him. It was dark in the back of the club and she didn't have a clear view of the guy.

The man crooked his finger at the dancer on the pole. The dancer—Shadoe didn't know her—stepped off the stage and toward him. With his focus entirely on the raven-haired Amazon straddling his hips, Shadoe stepped out from behind the pole and moved in closer, trying to blend in so she wouldn't be noticed.

He held on to the stripper's hips as she ground against his crotch, his head turned down to stare at her ass.

Come on. Look up. She needed to be sure.

When the dancer turned around so she could shake her boobs in the guy's face, he finally lifted his head. Grinned.

And then Shadoe was certain.

That man was a federal agent: one Jerry DeLaud from Washington, D.C.

FOURTEEN

YES! GOT HIM. THE DEPARTMENT HAD TOLD HER THAT THE national agency had no active cases in this area other than the one she'd been assigned to, so DeLaud had no business here. And she knew all the ones currently on vacation. He wasn't one of them.

Shadoe smiled at the same time her pulse picked up.

She knew she was right. She remembered DeLaud's agency photo from the endless files she'd studied before this mission. He currently sported a scruffy, unshaven lock, unlike his official agency photo. But it was definitely the same guy.

She had to tell Spence, but she hated leaving DeLaud. Then again, the song had another two minutes, and he'd paid for the lap dance, so it was doubtful he'd go anywhere. She took a few steps backward and rounded the corner, then hustled over to Spence.

He pulled her against him. "Where'd you go?"

She slid into his arms and put her mouth against his ear. "He's here."

He tensed. "Where?"

"The private room on the north side of the club. He's occupied with a raven-haired dancer. Don't know her name."

He drew back far enough to search her face. "You're sure about this guy?"

"Positive."

He took her hand. "Let's go for a walk."

Same as last time, they took the stroll nice and easy, smiling and nodding at customers who looked her way. Spence stopped her at the pole where she'd hidden before.

DeLaud was still the only one in the private room. Spence maneuvered Shadoe against the pole and nestled in between her legs, giving the impression that he was nuzzling her neck. That should give him a clear view of what was going on in the room.

"Thin guy, midthirties, shadow of a beard, wearing white polo and jeans?"

She clutched his shoulders. "That's him. Jerry DeLaud. He's a D.C. agent."

"He's early by several days. This deal isn't supposed to go down until at least this weekend."

"I know."

"Maybe he's checking out the club to see if there are any New Orleans agents."

"That would be my guess."

Spence wrapped his arm around her. "You need to go on in about fifteen minutes."

Shit. She'd forgotten all about her next set. "You're right."

"Go ahead. I'll alert Pax and AJ that our target has made an appearance. We'll keep an eye on him."

"All right."

He moved away, pressed a kiss to her lips, and she headed down the hallway toward the dressing area.

By the time she was ready to go on, DeLaud would be finished with his private dance. What would he do? Where would he be? From the stage, she'd be able to catch sight of him if he was still in the club.

Excitement skittered down her spine, her nerve endings tingling with the desire to spring into action. She had to force a calm she didn't feel, remember that she had to maintain her cover.

But damn, this was thrilling.

The game was on.

SPENCE HAD TO USE THE SIGNALS HE'D SET UP FOR PAX AND AJ to get their attention. He hung out at the bar, and Pax slid in next to him and ordered a couple beers. There was so much noise since the crowd was thick it was easy for the two of them to nod at each other and carry on a low conversation.

"Target's been acquired," Spence said, not making eye contact with Pax.

"Who and where?"

Spence had kept tabs on DeLaud since the agent had finished up the lap dance with the stripper. DeLaud had tipped her, then grabbed his drink and moved to one of the tables next to the stage.

"Solitary at a stage table, about ten o'clock. White polo, jeans, needs a shave."

Pax took the two beers the bartender slid his way, then turned around and leaned against the edge of the bar. "Got him." He pushed off the bar and walked away without another word.

Spence knew Pax would fill AJ in, and they'd do their job of helping him keep an eye on their rogue agent. He wanted to know everything about this guy—who he talked to while at the club as well as where he was staying in town. That way they could put him under constant surveillance since he'd decided to show up early.

DeLaud sat at the table alone drinking his beer and watching the dancers on the stage. No one approached him and he didn't seem to be looking for anyone.

The lights went out and Shadoe came out to do her dance. Spence took advantage of the darkness and the crowd gathering closer to the stage to move in around the side so he could get a better angle on DeLaud.

Unlike most of the guys at stage level who rushed up there hoping Shadoe'd come close so they could tuck money in her G-string, DeLaud watched calmly from his seat and drank his beer. The guy never took his gaze off the stage. He seemed to be mesmerized by Shadoe's performance, focused on her every move. He tilted his head to the side as if he was studying her.

Spence didn't like the way he watched Shadoe so closely, but maybe DeLaud just liked strippers. Still, there was something a little bit different in his eyes, the way they followed her across the stage. It wasn't raw interest, the out-there kind of enjoyment most of the men got. This was something darker.

Maybe it was because Shadoe gave the guys so much attention, making eye contact throughout the crowd. She scanned her gaze over DeLaud more than a few times, too, cocking her hip to the side after she'd discarded her clothes, turning around to shake her ass, then throwing a look over her shoulder. Spence caught the way DeLaud looked at her, the pure male appreciation in his eyes.

And Shadoe played to that, making sure she held his attention.

When her dance was over and she'd changed into a body-hugging minidress that barely covered her assets, she came out and bypassed Spence, working the crowd instead. Spence lingered in the background nearby, close enough that he could intervene if necessary, but not wanting to get too close to her.

She'd made some eye contact with DeLaud. He understood what she was trying to do, so he was going to stay out of her way and wait to see what happened.

Shadoe didn't approach DeLaud. She did what she had been doing since last night, which was make her way around the crowds, pausing to chat with guys at their tables or the ones who stopped to talk to her. Spence kept his focus between Shadoe and De-Laud.

DeLaud observed her the entire time. Another dancer had gone on stage, capturing some of the crowd's attention, but not DeLaud's. His hawklike gaze had zeroed in on Shadoe and stayed there. When Shadoe passed by his table, he motioned to her. She smiled, sashayed over to him, and he pulled out a chair for her.

DeLaud ordered Shadoe a drink and they started talking. No touching, nothing that would send Spence running over there. Just talking. He didn't smile much, and Spence would guess De-Laud was a fairly good-looking guy, so that hardass rebel look might be appealing to some women. Shadoe seemed to be en-gaged, keeping up her part of the conversation. She laughed a lot, talked a lot, made good use of body language to let him know she was interested in being there with him.

Dammit, he wanted to know what she was saying. That re-minded him she wore that communication device in her belly piercing. Time to get that baby activated.

She did a good job. She knew not to linger too long, instead just enough to finish her drink, pat him on the shoulder, and get up. Then she made her way to the next table. Spence let about twenty minutes go by before he caught up to her and stood be-hind her. She tilted her head back and winked at him.

DeLaud left about two-thirty. Pax and AJ took off right after him to follow.

An hour later, Shadoe had done all she needed to do for the club. "Ready to go?"

He nodded and she went to the dressing room to change. He went outside and climbed on the bike, pulled out his phone, and left a text message on AJ's cell.

Shadoe came out within a few minutes and they rode back to the hotel.

Once in the room, she tossed her bag on the chair inside the door and turned to him. "DeLaud is slime."

"Figured that. But hold off on any debriefing until Pax and AJ get here."

She cocked a brow. "They're coming?"

He shrugged. "Not sure yet. I texted AJ and told them to meet us here. They followed DeLaud out of the club when he left, so depending on where DeLaud went, they'll either be here sooner or later."

"Okay."

It turned out to be sooner, since they heard a knock on the door within thirty minutes of their own arrival. Spence opened it and let AJ and Pax in. They all slid into chairs in the sitting room.

"He's checked in at the Western Springs," Pax said.

Spence frowned. "Nice hotel. Downtown."

"And about equal distance between the club and the docks."

"Okay. You two check in there tonight."

"Already planning that," AJ said.

"Anything else?"

"Yeah," Pax said. "I bribed one of the bellmen to keep me informed if anyone goes to his room or if he leaves. I told him I think he's screwing my girlfriend so I want to know everyone going near his room or whenever he makes a move."

"Oh, good idea," Shadoe said. "So you'll have someone there to keep an eye on him when you can't."

"And all this time I thought I was the brains and he was just the pretty one," AJ said with a sly grin.

"No, I'm pretty *and* I have the brains, dickhead."

"No, I have the dick," AJ shot back. "That's why you need my help with the ladies. You reel 'em in with your face, I keep 'em in bed with my dick."

Shadoe snorted and looked over at Spence. "Are they always like this?"

He rolled his eyes. "Yeah." Spence stood and leaned against the wet bar. "Okay, so he's here early. We need to figure out why."

"AJ and I are gonna tail him tomorrow. We figure he isn't here to hole up in that room all day and wait around for the show at night. He's gotta leave sometime, and when he does, we'll be there to follow him."

Spence nodded at Pax. "Okay. Shadoe and I can step in and help with that, too."

"I don't know if that's a good idea, man," AJ said. "That's a risk to your cover. You're in good with the club now. Shadoe has a presence as Desi. You don't want to blow that. If he spots either of you while you're following him, this whole mission is screwed."

"Much as I hate to agree, since I'd love the opportunity to do surveillance, he's right." Shadoe laid her hand on his knee. AJ and Pax exchanged knowing looks.

Spence would hear about that later.

"Yeah, probably. But if you need me to step in, let me know."

Pax leaned back in the chair. "We can handle it."

"What did he say to you tonight?"

Shadoe wrinkled her nose. "Nothing much, really. Said he liked my act, that I had a nice body. Some general chitchat. Then he asked about my background, where I got my start, what clubs I'd danced in before. Really probing questions."

"Could be normal considering he's an agent and used to interrogation," AJ suggested.

"Maybe. But I've been trained, too, and I don't interrogate people I meet. It seemed to me he was really interested in getting to know me."

Spence laid a hand on her shoulder. "It could mean he's interested in you."

"Yes, I thought about that. He seemed really focused on me when I danced."

A lot focused.

"He might be the kind of guy that really gets off on strippers," Pax said.

"That could be. And it might be he takes a liking to them when he's in town and picks them up." Spence knew a lot of guys who traveled and had stripper girlfriends in different towns.

"That could work to our advantage if he likes me."

Spence frowned. "What do you mean?"

"Remember what I suggested before?"

"You and me breaking up?"

She nodded. "It could work here. Say DeLaud is interested in me. He's not going to make a move with you and I stuck together like peanut butter on bread."

"But if we're not a couple anymore . . ."

"Then maybe I can get close to him, see what I can find out."

Spence didn't like it. "He isn't going to tell you anything."

She shrugged. "I doubt he will, either. But one of us on the inside won't hurt, will it?"

He couldn't argue with her logic, and if he wasn't sleeping with her, it wouldn't make any difference to him.

But he *was* sleeping with her . . . or at least he had some kind of relationship with her. Sex, anyway. Hell, he didn't know. This was foreign territory, this caring for a woman. He knew it was going to cloud his judgment, and it had. He didn't want Shadoe to take on DeLaud, even if she was a trained federal agent.

But that was the man in him talking. He was a trained agent, too, and he had to do his job, which meant letting Shadoe do hers.

"Okay, how do you want to handle it?"

She arched a brow as if she hadn't expected it to be that easy. "Tomorrow night at the club we'll have a public breakup."

"What if DeLaud isn't there?" AJ asked.

"Word travels fast at a place like that," Spence said. "Even if he isn't there, the fact that Shadoe is now available will be known throughout the club within minutes."

"Especially if I make it known that this had been a long time coming, and that I'm not that broken up about it."

"Ouch," Pax said, shooting Spence a sympathetic look. "She's breaking your heart, man."

Spence rolled his eyes. "Just make sure it isn't the two of you trying to pick her up."

Pax slanted a look at AJ. "See how he ruins all our fun?"

Shadoe giggled. Spence shuffled the guys out of there and locked the door, then turned to face her.

"So, you're dumping me, huh?"

She stood and came over, leaned into him. God, he loved the way she smelled. She twined her arms around his neck. "Well, I'm breaking up with you at the club, but when we get back here I'll still fuck you."

He grinned. "You slut."

She batted her lashes. "Sweet talker."

He slid his arms around her waist. "Technically, you should get a separate room. That way in case he checks up on you, he'll know we're not still in the same room."

Her smile died. "Is it wrong that I don't like it?"

"No. I don't like it either." In a few short days he'd grown accustomed to having her around, to having her in his bed at night. That spelled the kind of trouble he didn't want to think about. Not when there were other things to think about, like the case.

She sighed. "Okay. When should I get a separate room?"

"Tomorrow after you leave the club. That'll make the most sense since we're going to stage our fight and break up then."

She laid her head against his chest. "I'm getting used to sleeping with you, Spence. I'm keeping my key to this room. Don't be surprised if I sneak in here and crawl in bed with you."

"If you do, you won't be sleeping."

She tilted her head back and smiled. "Sleep is overrated."

"Good, because you won't be doing much of it tonight, either."

"I thought you'd never ask." She lifted up on her toes, cupped the back of his neck, drew his head down, and pulled his mouth to hers.

He dipped and took her lips in a kiss that started off soft, but didn't stay that way for long. He was hungry for her. Watching her strip turned him on. Thinking of her with DeLaud, knowing what was going to happen, tripped possessive switches he didn't know he had.

He lifted her into his arms, carried her into the bedroom, and laid her on the bed. She kicked off her shoes. He toed off his boots and pulled off his shirt, then undid the button on his jeans. That was as far as he got before Shadoe pulled him down onto the bed with her.

"Kiss me. I need you."

He put his mouth on hers, slid his tongue inside, felt the heat ignite throughout his body. His cock was hard, throbbing, and he rubbed it against her. Even through denim he had to hiss at the contact, wished they were already naked so he could be inside her.

She made him feel like an anxious teenager, and he hadn't been anxious in a damn long time.

She lifted her hips, ground against his erection, and without saying a word told him she wanted him.

He lifted, pulled off her tank top and jeans, and looked down at her. She wore a lacy white bra and matching panties that were damn sexier on her than those black leather outfits she wore to strip. She lifted one leg and planted her foot flat on the mattress, kept her gaze firmly focused on his.

He laid his palm flat on her belly, roamed up over her rib cage, felt the pounding of her heart. Good to know it wasn't just his that slammed repeatedly against his chest.

He tired of women fast, especially after they had sex. With Shadoe, each time was a new adventure, each uncovering of her body like Christmas morning—a gift to open and enjoy.

In the back of his mind, warning bells clanged loud and clear—back off. He knew he was getting involved.

But he could handle it. He knew this was temporary. They'd both agreed, knew what they were doing. So he'd found a woman he enjoyed. That didn't mean he couldn't walk away when this was over.

He could.

He would.

SHADOE ALWAYS THOUGHT MEN WERE MINDLESS DURING SEX, BUT watching the play of emotions on Spence's face as he stared down at her, she knew that wasn't true.

Not for him, anyway. He was thinking. About what, she didn't know, but his mind was definitely working on something.

So was hers. Like on the way he looked, the intensity of his furrowed brow as he studied her body, then swept his gaze back up to her face. A mix of emotions, from desire to almost anger.

She understood his conflict. He had feelings for her and he didn't want to. Still, she couldn't help but be thrilled that he did, even though she knew as well as he did that it was for nothing. They weren't going anywhere beyond this mission.

But for now she was going to enjoy his hands on her, his lips on hers, and the hunger in his eyes.

She'd never felt so desired, wasn't sure she'd ever meet a man like Spence again. She wanted to savor every moment while she had it.

He leaned over her and pressed his lips to her belly, right above her panties. Her stomach quivered and heat pooled low and steady, flaming hotter as he moved lower, drawing her panties down as he kissed the top of her sex.

She shivered but she wasn't cold. Her skin felt on fire from the touch of his lips, the maddening sensation of his teasing tongue darting out to circle her hip bone, then slide along the crevice where her sex met her inner thigh.

Her clit trembled in anticipation, all nerve endings knotted up and waiting for the touch of his mouth, his tongue, desperate for that hot, wet heat that would send her over the edge.

She lifted her hips, slid her hand down to tangle her fingers in his hair. He raised his head.

"Please."

He smiled. "Okay."

He leaned in and pressed his mouth to her sex, and her head fell back against the mattress. She was lost in the oblivion he created with his oh-so-talented lips and tongue. He devoured her

senseless until she couldn't breathe, until she arched her hips off
the bed and fed her pussy to him, until her juices poured as she
came in wild abandon, bucking like a madwoman and not caring
at all that he had to hold her down to suck at her clit while she
climaxed on his face.

That he loved her body like this was phenomenal. That he
could give so much to her blew her mind. That she wanted to give
so much in return made her heart ache.

And when he stripped her completely, then himself, and slid
his body along hers, put on a condom and thrust inside her, she
welcomed him inside with complete abandon, her body bowing
with the need to fit more of him inside her—deeper than any man
had ever been.

As he moved in firm, even strokes, she raked his arms with her
nails and searched his face, desperate that he give her everything.
"More."

He pulled back, thrust harder.

Still, it wasn't enough. She felt restless, needy, wanted to give
him as much as he gave her. "More."

He dropped down against her, their sweat-slickened bodies glid-
ing against each other. "Tell me what you want."

His voice made her quiver. So dark, so dangerous, it was all the
things she never thought she'd wanted. With Spence, she did. "I
want it all."

He stilled, dug his fingers into her hip. "You sure?"

"Yes."

He dragged her to the edge of the bed, flipped her over onto
her belly, and drew her hair aside. He pressed his lips to the back
of her neck and bit down. Goose bumps raised up on her skin; her
nipples hardened to tight, aching points. She jerked her head up
and reached behind her to pull at his hair.

"More."

He smoothed his hand down her back, over her butt cheeks, and slid his finger down between the crack. She shuddered.

Yes, she wanted that.

"Ever done it?"

"No."

"You sure this is what you want?"

"Yes." She'd moaned out the word because he'd cupped her sex and began to move his hand back and forth, splintering her into a million pieces, teasing her by bringing her close to orgasm, then pulling away from her center.

He dropped to his knees, pulled her legs down farther, and spread her ass cheeks apart.

"Do you have lube?"

"Bedside drawer."

She was shaking, but not from fear. Excitement drilled her. She wanted this, both for her and for Spence. It was dark and thrilling and she'd never done it but always wanted to.

And, it occurred to her, she trusted Spence.

He spread her again, this time sliding his lubed fingertip between her cheeks, then circling her anus. The cool liquid made her shiver in anticipation, his finger driving wicked sensation through her. She gripped the sheets and held on while he continued to tease her, using one hand to play with her sex, the other to tease the puckered hole.

When he slid his finger partially inside, her lips parted and she moaned at the exquisite pleasure. She had no idea it would feel so good. He tucked his fingers inside her pussy and slid his other finger fully in her anus.

She tossed her head back and cried out in delight. To be touched front and back at the same time—her mind shot to AJ and Pax—the thought of two men pleasuring a woman simultaneously.

This was what it would feel like.

The sensations were incredible. Hot, tight balls of nerve endings exploding inside her.

"Yes. Oh, yes, that feels good." Unbearable pleasure shot through her like pulses of lightning. Spence had fingers buried in her everywhere, and his thumb circled her clit. She was so damn close to an orgasm she tightened all around his fingers.

But not like this. She wanted him inside her.

She reached behind her to grab his wrist. "Spence. Stop. Fuck me now."

Spence withdrew and she quivered, exposed, needy, and raw. He left her for only a few seconds, then returned, lubed up his condom, and settled in behind her. He cupped her sex again, slid his hand back and forth and drove her near to the brink of insanity.

"Breathe for me, baby," he said, his cock nestled at the entrance to her anus. "My dick is bigger than my fingers. Breathe out when I slide in."

She did as he asked. He pushed. It burned. It hurt. He thrust slow and easy, but it still hurt. And, oh, God it felt so good even as the pain seemed to set her on fire. He kept swirling his hand over her pussy while he buried his cock in her ass.

Then the pain dissipated, and his cock filled her. Never had she felt this full, this intimate.

"Christ," he whispered against her back, then began to move, and she just wanted to die, it was so good. He kept his hand pressed to her sex, his fingers inside her while he fucked her ass.

She was filled, going mad with sensation, and she began to move with him, rising up to buck against him as he met her stroke for stroke.

"Tight. So tight."

"More" was all she could say, blinded by this wild sensation.

"Fuck, Shadoe." His tone was sand and gravel. "Take it."

He pulled back and thrust hard, powering her with punishing strokes, using his fingers to push her over the edge. She teetered there for a fraction of a second, then toppled, screaming as she was blindsided by an incredible orgasm. She felt it everywhere, gripping Spence's cock, his fingers, and sending her sailing into mind-numbing oblivion.

Wave after wave shattered her, grabbed her by the throat and cut off her breath. She was seized with spasms so strong she couldn't see, could only feel Spence everywhere as he pummeled her with the sweetest sensations she'd ever experienced.

Spence pushed deep, groaned, and shuddered, then fell forward across her back, panting out deep, hot breaths against her neck while he rode out his orgasm.

She struggled for sanity, for breath. She had never imagined sex could be like this, that it could be this good. She'd known passion, but not so intense. She'd never in her life wanted to give herself so completely to a man.

Long, silent moments passed in which all she heard was the sound of each of them breathing. Through all that time Spence touched her, ran his hands over her legs, her arms, and kissed her neck. She never once felt like this was just sex for him.

Maybe that's what was so different—the way he touched her, connected to her. She didn't understand it, she just knew it meant something.

He finally withdrew and took them both into the bathroom, turned on the shower, and drew her in there with him. He washed her, held her, and kissed her. His actions were so tender it nearly moved her to tears.

He was so incongruous, this tough guy who had a heart he didn't want to expose, didn't want to share. But he had, just enough to give her a glimpse into the hurt little boy who longed for someone to love, and tried to mask his needs under a shield of armor. She knew all about those kinds of needs.

He needed her. Just like she needed him.

And she knew, deep down, that neither of them was going to get what they needed out of this relationship at the end.

FIFTEEN

SPENCE LEFT SHADOE TO HERSELF IN THE MORNING. HE GOT UP early and went to meet with AJ and Pax. AJ had texted him saying the bellman told him DeLaud was on the move.

He caught up with them at a restaurant off the docks. They sat in a corner booth. Spence slid in next to Pax, his back to the door.

"Where is he?"

AJ motioned with his head to the window. "Eating breakfast in the restaurant across the street. You can see him if you look through the window. First booth near the door."

Spence took a look, spotted DeLaud talking to a waitress. He was alone.

"Has he met anyone?"

Pax shook his head. "No. As soon as we got the heads-up from the bellman we hauled ass and followed him. He was on foot since this place is just a couple blocks, so he was easy to follow. He slid into that place and took a booth, so we came in here, figured we'd have a good vantage point to do surveillance without him making us. That way we can still hang out at the club tonight and watch him there, too."

Spence ordered breakfast, downed his first cup of coffee, and watched DeLaud eat and read the paper. By the time their food had arrived, DeLaud had finished eating but continued to drink coffee.

"I think he's doing the crossword puzzle," AJ said.

"Maybe we'll do it, too." Pax motioned to the newspaper sitting at the end of their table. "And if we come up with a word we can't figure out, we can run across the street and ask him to help."

Spence rolled his eyes, but perked up when a couple of guys who looked to be dockworkers came through the door of the restaurant and slid into the booth with DeLaud.

"We need a tail on those two," he said.

AJ nodded. "We'll split up when those two leave. I'll follow them. Pax can keep an eye on DeLaud."

Frustration ate at Spence as he watched the three across the street engaged in conversation. "This would be a lot easier if we could bug him."

"Hard to do unless you can shove a bug up his ass," Pax mumbled.

AJ grinned. "Maybe Shadoe can snuggle up to him and manage to get one up there."

Spence glared at him.

"Or, maybe not," AJ said, holding his hands up, then exchanged another knowing glance with Pax.

Spence knew what they were thinking.

"Be careful," Pax said. "We're kind of broke right now and we can't afford wedding gifts."

AJ snickered.

"Very funny. We're not getting married. We're not even dating."

"No, you're just fucking her. That's even worse, because it's obvious you're falling in love with her." AJ had a look of horror on his face that almost made Spence laugh, because it was the same look he used to give when he thought about relationships with women.

"I'm not in love with her. I hardly know her."

"You know her enough to be jealous at the thought of her being with someone else."

"We're on a mission."

AJ shrugged. "So? You've fucked women on missions before and never gave a shit what they did. Why is this one different?"

Why *was* she different? For a lot of reasons. For no reason. She wasn't different. It was just being here—New Orleans—that brought out all his damned emotions, something he normally kept well under control. And Shadoe bore the brunt of his rare display of feeling, that was all. It had nothing to do with her. She was just the bystander.

He took a long swallow of coffee. "It's nothing. We're not involved."

AJ exchanged another look with Pax.

"Would you two knock that off? It's fucking weird. You're like a hive mind or something."

Pax snorted. "You're just jealous."

Spence rolled his eyes. "Of what? The fact that the two of you have to share a woman all the time? That you can't manage to fuck one on your own? No thanks. I don't share. And what's that about anyway?"

AJ shrugged. "Something that just happened, and turns out we like it that way. It works for us."

"Why?"

"You don't get involved if you keep it fun. And doing a three-way is never serious," Pax said.

"You're that afraid of commitment?"

AJ laughed. "And you aren't?"

"I don't need to have another guy fuck a woman with me as a way to avoid being alone with her." Spence knew it had to be something more than that. Pax and AJ always did three-ways. Always. For as long as he could remember.

"You find something you enjoy, you stick with it," AJ said, then leaned back with his coffee cup in his hand.

"Whatever gets you off," Spence said, glad he'd managed to turn the conversation away from Shadoe and him.

Pax grinned. "It does."

DeLaud stood, dragging Spence's attention away from Pax and AJ. They all stared out the window and watched as DeLaud and the two other guys exited the restaurant, then went around to the alley. DeLaud's gaze roamed around as if he were looking for someone. Or maybe he wanted to make sure he wasn't being watched.

Once inside the alley, the three huddled close together, with DeLaud's back to them.

"Did you see that?" AJ asked.

"Yeah," Spence said, frowning. "Something exchanged hands."

"I didn't see what it was," Pax said. "Could be drugs."

"It might not be, though. We can't be sure."

"We're public and it's not like we could set up surveillance equipment here." Spence wished it were that easy, but it wasn't that kind of assignment.

DeLaud exited the alley and headed south. The other two guys went back toward the docks.

"I'll follow the guys," Pax said, standing. "If they're selling drugs, I might just be in the market for some. It should be easy enough to get a hit there. Drug dealers are always easy to spot. Maybe we can follow them up the food chain."

AJ stood, too. "I'm on DeLaud. I'll keep you posted."

Both of them shot out the front door and disappeared into the crowd of tourists, leaving Spence at the table with his coffee, and the check. He shook his head, smiled, and took the bill to the counter to pay.

SHADOE WAS NERVOUS. SHE KNEW UNDERCOVER WORK WAS AN integral part of her job, and she was about as undercover as an agent could get. After all, she was taking her clothes off every night.

But tonight, she was going to be required to put on an award-winning performance. She was going to have to act as if she hated someone she was growing to care deeply about. And she was going to have to walk away from him.

Then again, she might as well get used to it, since that's exactly what was going to happen when this assignment was over. She was going to walk away. So this would be good practice for the real thing, right?

Not even close, Shadoe. This was playacting. It wasn't time to leave Spence. Yet even the thought of that day—which was coming, all too soon—made her stomach clench. And that wasn't good. Because it meant she was growing attached, that she'd developed feelings for Spence, something she'd sworn she wouldn't do.

This was all supposed to be fun and games, no strings, just sex. It was turning into a lot more than that, at least for her. And no matter how she tried to talk herself out of feeling anything for him, she couldn't. She was going to have to figure out how to deal with that.

But not tonight. Tonight was performance night. And she didn't mean stripping.

DeLaud was there again, seated at one of the front tables, same as last night. He'd watched her intently during her first show, so she'd made sure to give him a lot of eye contact. And Spence had made sure to scowl, so much that she almost bought his pissed-off lover act.

She kind of liked it.

She changed clothes and came out wearing a red miniskirt and black skintight top with black stiletto heels. Damn high heels were going to be the death of her before this assignment was over. How did women walk in these all the time? She had a new appreciation for strippers.

Prepared for what was to come, she put on her best pissed-off look, lifted her chin, and strolled right past Spence. He grabbed her arm.

"I want to talk to you."

"Not now. Can't you see I'm working?"

"Now."

She jerked her arm free. "Look, we've been over this. You need to back down. Understood?"

"Loud and clear, bitch. But if you want me as your bodyguard, you can quit flaunting your affairs in front of me."

She laughed. "I'm not having an affair, Spence. That's just your deluded jealousy talking."

"I know what I see, Desi. And I'm not your trained monkey."

She turned to fully face him and crossed her arms. "I don't want a monkey. I want a man. And if you don't want this gig anymore, then quit."

Anger shot from his deep blue eyes. She'd never want to make him mad, because he played fury really well. "I don't need this shit from you or any woman."

"Then walk."

He stared at her for what seemed like an eternity. She stood her ground and stared right back at him until he turned and did just what she suggested—he walked, storming toward the bar. Shadoe made a show of looking hurt, then inhaled deeply, blew it off, pivoted around, and moved off in the opposite direction—in the direction of DeLaud's table.

He caught her gaze and motioned to her. She plastered on a fake smile and slid into the chair he pulled out for her. DeLaud signaled a waitress and held up two fingers, then turned his attention to her.

"Problem, Desi?"

"Kind of." She was going for reluctance rather than just spilling her guts right off.

"Want to talk about it?"

"No. That's okay."

He lowered his voice, calm and reassuring. "Tell me."

With a dramatic sigh, she said, "I just broke up with my boyfriend."

He frowned. "I'm sorry."

She shrugged. "It's been a long time coming. He's too possessive."

He stroked her arm with his fingertips. She wanted to shudder, but kept a straight face.

"A woman like you needs the freedom to do what she wants. After all, it's part of your job."

She turned halfway to face him. "I know. That's what I kept trying to tell him. I like people. I like talking to them. My job requires that I do it, but I really enjoy it. I don't know." She smoothed her hair away from her face. "I just think it was time we ended things. I'm ready for a fun new adventure."

His lips lifted. "Are you?"

Now she smiled. "Yeah. I enjoy my work catering to all the guys. I enjoy traveling and having the opportunity to experience new things. And I love men. I don't think I should have to be saddled with just one." She made sure to look into his eyes when she said that last line. She hoped he bought it.

From the look of utter lust on his face, she'd guess he did. He moved his fingertips along her shoulder and collarbone. "I think you should be able to do whatever you want."

The waitress brought their drinks and Shadoe sipped hers. Jerry downed his in two gulps, then ordered another. She supposed it would be too easy to assume she could get him drunk and he'd pour out all the information she needed.

No, he was too smart for that. But she also knew she was going to have to play this cool, not appear too eager to settle in with him.

"Thanks for talking to me. I needed someone to listen."

"You're welcome, honey."

She pushed her chair back. "I need to go work the room for a while."

"Come back and see me when you're done. We'll . . . talk some more."

Bingo. That's just what she wanted to hear. She gave him a bright smile. "Thanks. I'll do that."

She moved along and did her thing, avoiding Spence, who hung out at the bar. She didn't even make eye contact with him in case DeLaud was watching her.

"Hey, I saw what happened. I'm sorry."

Ariele wrapped an arm around her.

"It's okay. I saw it coming. I was just putting off the inevitable."

Ariele nodded, her expression serious. "Men suck sometimes." Then her face brightened. "But they can be fun, too."

Shadoe laughed. "And so easily replaced."

"One dick's just as good as another, huh?"

Shadoe caught sight of AJ and Pax giving Ariele the once-over. "Or in your case, maybe two?"

Ariele giggled. "They *are* fun to play with. And so damn good-looking they curl my toes."

"Yes, they are pretty, aren't they?"

"Honey, they're pretty all over."

Way more than Shadoe wanted to know about fellow agents, but she had to play the game. "I can only imagine."

Ariele turned to her. "Oh, you could join us sometime. I'm sure they wouldn't mind at all."

Ick. "Thanks, but I think I'll steer clear of threesomes for the moment. Or foursomes. Now that I'm free, I'm going to go man hunting."

"That good-looking dark-haired guy seems to have his eye on you."

She followed Ariele's gaze to see DeLaud looking at her. He winked. Shadoe wanted to gag. Yeah, he was good-looking all right. But he was dirty. And a dirty agent turned her stomach. "He *is* hot and he does seem interested."

"There's no better way to get over one man than to jump right on another," Ariele said, then winked. "I'm on next. See ya." She waved and moved off. So did Shadoe, who made her way over to AJ and Pax's table.

"Nice breakup scene," AJ said. "I nearly broke down in tears."

She settled into a chair and smiled. "Thanks. Spence and I should win an award for it, don't you think?"

Pax leaned forward. "I think so. And did our friend buy it?"

"Yes. He's offered a shoulder for me to lean on."

"Aww, isn't that generous of him. You know he wants to fuck you."

Leave it to AJ to be direct. "Yeah, I kind of get that, too. It's not going to happen. I'll have to spend time with him but put him off the sex."

"Why?" AJ asked. "You gave it to Spence."

She really should be insulted, but that was just AJ. "Yes, I did. But I don't 'give it' to just anyone. For instance, you're not getting any from me."

AJ laughed. "Okay darlin'. I get it."

Pax shook his head. "He really is an asshole. I don't know why I like him."

"Because I bring in all the women."

Pax rolled his eyes. She could already tell where this conversation was going. "Did you find out anything today?"

"I made new friends," Pax said. "Did a drug deal down on the docks. I'll go back later and see if I can hook up with them again."

"DeLaud went back to the hotel after he met with those guys," AJ said. "I stayed on him for the day, then had the bellman keep watch. He didn't leave the room."

Shadoe leaned back. "So he's involved with street dealers. That makes no sense."

"That's what I thought, too," Pax said. "Unless they're brokers or somehow connected to the big guns, and instead of DeLaud making contact via cell or in person, he's doing it through the middle man."

"For now," Shadoe suggested.

AJ nodded. "That's what we thought, too. Either way, with all of us on him, there's no way he can make that deal without us knowing about it."

"I'll stay as close to him as I can." As close as she could stomach. She had her limits as to what she was willing to do for her job. Having sex with a man she desired was one thing. Fucking someone as part of the job? She drew the line there. But she'd tease DeLaud and hold him on a long rope as long as she could.

She didn't linger with Pax and AJ, instead moved along to more tables, stopped and chatted with several guys, did everything she was supposed to do as a headliner.

She ran into Brandon as she made her way back toward one of the darkened corners. He slipped his hand in hers, which surprised her since he'd never touched her before.

"I saw what happened between you and your boyfriend."

"Yes?"

"I'm sorry. That was rough on you, I'm sure."

She breathed out a sigh of relief. She'd been certain he was going to jump on her about causing a scene.

She shrugged. "It's fine. We used to have blowups all the time, and frankly, I'm fed up with him."

"He's still here."

"I know."

"Want me to have him tossed?"

She shook her head. "Not at all. He can hang here if he wants to. If he causes problems, I'll let you know."

"You'll need another bodyguard."

"Your bouncers do a really good job of keeping the grabby ones away."

Brandon smiled. "Yeah, they do. But they can't always be by your side."

"I'll hire a replacement soon enough. Thanks for looking out for me."

"Hey, just doing my job. You're doing great out there. We've been packed in every night since you started, and your PR skills are top-notch."

"Well, thank you. I'm glad your business is doing well and that I'm helping out with that."

"You're welcome here anytime, Desi."

He walked away and she was relieved to have one less thing to worry about. Now it was time to work her magic on DeLaud and see if she could find out anything about this mystery man.

As she scanned the room, she noticed Spence had moved away from the bar and was hanging out with Spitfire, the talkative red-head. Seeing the two of them lean into each other and laugh, she was instantly hit with a stab of jealousy, but knew she had no right. She had to turn away, refuse to glance at him, and focus on her job. Spence was doing exactly what he should. She needed to do the same thing.

"Already got the next meat on the hook?"

She spun around and frowned at Cheri. Dressed in . . . well, what she wore could barely be considered "dressed," since it was some diaphanous outfit that went to the floor like a nightgown, nearly see-through, and the only thing she wore underneath it was her G-string. Really, the girl knew nothing about leaving a little mystery. They gave enough of themselves out on the stage. When wandering around the club it made sense to make the men ache for what was underneath their clothes, not put it all out there for them to ogle.

"I have no idea what you're talking about."

Cheri rolled her eyes. "Oh, please. You dumped your boyfriend and you're already hitting on Brandon."

"Excuse me? I am not."

"I saw you chatting him up in the corner. Trying to get yourself a permanent position at the Wild Rose?"

Yeah, that would be her greatest ambition. Not. "Shouldn't you be out working the customers instead of me, Cheri?"

"Stay away from Brandon. He's not going to hire you. I'm going to be the star here."

She'd had enough. "Fuck off." She started to walk away, but

Cheri grabbed her arm and dug in her nails. Reflex took over. Shadoe grasped Cheri's wrist and wrenched it behind her back, whipping the woman around faster than Cheri could suck in an outraged breath. She shoved the front of Cheri's body against the wall, using leverage to hold her there.

Shadoe knew this caused a scene, but she had to establish her own dominance here or others would walk all over her.

"Stay the fuck out of my business, Cheri. You understand?" To prove her point, she jerked upward on Cheri's arm, enough to cause discomfort, but not hurt her.

"I got it. Ow, bitch, yes!"

Shadoe released her and took a quick step back, her body tensed and prepared to do battle if Cheri decided to launch at her.

"What the fuck are you doing?"

Instead, Lance came rushing down the hall to glare at his wife.

Cheri adjusted her clothing and walked over to her husband. "Nothing. Me and Desi just had a little disagreement."

Brandon had arrived, too, along with half the club's male population, no doubt hoping to see a catfight.

"What's going on?" Brandon asked.

"Just a little meeting between Cheri and me."

Brandon shot Cheri a warning glare, then he slanted a concerned look at Shadoe. "You okay, Desi?"

Cheri squealed her outrage. "Is *she* okay? She damn near twisted my fucking arm off! Why don't you ask if I'm okay?"

"Lance, bring Cheri into my office. I'd like to talk to her."

Lance nodded and escorted a somewhat unwilling Cheri from the area.

"I'm sorry," Brandon said, while the bouncers shuffled everyone out of the corner.

Shadoe shrugged. "Don't be. It's not my first girl fight. Won't be my last. I can take care of myself."

Brandon grinned. "I guess you can. But I'll deal with Cheri."

"She didn't do anything, really. Don't worry about it."

But he just winked and walked away. Whatever. Cheri was his problem to deal with, not hers. She had her own agenda.

"Are you all right?"

A hand on her shoulder, and a familiar voice. Not the one she wanted for comfort, but it played right into her agenda. She turned and smiled at Jerry DeLaud.

"I'm fine. Just a tiff between me and another dancer."

He arched a brow. "Is she jealous?"

Shadoe laughed. "I think she might be."

He held out his arm and she linked hers through it.

"She should be. You're one of the best dancers up there."

"And flattery will get you . . ."

He looked at her expectantly.

"Well, we'll see where it gets you."

He laughed and led her to a table in one of the private corners. "I thought we could talk without being interrupted, unless you need to go back to work."

She took one of the padded seats. "I think I've worked enough tonight. I need to kick back and relax for a while."

He sat next to her. "Good. I'd like to get to know you better."

A waitress stopped by and he started to order drinks.

"I'll have water, please."

When he looked at her in question, she said, "Dancing dehydrates me. I need to drink a lot of water."

He nodded and put in his drink order. "You're not a lush. I like that about you."

"I'm glad. I need all the friends I can get, since I seem to have made a few enemies today."

"That woman and your ex-boyfriend."

"Yes." She looked down at her lap and tried to look sad.

He tipped her chin up to face him. "I'd like to be your friend."

What a creep. "That's really nice. I could use some new friends. But I don't really know you."

He held out his hand. "Jerry."

She shook his hand. "Nice to meet you, Jerry. Do you live here in New Orleans?"

He shook his head. "No, but I come here on business periodically."

"Great place to travel to. What do you do?"

"I'm in the import business."

I'll just bet you are. "That sounds exciting."

"It can be."

"So where are you from?"

"Los Angeles."

Liar. "Ohh, how wonderful! I'd love to go to L.A. sometime."

"I'd love to have you come out and visit me sometime. Where are you headlining next?"

"I have a gig in Shreveport, then Dallas, then Houston. After that I'll have to check my schedule."

"You like to travel?"

She grinned. "I love to."

"And where are you from, Desi?"

"Tulsa, originally, but I've lived all over the place. I left home when I was sixteen and traveled with some friends, got a job at eighteen in a strip club and never looked back."

"You enjoy this life."

"Yes, I do." It was amazing the bullshit she could make up on the fly. She was getting good at this.

"I like a woman who knows what she wants."

"I love entertaining."

"Ever do private parties?"

She lowered her lashes. "I did a little of that. I hooked up with one of those companies that offered strippers for bachelor parties."

"Lucrative."

She shrugged. "It depends on the company. The one I worked for was shady. I got screwed on wages."

"You should be able to call your own shots, set your own price."

"That would be nice. At some point I hope to have a good manager, set up my own company, and hire on others to work for me."

He reached out and smoothed his hand over her hair. "Beautiful and a head for business, too."

"Well, thanks. I'd like to think so."

"Ever do drugs?"

Interesting question. She wondered where he was going with it? "Is that an offer or just a background question? Hey, you're not a cop, are you?"

He tilted his head back and laughed. "Sorry. No, I'm not a cop. You just seem so clean-cut."

"I am, but I wasn't, once. I did the whole drug thing when I was younger. It messed with my head so I don't do them now."

"Hate them, huh?"

She shrugged. "They're fine for whoever wants them and can handle them. I just prefer to keep a clear head."

"So you don't judge others who use?"

"As long as they don't mess with me while they're loaded, or steal from me to buy their shit, I couldn't care less what anyone else does. It doesn't affect me."

He nodded. "Good attitude."

"I'm not judgmental, Jerry. I was judged way too often in my past. I think people should be allowed to do whatever makes them happy."

She hoped she was giving him all the right answers.

"Would you like to go grab something to eat?"

She supposed she'd passed the test. "Sure. I can't stay out too long. I need my beauty sleep."

"I understand. I'd just like to get away from this noisy place."

"You and me both."

She knew Spence or AJ and Pax would follow, so she felt safe. She was wired, too, with the transmitter in her belly button, and she and Spence had tested it earlier in the day. They knew tonight might provide an opportunity to use it, so Spence would be listening in. Plus she had her piece in her purse, which she grabbed after she changed into jeans and a tank top. She met Jerry through the side door and slid into his car, a sporty model that smelled new. Rental, probably. Harder to trace to him that way.

"Nice wheels."

"Thanks."

He drove her out of the French Quarter and into the city. They stopped at an all-night breakfast place, ate, and had coffee.

"How long will you be in town on this trip, Jerry?" Shadoe pushed her plate away and poured more coffee from the refill pot the waitress had left on their table.

"About five days. I have some meetings and a key deal going down in the next day or so."

Her brows lifted. "Really? Something good for business?"

He placed both palms around his coffee. "Something very good for business."

"You must do very well at it."

"Why do you say that?"

She nodded toward him. "You dress well. You wear expensive shoes. You drive a hot car that's worth some money."

He cracked a wry smile. "You taking inventory?"

"No, but it's my job to be observant." That much was true. It was her job. Her real job.

"You observe very well."

"It keeps my customers happy if I notice things. It can't always be about me flashing my boobs."

"Well, those are very nice."

She laughed. "Thanks, but I've found men like talking about themselves, too. Not just how nice my breasts are."

"Do you dabble in psychology, too?"

"One of my favorite courses in college."

He tilted his head to the side. "You've been to college?"

She already had an answer for him. "I told you, I don't intend to just strip, though I do love it. If I want to run my own business someday, I knew I'd need to go to college to figure out how. That's why I'm as old as I am and just now making it as a head-liner."

"Got it all planned, do you?"

"It's important to have goals."

His wide smile and nod said she'd charmed him. She hoped so. "I like you, Desi."

"I like you, too, Jerry. You made a miserable evening turn out really nice. I appreciate that."

"The evening doesn't have to end."

Oh, hell yes, it does. She reached out and slid her hand across his cheek. "Your offer is tempting. I'd like nothing more than to lose myself in your bed tonight. But I need to check out of my boyfriend's room and get one of my own. And then I need some sleep."

"I understand." He paid the check and took her to the hotel, opened her door, and turned to her.

"Thank you, Jerry. Will I see you again tonight?"

"I wouldn't miss it." Before she could move away, he pulled her into his arms and kissed her, sliding his tongue inside her mouth. She couldn't very well fight him off, so she leaned into him, laid her hands on his shoulders, and kissed him back, even when he reached down to knead her buttocks with his hand and pull her against his erection.

He released her mouth. "I really want to fuck you."

She pretended to pant. "You'll give me something to think about all night." She pressed a quick kiss to his lips, smiled, and walked away.

She got another room at the front desk, pocketed the key. Once inside the elevator, she wiped her mouth with the back of her hand, reached into her bag, and grabbed a breath mint.

"Grab-ass bastard," she muttered. She fished out the key to Spence's room and hit the button for his floor. When she got into the room, he wasn't there. She sighed, feeling lonely without him there. She packed up all her things and moved them down one floor to her new room.

She'd no more finished unpacking than her phone rang.

"What's your room number?"

It was Spence's gruff, no-nonsense voice. She gave him her room number and he hung up immediately.

She knew why. She paced in front of the door, waiting.

It didn't take long. Within a minute there was a knock on the door. She pulled the door open and just seeing him made her breath catch. She'd missed him, had had a miserable time with Jerry, loathed having his hands and mouth on her even though she'd only been doing her job.

Spence walked in and shut the door.

"I watched him touch you, heard everything he said to you. He kissed you," Spence said, his voice tight with strain, his body tense. "I didn't like it."

"I hated it." She moved closer and tilted her head back to gaze into Spence's gorgeous blue eyes, opening herself up to him. "Erase his touch."

Spence wrapped his arm around her and jerked her against him. His mouth came down on hers hard, his tongue entering her mouth in the same way Jerry's had. Only this was so different. She welcomed Spence's kiss, craved his mouth on hers, his tongue licking against hers, the hungry way his hands traveled over her body, pulling her clothes off everywhere he touched. He backed her over to the bed.

She reached for his shirt, pulled it out of his pants, and slid her hands underneath to touch his skin.

It was hot, smooth, the muscles of his stomach rippling under her touch. Spence let out a light groan and the sound of it made her wet.

Oh, hell. She'd been wet from the moment he'd opened the door.

"Put your mouth on me. Touch me." She was breathless and she wasn't fully undressed yet. Just touching him did that to her.

Her jeans were unsnapped, unzipped, partially down and open for his hand to slide down and cup her sex. She cried out, arched against his touch. He slid a finger inside her and slid the heel of his hand back and forth over her clit, his movements relentless as he looked down on her with a fierceness that made her quiver inside.

She wanted him naked, inside her. She wanted to be free to touch him, to let her hands roam over his magnificent body. But she was frozen to the mattress, her entire body focused on the movements of his hand as he brought her to a quick, blinding orgasm that had her lifting up her butt and grasping his wrist to shove his finger deeper inside her.

"Yeah," he murmured, before he took her mouth again and

dipped his tongue inside, driving her to the brink yet again with the smooth movements of his hand and fingers.

But then he stopped, withdrew, and she didn't know whether to be relieved or frustrated.

He crawled off the bed to undress, and she rolled over to her side and propped her head on her elbow to watch the unveiling. Tanned, smooth skin rippling with muscle, flat abs, broad shoulders—she'd never tire of looking at his body. Scars and all, he was perfection to her. He gave her butterflies in her stomach and made her toes curl, and as he turned around, she realized he had a mighty fine ass, too. She got on her knees and pressed herself against his back, kissing the tattoo on his shoulder blade.

"That feels nice," he said, tossing her a look that made her melt inside.

"The kiss?"

"Your tits against my back."

She laughed and rubbed back and forth, her nipples tingling as they slid against the smooth skin of his back.

He turned around and pushed her onto the mattress, grabbed her wrists, and lifted them above her head. He swept the palm of his hand over her distended, sensitive nipples. Her lips parted and she let out a gasp at the contact, the sensation shooting between her legs and ratcheting up her need to feel him inside her.

He rolled her nipple between his fingers, plucked the bud until she arched up.

"More."

That seemed to be her favorite word whenever Spence made love to her. Whatever he gave her, she wanted more of it. She was drawn to him in a way she'd never been with any other man. His touch set her on fire and she craved more of it every time.

He bent down and took her nipple in his mouth, using his hand to cup her flesh and hold it while he licked and sucked the bud, rolling his tongue over it, nibbling at it, every single lash of his tongue and teeth sending shooting sparks to the nerve endings in her clit.

He'd released her wrists and she cradled his head between her hands, letting her fingers roam in his hair. She held him while he loved one breast, then the other.

"Please. Fuck me."

She couldn't wait, slid her hand between them to encircle his cock and grab tight. His head jerked up to meet her gaze, his eyes glassy with passion and need. He hissed out a breath as she stroked him, then pulled away to put on the condom, obviously as anxious as she was.

He rolled her to the side and lifted her leg over his hip, thrusting inside her even as he grabbed on to her and dug his fingers in her flesh.

Heaven. Hell. Torture and pleasure mixed as he powered against her with deliberate strokes made to caress, to tingle, to drive her mad. With one hand he held on to her hip, the other he slid behind her head to bring her into a kiss that melded the two of them into hot passion and tender emotion, the mix almost unbearable.

She tried to focus on the sex, the slick melting of her flesh against his, but the way his lips moved against hers seemed to be more than purely physical.

Maybe it was only her, but the connection she felt went much deeper than just a joining of their bodies.

Stop thinking. Enjoy this. There's nothing more.

She pushed away the lingering emotion, the involvement of her heart, the way his eyes seemed to penetrate her soul as he moved against her. She wasn't going to get involved.

She wasn't falling in love with him. This was just sex.

"Come for me, Shadoe." He rolled his hips, his shaft sliding along her sex, leading her along the path to orgasm. He did it slow, deliberate, grinding against her and shredding her control until she splintered around his cock with spasms of wild pleasure.

He held tight to her while she spun in a vortex of intensity. Her climax grabbed her in its clutches and wouldn't let go, shooting through her with pulses of incredible sensation that kept going on long after she thought it would stop. She was dying from the sheer pleasure of it, held on to Spence, cried out his name as he continued to pump inside her and took her over the edge again, this time going along for the ride with a loud groan and a shudder.

Shaken, she laid her forehead against his, her body continuing to tremble with aftershocks. Spence stroked her back, kissed her, and her eyes filled with tears. She blinked them back, feeling weak and emotional, and she wasn't the weak, emotional type. She was tough, dammit. She could handle this. Soon he would get up and leave and go back to his room.

He got up, went into the bathroom, and came back, then climbed onto the bed with her and gathered her into his arms. She laid her head on his chest, content to feel his hands stroking her skin. Her eyes began to drift closed but she kept jerking herself awake.

"What are you doing?" Spence whispered.

"I don't want to fall asleep."

"Why not?"

"I want to be awake when you leave."

"Leave for where?"

"To go back to your room."

He tipped her chin up with his fingers, made her meet his gaze. "I'm not sleeping without you tonight."

She shuddered out a sigh, wanted to cry, and hated that she wanted to. "Oh."

"Relax and sleep, Shadoe."

It was all too good. Too perfect. A million things flitted around in her mind. The what-ifs, the impending end of whatever this thing was that was going on between Spence and her.

The fact she was falling in love with him, and knew how fruitless those feelings were.

But for now, he was here. In her room. He'd come to her.

Did anything else matter?

She allowed sleep to take her over.

sixteen

Shadoe awoke alone in her room. It was late, afternoon she'd guess. God, she was going to be so screwed up when this assignment was over. Staying up all night, sleeping all day. Bleh. Her time clock was messed up. She slid her palm along the side of the bed where Spence had slept, and felt a moment of melancholy sadness.

Get over it. Soon enough your life will be like this again. Sleeping alone.

When she got out of the shower her phone rang. It was Spence, saying AJ and Pax were at his room and she needed to come up. She dressed in a hurry and rode the elevator up one floor to Spence's room, used her key to slide in, and closed the door behind her.

Pax and AJ were having coffee and breakfast in the sitting area. Spence was pacing. Shadoe poured a cup from the room service cart and grabbed a roll to nibble on. "What's up?"

"Guess who visited DeLaud's room last night?" Pax said.

"Who?" she asked, sliding into one of the chairs.

"Lance."

Her gaze shot to Spence. "Cheri's husband? Why?"

"Good question." Spence frowned. "We're trying to figure that out now."

"Maybe he's buying drugs."

Spence shook his head. "He could do that from a lot of people, including the two guys you bought from yesterday, Pax."

Shadoe scrunched her nose. "You think Lance is DeLaud's connection at the club?"

Spence nodded. "It makes sense. We've suspected all along that DeLaud had a connection to the club, someone on the inside to help him make contacts in a legitimate location away from the docks."

Shadoe thought that made sense, too. "He's pretty high up on the food chain there. Brandon told me Lance takes over for him as manager whenever he's away or unavailable."

"So he would have keys, access to everything at the club," AJ said.

Shadoe nodded. "You know, Brandon offered me another bodyguard after Spence and I had our very public breakup last night."

"I'll bet you think Lance would make a good bodyguard," Pax said.

"Why not? I'm already in with DeLaud. If I pick up Lance as a bodyguard and those two are thick as thieves, it'll be perfect."

Spence frowned.

"You're right," AJ said. "You'd be close to both of them."

Spence still hadn't commented.

"I'll be fine."

"I don't like it. It's too dangerous. What if the deal goes down and you're right in the middle of it?"

"Isn't that what we want?" she argued.

He dragged his fingers through his hair. "I guess so."

"You'll all be there to protect me, Spence. And besides, I'm a trained agent. This is my job."

He nodded. "Yes, I try to remember that."

He looked as if he wanted to say something, then slid his gaze over to AJ and Pax, who watched him expectantly. He closed his mouth and walked through the bedroom and outside onto the balcony.

"Dude, that was interesting," AJ said.

Pax shrugged. "Never seen it before."

Shadoe's attention flitted between both of them. "What?"

Pax stared at the balcony doorway, then brought his attention back to her. "He's bugged."

"About?"

"You," AJ said.

"Me?"

"He cares about you."

She let her gaze drift down to her lap, to the cup of coffee balanced there. "Oh. Well, yeah."

"Yeah is right. He's about as fucked up about it as I've ever seen him. The mission is primary to Spence. Always has been."

"Until now," AJ said. "You've really messed him up."

Shadoe snapped an angry glare at AJ. "What the hell does that mean?"

AJ's eyes widened. "Hey, don't get all female on me. I just meant you've messed him up in a good way. He needs someone to care about him."

"He has all of you guys."

Pax laughed. "Yeah, but we don't fuck him."

Her face flamed hot, but she couldn't help but laugh. "I sure hope not."

"Look," AJ said, keeping his voice low. "This is screwing with his head. He feels something for you. He's protective and concerned and he doesn't know what to do with that. Normally he wouldn't care if a fellow agent put herself in harm's way. That's the job, ya know?"

"Yes. It is my job."

"But your job could get you killed. And he cares about you. As mission leader, he's giving the okay for you to put yourself in danger. He's conflicted."

"Whoa. You studying psychology in the bathroom, AJ?" Pax looked appalled.

AJ snorted. "Yeah, I sneak in Advanced Psych textbooks under my *Hustler* magazine."

Shadoe shook her head. But what the guys had said gave her pause. She'd thought her feelings were one-sided.

Maybe they weren't. Which didn't change things at all. When the mission was over, they were history.

But maybe she wouldn't be the only one upset about that. It gave her a little bit of comfort to know that Spence might actually care as much as she did.

She stood and put her coffee cup on the table. "I'll go talk to him."

Spence was leaning over the balcony, staring down onto the street. Shadoe came up next to him and laid her hand on his back. "I'm going to be fine. I know how to take care of myself."

He turned his head and smiled. "I'm sure you do."

"Do you know I'm trained to kill a man with my bare hands?"

"I'm glad I haven't pissed you off, then."

She laughed, leaned in, and kissed him. "I'll have a weapon on me at all times. I'll be fine."

"And we'll have your back. I'll be listening in via the transmitter attached to you. I get all that. But it doesn't mean I won't worry about you."

She didn't want him worrying, but she liked that he cared that much. "Thanks."

He straightened and faced her. "I worry about everyone on my team. It's my responsibility if something happens to you. I have to plot all this out so I can . . . minimize the potential for losses."

"I see." Now he was trying to pretend she was just one of the guys, that he didn't worry any more for her than he would for anyone else on his team. "Good to know I'll have you as backup, then."

She didn't want to push him, but she didn't want him to pull away either.

She didn't think she was going to be able to have it both ways.

After a long tactical conversation about the possibilities and restrictions of what Shadoe could and couldn't do with both Lance and DeLaud, AJ and Pax left. Pax was off to see if he could follow up on the drug deal he'd made yesterday, and AJ to keep an eye on DeLaud. Spence decided to go with AJ to provide backup in case he needed it. Shadoe wanted to spend a few early hours at the club today to see what she could dig up from the girls. Spence said he'd stay wired to her in case anything went down he needed to be aware of.

CHERI WAS ON THE STAGE WORKING ON HER MOVES. SHE SHOT Shadoe a dirty look. Shadoe didn't bother to acknowledge her. Lance winked at her though, and she gave him a wide smile. Shadoe waved to Brandon, who was behind the bar helping the bartender unpack bottles of liquor. She went into the back room and found Star, sullen and quiet as usual, and Spitfire, talking Elan's ear off while Elan sat patiently listening and smiling.

"What's up today, ladies?"

Spitfire looked up, sniffed, and grinned. "We're chattin', darlin'. Come join us. Would you like some coffee? Or maybe a drink, though I think it's too early to indulge but maybe not for you. Some people like to start their cocktail hour sooner than others. Not me, though. Nuh-uh. I don't drink alcohol. Straight soda or water for me. Anyway, I was tellin' Elan about this great sale on shoes. I got me a new pair. See?"

She lifted her foot to show off a pair of clear acrylic fuck-me shoes. Shadoe blinked, first at the rapid-fire conversation, then at the amazing six-inch heels. "Wow, those are cool."

"I think so, too. And they were half-price. I bought a pair in red patent leather, too. I need to get me a new act and I want to go all red to match my hair. Wouldn't that just kick ass? I could so see me in a red leather G-string. Did I mention how much I love your black leather getup, Desi? Wow, the guys just drool over your costumes."

"Thanks." Shadoe moved to her locker, watching Spitfire turn back to Elan, who must have the patience of a saint to sit and listen to Spitfire's nonstop, all-over-the-place jabbering. And the way Spitfire constantly rubbed her nose, and the glassy-eyed look about her led Shadoe to believe that it wasn't the redhead's natural exuberance that made her chatty.

Spitfire was on something. Cocaine or meth would be Shadoe's guess. She wondered if Spitfire was involved with DeLaud or with Lance in any way. She'd have to keep her eye on the girl tonight, see if she engaged the two men at all.

She visited with all of them for a while. Spitfire, of course, was the most talkative, but she was one of those people who talked nonstop without really saying much. It was hard to get her to focus. When Shadoe quizzed her about what she did on her off-time, she said she "partied," then crashed, that she had lots of friends, rattled off a ton of names unrecognizable to Shadoe, so it wasn't helpful at all. Shadoe couldn't badger her, so she let it go.

She hung out with Ariele for a while, who said she liked to spend a lot of her free time in dance class—or having sex with AJ and Pax. And *that* she didn't want details about. Ariele didn't seem to be a likely suspect, so Shadoe left the dressing room and went out into the club area, where Lance greeted her while he watched Cheri dance.

"I hear you're in need of a new bodyguard."

She smiled. "Yes, Spence and I broke up last night."

"I'm sorry. That's rough."

"Nothing you have to worry about, though. It must be nice to be able to take care of your wife and work with her, too."

His smile died. "Uh-huh."

Hmm, maybe Lance and Cheri's marriage wasn't all paradise. Shadoe could play on that. "So are you offering your services as bodyguard?"

"Well I'm here, I've got the time, and I'd be happy to look out for you. You're pretty popular so you need someone to watch over you."

"Thanks." She directed him over to a table. They went over hours and money and they came to a quick agreement. Cheri darted scathing looks in their direction every few seconds, but Brandon had walked to the front of the stage to talk to her when her dance ended, which prevented her from storming over and causing a scene. Good, since Shadoe didn't want that. She needed to hook up with Lance as her bodyguard for tonight, then see what happened after that.

"Is this going to be a problem?" she asked when they stood.

"What?"

"You being my bodyguard. Cheri doesn't look happy."

He let out a short laugh. "You let me worry about Cheri."

"Works for me." They shook hands and Shadoe went to find Ariele. They grabbed something to eat before the crowd started to arrive, then came back so Ariele could get ready for her first show since she went on much earlier than Shadoe.

Which meant Shadoe could actually wander around for a while before she had to dance.

When the doors opened at four P.M., people came in. Kind of early, and it wasn't a heavy crowd, but apparently men and women both were thirsty and happy to get out of the sweltering heat and have a seat to watch the dancers.

Shadoe sat at the bar and nursed a diet soda, visited with the bartender and Brandon, who remained back there to help since the second bartender wasn't due to come in until seven.

"So you hired Lance?" Brandon motioned with his head toward Lance, who had already taken position nearby, discreet but close enough to come to her aid if she needed him.

"Yes. He offered and it's convenient since he already works here. I hope that's not a problem."

"Not at all. If it keeps our star dancer safe, I'm for it."

Brandon frowned when the door opened and sunshine spilled in along with a throng of new people. Shadoe swiveled in her seat and fought a smile.

Spence came in with the group. She turned away to face the bar.

"Why does he keep coming back in here if the two of you broke up?" Brandon asked.

She shrugged. "Probably to piss me off, though I think he's taken with Spitfire, too."

"Does that bother you? Because I'll toss his ass out."

She laughed. "No, really, don't. I don't care what he does. I don't feel anything for him anymore, so he can do whatever, or whoever, he wants."

"Okay, but if he causes trouble for you, he's history."

"Thanks, Brandon." She turned back around in her chair and gave Spence her best smug smile when he walked by. He arched a brow, said nothing, and grinned when Spitfire threw herself at him and kissed him.

It was a good thing Shadoe figured Spitfire was a drug user and Spence was just trying to get information from her, or at least have a good reason to be here at the club. Otherwise she might care that the gorgeous redhead was rubbing her breasts all over her man's chest.

Her man. He wasn't though, was he?

She refused to think about it. It made her head—and her heart—hurt.

Spence moved off to a table with Spitfire, and Shadoe forced her attention elsewhere. She studied some of the newer dancers' acts since they went on early, then her gaze wandered to Lance, who nodded at her from his position against the pole near the bar. Cheri walked by, clearly irritated at her husband, since she lifted her chin as she strolled in front of him. Lance didn't seem overly happy with his wife, either. Cheri stopped at the other end of the bar and crooked her finger at Brandon, who sighed and walked over to her, listening while she whispered in his ear. He frowned at whatever she said, shook his head, and started to walk away, but Cheri latched on to his wrist and held it, said something else. Apparently whatever she wanted was urgent—at least to Cheri—because there was fire and anger in her expression. But Brandon jerked his arm away, much to Cheri's irritation. She pivoted and flounced away, this time not even glancing at Lance. Lance was looking at her, though, and he wasn't happy, probably because she was causing shit with the club owner.

Whoa. What drama. And what a diva. Guess Cheri wasn't going to be happy with anyone tonight, was she? She really wanted to get the scoop from Brandon on what all that was about, but didn't want Brandon to think she was digging up gossip.

As the crowd thickened, she slid off the barstool and mingled, chatting up the guys at the tables. Lance did a good job following her around but maintaining a discreet distance. Shadoe couldn't find Spence so didn't know and tried not to care where he'd gone off to. AJ and Pax had slid in a few minutes earlier and taken a table in the corner with a good view of the entire club. She went over to say hello to them, but then Ariele came by and Shadoe moved off, so she didn't get a chance to ask them if anything happened today. She'd have to do that later.

She tingled with anticipation, as if something major was going to happen tonight. She had no idea what, and maybe it was because the wheels had been set in motion and she was right in the middle of it all. The atmosphere felt charged with energy.

"I want to talk to you."

She turned at the sound of Spence's voice, tinged with anger. His gaze flitted to Lance, who had started to make a move toward her. She held up her hand. "It's okay, Lance."

She walked over to a corner, her arms crossed, her expression fierce. "What's going on?"

Spence kept his own anger as he bent and whispered. "Wanted to give you a heads-up. We followed DeLaud to the docks today. The ship is in."

She tried to keep the surprise off her face. "Did he meet with anyone?"

"No. He just walked by, but nodded at the two guys he had breakfast with the other day. I expect the deal to go down tonight."

Instead of nodding, she shook her head as if they were arguing. "Do you think DeLaud will be in here?"

"This is allegedly the place where he brokers his deals." He grabbed her arms and she pushed him away. "Be careful."

"I will. You, too." She turned and walked away. Lance came to her side.

"You all right?"

"Yeah. Just a little argument about money he thinks I owe him."

Lance cast a glare at Spence over his shoulder. "Want me to take care of him?"

"No. He's all talk."

Lance stopped, turned to face her. "If you need my help, I'm here for you."

"Thanks, Lance, I appreciate the offer, but I'll be fine, really. I can handle Spence. We've fought on and off for years. I should have just broken it off before I came to the Wild Rose, but I didn't want to come alone. Stupid, really. Now I'm embarrassed he's causing this shit with me here at the club."

She sniffled and Lance put his arm around her. "It's okay. You're not alone now."

He caressed her back, then let his hand drift lower. She allowed it, mainly because Cheri came out right then, spotted them, and walked by as if she didn't care.

Shadoe pulled away then. "I need to go get ready. Thanks, Lance."

He looked at her like she was water and he was dying of thirst. "Anytime."

She went through the doorway toward the dressing room and blew out a breath. Wow. For a couple supposedly married and in love, Lance and Cheri didn't seem to be very happy together. Maybe Cheri's ambitions were getting to be too much for Lance. And then again, maybe Lance's attention was focused elsewhere.

By the time she came out to do her first show, Jerry DeLaud had arrived and was seated at one of the tables near the front of the stage, but he wasn't alone. The two guys from the docks were there with him. As soon as she moved to the front of the stage, he nodded and the guys moved to the back of the club. As Shadoe did her routine, she noticed AJ got up from the table, bought a beer, then circled around so that he now covered the front door while simultaneously keeping watch over the two guys. Shadoe focused her attention on Jerry, gave him a smile and a wink as she did her show. When she finished, she changed into a miniskirt, body-hugging top, and heels, and went out to see Jerry. She slid onto a chair at DeLaud's table and gave him a bright smile.

"I'm glad you came tonight."

He took her hand and folded his over it. "Did you think I wouldn't?"

"I never count on anything."

He linked his fingers with hers. "I like your act. I wouldn't miss it."

"Only a few more days and I'm done here. Time to move on."

He nodded. "Me, too. My business will be finished here to-night and I'll be leaving."

She affected a pout. "So soon? I thought you were going to be here longer."

"So did I, but it turns out my . . . import deal will wrap up quicker than I thought."

Just what she needed to know. Excitement shot through her and she found it hard to sit still and play the part. But she put on a disappointed pout. "And we were just getting to know each other."

"I could maybe stay an extra day, if you convince me."

Arching a brow, she said, "And how could I convince you of that?"

"Have dinner with me."

"I'd love to."

"How much time before your next show?"

"Two hours."

He looked at his watch. "I have an . . . appointment in about an hour, so that would give us some time alone."

She didn't even ask why he would have an appointment after midnight, but she knew what for. And she wanted to wrangle time with him, possibly arrange to somehow be with him when it went down. "So what are we waiting for?" She leaned in, letting her breast brush his arm.

He stood and held out his hand for her. "Let's go."

Perfect. "Let me change clothes."

"No need. You look beautiful as is."

She laughed. "This is strip club attire, honey. Not really suitable for a restaurant."

"We aren't going to a restaurant. We're going to my hotel room."

She cocked a brow. "That sure of yourself, are you?"

He slid his thumb over her hand. "I think we both know what we want."

Gag. "I need to grab my purse. It has my cell phone and I need to stay in touch with the club."

He hesitated, then nodded. "Go ahead, then."

"It'll just take me a second."

She hurried to the dressing room, grabbed her purse, and shot off a quick text message to Spence, then ran back out to Jerry. She linked her hand with his. "Let's go."

She was waylaid by Lance, who stepped in front of her. "What are you doing?"

"I'm going to head out and have dinner with my friend Jerry here."

Lance frowned. "Not a good idea."

"Why not?"

"You . . . have a show to do."

She glared back at him. "You're my bodyguard, Lance. Not my keeper. You don't get to tell me what to do. I'll be back in plenty of time for my next show."

He opened his mouth as if to say something, looked around her to stare at DeLaud, then closed it and stepped aside. She smiled at him. "Thanks for worrying about me, but I'll be fine, really. And I'll be back soon."

"You be careful." He turned and walked away.

Was he partners with DeLaud? Did he know what was going down tonight?

She hoped Spence would get her message, and that she'd somehow be in the middle of Jerry's deal when it went down. Her skin prickled again with the anticipation that something big was about to happen.

Playtime was over. It was time to put on her agent hat.

They drove to Jerry's hotel, and he led her up to his room. He laid his hand on the small of her back as he opened the door, then closed and locked it behind him. The sound of the click echoed like a prison lock in her ears. She remembered the gun in her purse. She'd be fine. She was trained for this and could take care of herself. She palmed the piercing at her belly, knew Spence would listen in.

If there was any trouble, he'd be here.

"Champagne?" he asked.

She turned to him and smiled. "I'd love some."

He picked up the phone, ordered a couple bottles of champagne along with appetizers. Good. She could kill some time with eating, because no way in hell was she going to have sex with him.

It didn't take long for room service to bring the cart. Jerry popped open a bottle of champagne and poured two glasses, then pulled the lid off a sampler of shrimp, crab, and other snacks. She wasn't hungry at all, but she grabbed a plate and piled on food.

"I'm starving." She kept stuffing food in her mouth, hoping she could stave off his advances.

"Sit beside me." He patted the brocade sofa, giving her no choice but to grab her plate and glass and take a seat next to him. When he took her plate and set it on the table, she took a long swallow of champagne to lubricate her parched throat. Then he took her glass away and leaned in.

Blech. She was going to have to kiss him. She hoped he'd be turned off by her fish breath.

No such luck. He gathered her into his arms and plunged his tongue inside her mouth, ravaging her lips with a deep kiss that utterly revolted her. Jerry was a young, good-looking guy with a great body, but he was also a criminal. That alone repelled her. Yet she still had to do her job, so she kissed him back, trying to envision herself in Spence's arms, with Spence touching her. That made it easier, though Jerry didn't touch her or kiss her like Spence did. There was no finesse, no passion between them like there was between her and Spence. Her heart, her emotions, weren't invested. That made all the difference.

She didn't love Jerry like she loved Spence. She whimpered.

"Oh, yeah," Jerry murmured against her lips, thinking she whimpered because of his kiss and his touch.

He was so wrong. And when he reached up to slide his hand inside her shirt and pinch her nipple, she drew back. There was only so much she'd allow.

"I think we—"

She was interrupted by a knock at the door.

"Fuck!" Jerry stood and looked down at his watch, then smiled at her. "Whoever it is, I'll get rid of them."

She turned on the chaise and watched as he unlocked and opened the door. A young guy came rushing in.

"It's on."

Jerry shot a gaze over his shoulder. "I have company."

"Oh. Sorry. But I need to talk to you. Now."

"I told you I'd call you. We'll talk later."

The guy was jittery, balancing back and forth on the balls of his feet, his hands jammed into the pocket of his baggy jeans. He wore a ball cap and had on a jacket that looked like it was two sizes two big for him. He was young, midtwenties maybe. Shadoe had seen him in the club before, had talked to him after her show. But he wasn't one of the dockworkers, at least not one she'd seen that day. This guy might be DeLaud's contact for the drug deal.

Jerry dragged his fingers through his hair, looked at Shadoe, then back at the guy. "Now?"

The guy nodded, leaned in, and whispered. But Shadoe caught what he'd said.

"The launch has already docked beside the ship. They're ready to transfer."

Shadoe stood. "Should I leave?" She did her best to affect a disappointed pout.

Jerry held up his hand. "No. Give me a second to think. My appointment is just earlier than I thought it would be."

Perfect. "I could go with you, then maybe we could take a ride in your car." Men loved car sex. It was public and naughty.

His lips lifted. "If you don't mind waiting in the car while I have a short meeting . . ."

She shrugged. "I don't mind at all. As long as we bring the champagne with us." She grinned.

He smiled back. "Okay, then." He turned to the guy. "I'll meet you there."

The guy took off and DeLaud grabbed his keys. Shadoe picked up her purse and met him at the door.

"Thank you for being so understanding."

She pressed a kiss to his lips. "I don't mind at all. You're worth waiting for."

She knew where they were going.

To the docks. The deal was about to go down.

seventeen

THEY ARRIVED AT THE DOCK GATES AND JERRY TURNED TO HER. "This won't take long. Just a mix-up with import paperwork and it needs to be taken care of before the shipment departs."

She held up the bottle in her hands. "My friend and I will be fine here. Don't worry about it." She poured more champagne into her glass and kicked off her shoes, purposefully let her skirt ride up, giving him a shot of her G-string. He took a long look between her legs, leaned in to give her a kiss, closed the door, and headed toward a building near the gates, then was swallowed up by the darkness. Damn, she wished she could see where he was.

As soon as he was out of eyesight, she pulled out her cell phone and dialed Spence's number.

"We've got you covered. We're just outside the dock fences, east of your location."

They must have followed her the entire time. The jitters in her stomach relaxed.

"They went on board a red and white ship named *The Royale*."

"You're fucking insane for leaving with him."

She ignored his irritation. "I had an opening to go with him and I took it. I think the deal is going down right now so hurry your ass up and get over here."

"On our way."

She stepped out of the car and spotted Spence giving her a short wave. He had hidden behind a set of tall piers. Dammit, she really wished she had her jeans and flat shoes on instead of a miniskirt and stilettos. She kicked off her shoes and left them, then went running in her bare feet, thankful she didn't have to do it on gravel. She ducked down beside Spence.

"Where are AJ and Pax?"

"They've moved to the other side. DeLaud and his friends are on the ship. Pax said they moved up the gangplank and went inside."

"They didn't see you?"

"Please. We're using high-powered binoculars to track them."

Okay, so they knew what they were doing. "Do we know who else is on board?"

"Unknown."

She nodded, figuring there would be variables involved. "What about calling the other Feds in?"

"After we know for sure the deal is going down. Not until then."

"I disagree. What if there are fifty men on board? The four of us can't handle that many alone."

"Feds are on standby and have been all week, ready to roll at a moment's notice. If I give the signal that we need backup, they'll be here."

She still didn't like it, but understood the need to wait. If they sent in the Feds before confirming the deal was actually in progress, they'd lose credibility—and the opportunity to nab DeLaud. They knew more than they had a few days ago—the possible rogue agent and the ship responsible—but they still had to lie low to see what happened.

The deal was going down early. The shipment wasn't supposed to be in until this weekend at the earliest. The timing was thrown off. Maybe that's how DeLaud and the Colombians got these deals and shipments in, throwing off timetables and expectations and giving the Feds the runaround, making them show up at the wrong time, after the deal had already gone down and the shipment had been off-loaded, distributed, and the ship had left port.

She wondered how DeLaud planned to bypass all the security and get the shipment of drugs off without being caught.

When three couples came down the gangplank, she had her answer.

Decoys. Shipyard security went over to investigate them. Shadoe recognized the girls from the strip club—they had auditioned for Brandon the other day, so they were new and no doubt plants put in there by DeLaud.

The girls did a fine job distracting security, flirting with the guards. The guys were belligerent, the girls acting like drunken partiers who were there just to have a good time with their boyfriends. It was innocent but out of hand and security had to call for backup, which meant the yard wasn't being covered like it should. Shadoe could hear security arguing about how they weren't supposed to be on board the ship, the guys saying they wanted to give their girlfriends a tour, the girls trying to act innocent and laughing.

"They're unloading the shipment somewhere else," Spence said.

Shadoe nodded. "Probably off the side of the ship. The guy who came to the door said the launch was in place and the shipment was ready to be off-loaded. My guess would be a waiting boat."

Spence took off like a rocket; the rest of them followed, not easy to do since the last thing they wanted was to capture security's attention. They had to run all the way to the end of the docks, then head up toward the water.

"We're going to have to cut through this fence," Spence said.

AJ reached into his cargo pants. "Not a problem."

Shadoe arched a brow at the tiny bolt cutters no bigger than a set of pliers. "You think those are going to cut through this thick fence?"

AJ didn't bother to look up. "I know so."

He was right. It took less than a minute and he was through. He then cut a hole large enough for them to fit through, which they had to do carefully so the sharp pieces wouldn't cut skin or clothing. Pax held the top while they eased through the opening. When they were through, they pulled the fence closed so it wouldn't look cut.

"Head back this way."

They followed Spence along the narrow dock barely wide enough for one person. Shadoe could see the ship ahead. In the dark, it was hard to tell what was going on.

Until they got close enough to see a black boat moored alongside it, a rope ladder connecting it to the ship's rails above. They weren't using any kind of light, so Shadoe had to squint to make out the action.

"I see movement above," AJ said, crouching down and pointing, sending them all into a sudden halt and scramble for cover.

Someone came down the rope hauling a bag strapped to his shoulder.

Filled with drugs, no doubt. They dumped the bag once they got about ten feet to the boat, then scrambled back up the ladder.

"I'm alerting the Feds. We don't have confirmation this is the drug shipment, but whatever they're doing here, it can't be legal."

Spence pulled his phone and made the call.

Now they just had to make sure these guys didn't leave before the Feds showed up.

"I've got an idea," Shadoe said. "I'll head around front and go looking for Jerry. It'll alert security that there's someone on board."

Spence paused, then nodded. "It's plausible enough. Go. I'll back you up." He looked to AJ and Pax. "Make sure that boat doesn't leave."

Pax narrowed his gaze at the black beauty bobbing in the water. "Done."

Spence and Shadoe snuck down the back dock, then once they turned the corner and made their way through the cut fence, she took off in a run to get back to the car. She turned toward Spence as she slipped her shoes back on and straightened her skirt, then grabbed her purse. "Okay, I'm going in."

"You be careful. Don't do anything stupid."

"I'm not planning on it. I just want to cause a ruckus so we can capture DeLaud's attention and delay things a bit."

He nodded and pulled his piece out of the back of his pants. "If anything goes wrong, you duck."

She patted her purse. "If anything goes wrong, I intend to be the first one to start shooting."

She moved around the car and headed toward the shack, then through the open gate. It took awhile for security to notice her, since they were still trying to sort out the mess with the group already there. She decided to announce her arrival.

"Jerry! Oh, Jerry, are you in here somewhere?"

She tried to be as loud as she could, and weaved side to side for effect, so maybe security would think she was drunk.

That got their attention. They turned and headed in her direction. "Ma'am? Ma'am, you can't be here. This area is off-limits."

She stopped and pursed her lips. "But my boyfriend is on that ship and he told me to wait. And I waited a really long time and he hasn't come out yet and now I have to pee."

One of the men frowned. "He's on what ship?"

She pointed. "That pretty red and white one?"

"Is he the captain?"

She giggled and hiccupped. "Nope. He's a . . . importer or somethin'. Said he had a meeting. Can I go somewhere and pee now?"

The first guy called to the second guy; they bent their heads and whispered and there was a lot of finger-pointing to her, then to the ship. Then they got on their walkie-talkies and rapid-fire conversation ensued. The group behind them started to look really nervous, and began to tiptoe their way to the nearest exit.

"Hey guys, those people are leaving. Do they know where the bathroom is?"

One of the security guards pivoted, pulled his weapon, and ordered the six to freeze and hit the ground. They did. Shadoe tried not to smile.

"Uh-oh. Are they in trouble? And, sir, I still have to pee."

"Ma'am, I can't help you right now. Please leave this area immediately."

She supposed security had more pressing matters than finding a drunken stripper a bathroom, because they hightailed it toward the ship and rocketed up the gangplank. Which was fine with Shadoe, because she was going with them. She saw Spence pull out of his hiding spot near the building and she met up with him after kicking her shoes off.

"Not sure how well trained these security guards are, but I'll bet whoever is inside has better weapons than they do."

She nodded at Spence as they ran up the gangplank. She pulled her badge and her gun and discarded her empty purse, hoping like hell they could pull off this arrest without anyone dying in the process.

She heard voices. Spence got in front of her and she followed his lead up a set of stairs and onto the main deck. They stayed low so they couldn't be seen, but they could hear.

Security hadn't had much luck, and had run into DeLaud and his friends. Shadoe peeked up above the metal rim of the captain's bridge to see a group of six men holding guns on the entire security team.

Not good. DeLaud said something to his guys in rapid-fire Spanish, and they pointed their weapons to the stairs on the other side of the bridge. Security, hands held high, began to descend. Spence looked over at her, then motioned with his head behind her. She pivoted and saw AJ and Pax coming up the other side.

Four of them versus a horde of bad guys. Where were the Feds? She tapped her wrist and Spence held up five fingers.

In five minutes this could all be over with. And a lot of innocent people could be dead.

Spence motioned for her to stay put, indicating he was going around to the other side. He wanted her to supply backup. She nodded and stayed in position while he crawled behind her and around the back of the bridge. Now they had coverage on all sides except the front where DeLaud and his men stood, and where the drug shipment was being unloaded.

She hated doing nothing but watching, especially since the security guards were in danger. She knew what was going to happen to them—they were no doubt going to be either killed or tossed overboard once the boat holding the drugs left port, so there'd be no witnesses. Shadoe couldn't let that happen. And sitting around here waiting for the Feds to arrive made her crazy. Every second that ticked by wasted time, and could possibly cost those men their lives.

She took a few steps back, intent on finding Spence and hatching out a quick plan to rush DeLaud and the others, but she was swallowed up by arms across her and a hand around her mouth.

"What the hell are you doing here, Desi?"

Lance.

Where had he come from? She tensed, struggled, unwilling to let him overpower her. She couldn't stay silent, couldn't let this happen. A rush of adrenaline made her flush hot, break out in a sweat. She pushed against him but he held tight to her.

Unfortunately, their fight caught the attention of DeLaud and his men.

"What's going on over here?" DeLaud and two of his men ran over to the side and saw Shadoe fighting off Lance. DeLaud pulled a gun and aimed it in their direction.

"Desi? What are you doing here?"

"That's what I'd like to know," Lance said, grunting with the effort to hold her still. "Desi, stop struggling."

She bit down on Lance's hand covering her mouth. With a loud curse he released his hold over her mouth.

She knew she was in deep shit when DeLaud raised the gun and pointed it at her. She was expendable, nothing to him. A rush of panic overcame her and she fought to remember her training. She jammed an elbow in Lance's ribs and ducked down as soon as Lance let go of her. DeLaud fired and Lance went down, giving her a split second to pull her own gun and fire at DeLaud.

Then all hell broke loose. DeLaud grabbed his middle and

dropped to his knees. Spence came flying over the top of the bridge and landed on top of DeLaud's men. AJ and Pax came around the other side at the same time Shadoe regained her momentum and stood, running around the corner. She took out two of the men; AJ and Pax took four.

The Feds came in around the same time, high-powered rifles drawn and bullhorns announcing that they were Federal agents. In both English and Spanish they gave the order to drop weapons. She heard them below so she was sure—or hoped—that they'd gotten the drop on the men in the boat.

DeLaud's men surrendered, dropped their guns, and hit the ground. Shadoe pointed the barrel of her gun to the floor, kept her finger on the trigger, and carefully approached DeLaud, who lay facedown on the deck. She kicked his gun out of his reach, bent down, and checked his pulse.

Still alive.

"We need an ambulance here," she shouted. "This is our prime suspect and he's still breathing but he's bleeding bad." She turned him over and saw a field of red spouting from his side. "See if there's a first-aid kit on the bridge," she said to AJ, who nodded and ran off, coming back a few seconds later with one.

She grabbed a handful of bandages and pressed them on the wound to stop the bleeding.

"Lance is dead," Spence said, coming over to kneel at her side.

She grimaced, wishing that hadn't happened. She wanted to know how deeply he had been involved with DeLaud, and now they'd never be able to find out. But at least they knew who the inside person at the club was.

Strange that Lance had shown up so late for this transaction, or at all. So much she didn't understand.

"Are you all right?"

She looked up, nodded at Spence. "It went down so fast."

He rubbed her back. "It always does. No time to think, only react. You did good."

"I'm shaking."

He grinned. "That's normal."

"I might want to throw up later."

He laughed then. "That's normal, too."

"I still don't understand the whole connection to the Wild Rose," Shadoe said.

"My guess is they used the club as a distribution point for the drugs. That's how Lance was connected."

"Which means the Feds will need to do a little more investigating on the distribution end of the deal."

"Yeah."

But at least they'd figured out who the rogue agent was, and who was working the inside at the Wild Rose. "I need to go talk to the Fed in charge."

She nodded. "I'm going to stay here with DeLaud until the ambulance arrives. I want him to live."

Spence arched a brow. "Care that much for him, do you?"

She snorted. "I want him to live long enough to tell us what we want to know, then go to prison. He can die there, not tonight."

"Good thinking." Spence stood and moved off to find the DEA agent in charge. The paramedics arrived and took over, leaving Shadoe to stand over them and watch as they stabilized DeLaud, then lifted him onto the gurney and took him to a waiting ambulance. She instructed two agents to follow and provide constant guard over him. She wasn't going to lose him, just in case someone had the idea to break him out of the hospital.

If he lived.

She blew out a breath, dragged both hands through her hair, and went off to find Spence.

He was busy with the head agent, so she informed AJ she was going to take DeLaud's car and head back to the club, that she'd notify Lance's wife of his death. Plus it was time for her to reveal who she was and tell Brandon his feature stripper wasn't going to be stripping anymore.

She was glad that part was over. She was more than ready to keep her clothes on in the future. She parked in front of the club. It had just closed, so she went to the side door and knocked. Ariele let her in.

"You missed your second show."

"I know. Where's Brandon?"

"In his office."

"Is Cheri still here?"

"Yeah. She's in the office with Brandon."

Perfect. Brandon could help her support Cheri when she delivered the bad news. She went through the club and to the other side where Brandon's office was. The door was closed. She wondered if they were having a meeting about Cheri's performance, or attitude. Hell, it could be anything. She didn't want to interrupt, but had no choice. She knocked.

It took a few seconds for Brandon to answer. "What?"

His tone was curt. "It's . . . Desi."

"Can it wait?"

"No. It's urgent."

She leaned against the wall and waited, then the door opened and Cheri walked out. Her face was flushed and she shot a vicious glare at Shadoe.

"What the fuck do you want? You missed your second show. I hope he fires your ass."

"Actually, I need to speak to both of you."

Cheri arched a brow.

"Can you come in here with me?"

"What for?"

"It's about Lance." She didn't wait to explain any more, just stepped into Brandon's office and figured Cheri would follow.

She did, and Shadoe shut the door behind her.

"What's this all about, Desi?" Brandon asked.

She didn't sit, instead stood as Cheri took a seat in the chair across from Brandon's desk. She'd never done this before—delivered bad news. She didn't like it, didn't want to, but she had no choice. "First, my name is Shadoe Grayson and I'm an agent with the Department of Justice." She showed them her badge and ID.

Cheri's gaze shot to Brandon, then back to her. "What?"

Brandon just stared at her. "What are you talking about?"

"We've been monitoring drug shipments coming in from Colombia, and the involvement of a Federal agent. I was sent to work undercover because we suspected the drug deals were somehow connected to the Wild Rose. Our agent was known to be hanging around here. He was using someone with a relationship to the club and the docks as an inside contact, and the drug deal went down tonight. We believe Lance was involved in all this, because he showed up in the midst of the deal."

"What was Lance doing on the ship?" Brandon asked.

"We have reason to believe he was the inside contact for De-Laud here at the club."

Cheri's gaze shot to Brandon's again, then back at Shadoe. "No. That can't be. My Lance wouldn't be involved in . . . drug dealing." Cheri stood. "Where is he?"

"He was shot during an altercation with DeLaud. I'm very sorry to have to tell you that he didn't survive."

Brandon stood. "What?"

Cheri's eyes widened. "No." She blinked several times, then crumpled forward in the chair and covered her face with her hands. "Oh, no. Not Lance."

Brandon came around the desk and stood behind Cheri, placing his hands on her shoulders. "I don't understand any of this. My club was being used to transport drugs? How could I not know about this?"

"These people are good at covering their tracks. And they had . . ." She looked down at Cheri, who sobbed into her hands. ". . . they had an inside person."

Cheri began to wail.

"I need to get her out of here," Brandon said, helping to lift Cheri from the chair. "Come on, honey. Let's go get you a drink, calm you down, then I'll take you home."

Shadoe moved out of their way, feeling helpless. Was it always like this? The grieving ones fell apart and she would be able to do nothing but stand by and apologize? "I'm very sorry for your loss. I'll just clean out my things and be off. Brandon, a Federal agent will be around probably tomorrow to take a statement from you and from the girls."

Brandon nodded.

Cheri didn't uncover her face, instead laid her head against Brandon's chest and let him lead her from the room. Shadoe followed and went back to the dressing room, cleared out her locker, and loaded her things in her car. She wanted to say good-bye to the other girls, but they'd all taken off. She'd come back tomorrow and do that before they left town and headed back to Dallas.

The mission was over. The rush of adrenaline had passed, the excitement of wrapping up her first case evaporating as fast as a short burst of rain on parched pavement. Her head began to clear as she realized what this meant.

She and Spence would soon part. She'd report back to Washington to file her report on this case, and receive her next assignment. Spence would be off on his next adventure, too.

They were done.

The ache in the pit of her stomach intensified, and she suddenly wanted nothing more than to spend the night with him, to feel his touch, his arms around her, his mouth on hers, and his cock buried inside her.

How was she ever going to be able to walk away from him?

She slid behind the wheel and reached for the ignition, then paused, looked as the blinking neon light for the Wild Rose was shut off. She leaned back in the seat and pondered.

And pondered some more.

Something clicked. Cheri leaning over the bar to whisper at Brandon. The fierce way he held her wrist. The looks exchanged between them. The flushed look on her face when they were interrupted tonight.

The way she covered her face when she found out about Lance.

Shadoe hadn't seen any tears. Brandon didn't seem all that upset about Lance. It had all gone down so fast. They hadn't asked a lot of questions about the drug dealing or the club's involvement. He'd wanted to hurry Shadoe out of there.

Why?

And Brandon had asked what Lance had been doing onboard the ship.

Shadoe didn't recall mentioning everything had gone down on a ship. She was almost certain she hadn't.

She suddenly had more questions. Maybe it was nothing at all, but after putting the pieces together, some things didn't fit right.

She needed to talk to Brandon and Cheri again. She opened the car door and tried the side door of the Wild Rose.

It was still open, so she went inside and through the dressing room, peering through the windowed doors into the club.

There, sitting at the bar toasting each other with champagne, were Cheri and Brandon.

Smiling, laughing, leaning in to kiss each other.

That was no grieving widow, nor a club owner upset that his club had been used to transport drugs.

She eased one of the doors open just enough to hear what was being said.

"We should send a thank-you note to the Feds for getting Lance out of our way," Cheri said with a wide grin.

"That's what he gets for wondering what DeLaud was up to. If he hadn't been so nosy, trying to make the connection between us and DeLaud, he wouldn't be dead now."

"Then I guess it's a good thing my poor dead husband saw a mystery and went to figure it out, isn't it? He's the fall guy and we're in the clear."

"It couldn't have worked out better. If they'd traced the drugs back to us, we'd be doing jail time now."

Cheri nodded, then downed the rest of the champagne and laid her glass on the table. "We have nothing to worry about, baby. Everyone else took the fall. DeLaud and Lance and the guys on the ship. We're in the clear."

"But we've lost the shipments and all the money."

Cheri shrugged. "The Colombians still need distributors. We'll figure something out. Maybe I'll get a gig at another club and set something up there."

Brandon leaned his elbow on the bar. "I don't know. It was perfect having an inside man at the Feds like DeLaud."

"Hey, there's money in a deal like this. There will be someone else like DeLaud come along. We'll make it work again."

He laughed. "I guess you're right. At least we came through this free and clear."

"And we have each other now." She slid off the barstool and moved in between his outstretched legs, twining her arms around him. "I didn't even have to divorce Lance."

Brandon wrapped his arms around her. "Or kill him."

She laughed.

Shadoe shook her head. What unbelievable scum. They thought they were in the clear? They were wrong. She reached around for the gun tucked into her waistband, but as she did, the door creaked, and both Brandon and Cheri spotted her.

"What the fuck is she still doing here?" Cheri screeched and took off running after Shadoe. Shadoe pulled her gun and pushed through the doorway, but before she could get set Cheri leaped on her, knocking the gun out of her hands. Cheri landed on top of her, knocking the breath out of her. Brandon grabbed the gun and stood over her, pointing the barrel at her face.

She struggled to suck in oxygen. Cheri sat on her stomach, and Brandon loomed over her, a murderous look on his face.

"You're dead, bitch," Cheri said.

This wasn't looking good. Shadoe was in deep shit.

Cheri reared back and the last thing Shadoe saw was a fist coming toward her face. She braced for impact.

eighteen

Spence hated cleanup, the part after a case had come to an end, and all that was left was tying up all the loose ends, followed by paperwork. The paperwork would come after they returned to Dallas, so at least he didn't have to worry about that right now. But there were interviews, talking to all the players, liaising with the head Fed in charge, and doing verbal reports.

All of those things kept him from doing what he loved best, which was the action. None of this standing around and bullshitting was action, but it was a necessary part of his job.

Right now they had amassed the group of DeLaud's henchmen and were conducting on-site interviews to see if any of them would spill their guts before they decided to lawyer up. Sullen, silent, they stood cuffed and separated from each other, each being interviewed by a separate DEA agent and an interpreter. Spence wandered among them all, listening in on snippets of the interviews. So far not much was going on. He stopped to talk to John Jacobs, the agent in charge.

"Anything?"

"This one here looks scared shitless. Says he has a wife and four kids back in Colombia and wants to make a deal. Considering we don't think he has much to offer, we're willing to listen first and see if he has anything of value."

Spence decided to hang nearby to hear what the guy had to say. He was pretty young for having four kids, but what did Spence know? Maybe the guy started early? The interpreter asked the questions, and the guy shot back in rapid-fire Spanish, gesturing wildly. The interpreter listened, then turned to John.

"He says DeLaud was definitely in charge, reported back to Captain Morales. They've been doing these shipments for about three years now, and the ship would come in three times a year with cocaine and heroin. They'd off-load to the waiting boat, then the boat would deliver the drugs in booze boxes to the Wild Rose. The booze boxes would be tossed out back as empties, to be picked up by the club and distributed from there."

"Nice setup," Spence said.

"Yeah."

The agent asked questions through the interpreter. The guy started talking some more, and the interpreter arched a brow and turned to John. "He says he's never seen that dead guy before."

Spence went cold. "Lance?"

"Yeah. He said they dealt with the club owner."

"That would be Brandon."

The guy nodded. "*Sí*, Brandon." Then he started talking again, the interpreter listened, and turned to John when he was finished.

"He also said some tall blond chick was usually around. One of the strippers. She was Brandon's girlfriend. Cherry or something."

"Cheri?" Spence asked. "That's Lance's wife."

Spence did an about-face, searching the deck. His skin prickled with unease as he looked for Shadoe, but didn't see her.

"Have you seen Agent Grayson?"

The agents around him just shrugged.

Not good. He spun on his heel and ran the entire deck until he found AJ. "Where did Shadoe go?"

"She took DeLaud's car and went back to the club to tell Cheri about Lance and let Brandon know everything that went down."

Spence's heart slammed hard against his chest. "Sonofabitch. Brandon and Cheri are the inside people."

AJ's eyes widened. "What?"

He jammed his hand in his pocket where he'd shoved his ear-piece earlier. He slid it into his ear now.

He heard heavy breathing. Moaning. Then voices.

"Let me kill her and get it over with."

"Not yet. I want her to wake up first. Then I'm going to have some fun."

Brandon's voice. Cheri's. Fuck.

"Grab Pax. She's at the club with them. Hurt. We've gotta go now."

FOR SOMEONE TALL AND SLENDER, CHERI WAS SURPRISINGLY strong. Shadoe was no lightweight, but she'd had the wind knocked out of her so Cheri had the advantage landing on top of her like that. And the first punch to her face had knocked her senseless.

Cheri was obviously a street fighter, and didn't mind getting her knuckles bruised. Shadoe was still trying to regain her senses when Brandon grabbed her by the shirt and hauled her to her feet. Dizzy, disoriented, she could barely stand upright when Cheri hit her the second time. She went barreling backward through the double doors leading to the dressing room, tumbling end over end and thankful for the thick carpeting when she hit her head.

Jesus, that hurt.

She had to focus, had to grab her wits. She was damn lucky Brandon—who now had her gun—hadn't just shot her.

"Quit fucking around. Let me just kill her," he said.

"Hell no. This bitch has had it coming since the minute she stepped foot in our club. I'm going to beat her until she's dead."

Fine with Shadoe. Fists she could handle. A bullet was a much more permanent solution, so the longer she could put that off, the better. When Cheri came for her this time, Shadoe was a bit more clearheaded—and sufficiently pissed off.

Shadoe dodged her and Cheri went sprawling facedown on the carpet. Now it was her turn to jump on top of Cheri. She wrenched her arm behind her back and gave a quick jerk.

Cheri screamed, kicked her feet back, and tried to buck Shadoe off, but Shadoe had her weight on top now and she wasn't about to budge.

Until the butt end of a pistol whipped the side of her head. Pain knifed through her skull and she let go of Cheri's arm, grabbed her head with both hands, and Cheri threw her off. Shadoe crashed against the wall and landed prone.

"Goddammit, that hurt." Hot, sticky wetness trickled down her fingers.

Blood. Shadoe pressed her fingers against the wound. Great. Now she was dizzy, nauseous, and everything was growing fuzzy. She forced herself to stay conscious. She glared up at Brandon, determined to do whatever it took to stay alive for as long as she could. "Don't think your girlfriend can take care of herself?"

Brandon, who she'd thought was such a nice guy, leered down at her now. God, she'd gotten that so wrong.

"Doesn't really matter what you say. You're not going to live through the night." He raised the gun but Cheri scrambled to her feet and grabbed his arm, pushing the barrel away from Shadoe. She'd like to be grateful, but she knew it was only temporary.

"No, dammit. Not yet. I'm not finished with her."

Panting, disoriented, and just plain sick to her stomach, Shadoe dragged herself to a sitting position, refusing to let this skank get the best of her. She had to clear her head, had to think about how she could get Cheri out of the way, then disarm Brandon.

Not easy with a bleeding head wound and already beaten by the crazy woman. The odds weren't in her favor. No one knew about Brandon and Cheri's role in the drug-smuggling operation. Spence would be busy with the Feds on board the ship for a while and would expect her to return there . . . eventually. They weren't going to come looking for her.

She was dead and she knew it. But she wasn't going to let them kill her while she just sat there. She pushed herself up the wall and braced herself against it—no easy feat considering she no doubt had a concussion. Cheri watched her, a smug, victorious smile on her face.

"Finish this, Cheri," Brandon said. "Or I will."

The room spun, and Cheri did, too, actually. Shadoe knew it was a product of her head wound, but there wasn't much she could do about it. She thought about pushing off the wall and launching herself at Cheri, but knew that would be pointless as she'd either fall on her face or miss the woman entirely. So she waited, her right hand tucked behind her, fingers curled into a tight fist. She didn't have a lot left, but she reserved it for Cheri's attack.

When Cheri came for her, Shadoe resisted the urge to sink down, to sidestep. Instead, she waited until just the moment when Cheri was in range. Then she pulled her arm out, hauled it back, and used every ounce of strength she possessed to slam her fist right in the middle of Cheri's face. Bone crunched as her knuckles connected with the cartilage in Cheri's nose. Blood spurted everywhere, and her hand hurt like a sonofabitch.

But she'd hit the spot. Cheri's eyes slid back in her head and she crumpled like an accordion, hitting the floor with a dull thud.

Shadoe didn't even look at her. She bent down, grabbed one of her stilettos, and while Brandon was busy gaping down at his girlfriend, she took the heel end of her shoe and slammed it down on top of his head. The action caused him to raise his gun arm, which she reached for with both hands. Weakened, she didn't have much strength to fight him, but she intended to hold on as long as she could.

At least she'd wounded him. Blood poured down his face, into his eyes, forcing him to fight her for the gun and drop his forehead onto his upper arm to wipe away the blood.

Strengthened by Brandon's weakness, she fought harder, using everything she had at her disposal. She kicked him with her remaining shoe, pounding down on the top of his foot. He groaned out a curse, pushed against her. She elbowed him in the ribs but he was stronger, finally pushing her hard enough that she lost hold of his arm. She went flying to the ground and immediately rolled over, intent on pushing to her feet.

But it was too late. He had one hand over his face to wipe away the blood, the other pointing the gun at her.

She braced herself for the bullet, praying it would be quick and painless. The explosion of gunfire deafened her and she jerked.

But it was Brandon whose eyes widened in shock. His chest spread with crimson. He flew backward and hit the ground, even in death his eyes still bearing that surprised look.

She was pretty damned shocked herself, had the urge to check her arms and legs and body to determine where the bullet hole was. But other than her throbbing head and bruised body, she hadn't been shot.

The gunfire had come from behind her. She craned her neck around to see Spence holding a gun, AJ and Pax flanking him.

Relief sent her reeling; the tension drained immediately from her body.

He'd found her. He'd come. How had he known?

Spence pocketed the gun and ran to her side, dropping to the floor. He scooped her against him and cradled her in his arms.

"Jesus, you're a mess."

She smiled up at him. "Thanks."

He wasn't smiling. "Are you okay?"

Now that it was over and she was safe, she felt oblivion coming. She struggled against it. There was so much she wanted to tell him. "I don't feel so good."

That was all she managed before blackness descended.

SPENCE PACED OUTSIDE THE HOSPITAL ROOM, STOPPING AT THE closed door to glare at it.

Not that it did much good.

They'd had her in there for eight hours—minus the time they'd wheeled her out for a CAT scan, and he hadn't had a second to even see her. He'd sent Pax and AJ back to Dallas. He wasn't leaving. Not until he knew what was going on.

Damn doctors never told you anything.

And the Department of Justice had already informed him that as soon as the doctors cleared it they were moving her back to D.C. to a hospital there.

Not back to Dallas. Not with him.

She wasn't his, after all.

Goddammit.

He went to the nurse's station outside the emergency room for the fiftieth time. The same stern-looking woman glared back at him.

"No, you still can't go in. They're running tests."

"That doesn't tell me anything."

"I'm sure they'll be finished soon."

This was such bullshit.

He'd never felt so powerless in his life.

He leaned against the counter as one of the guys in the white coats who he'd seen in Shadoe's room came up bearing a clipboard.

"They're releasing Ms. Grayson to the waiting private ambulance, where she'll be flown by jet to D.C. I've signed off."

"Thank you, Doctor."

Spence stepped up. "How is she?"

"She's stable. She has a severe concussion and a lot of bruising."

"But she'll be fine."

"She'll recover, yes. She's stable enough for transfer." The doctor handed the chart to the nurse.

"Can I see her for a minute before she leaves?"

"A minute. No more."

"Thanks."

That was all he needed. He tried not to run, but he walked really damn fast and inched the door open.

The lights were dimmed, but enough that he could see her.

Christ, she was pale. His heart dropped. Her eyes were closed and her arms against her sides. She was hooked up to an IV and some kind of monitor that beeped stuff on a screen next to her bed. He stepped fully into the room and shut the door, walked as easily as he could and stopped next to the bed.

Her face was swollen and bruised, didn't even look like her. She had cuts and bruises on her arms and neck, the only parts of her body he could see.

This was his fault. He hadn't paid attention, hadn't been there for her. They were partners, he was supposed to be at her side, instead of wrapping up the investigation.

Why had she gone off alone?

He slid his hand underneath hers. Her fingers were cold.

Her eyes opened.

She smiled. "Hey."

It didn't even sound like her.

"Hey. How are you?"

"I feel beat up."

"You look beat up."

"I think the other guy is worse."

He laughed. "The other guy is dead."

"Thank you for that." She squeezed his hand. "You saved my life."

He didn't deserve her thanks. If he'd been there with her, this wouldn't have happened.

"Cheri?"

"They're patching her up and then she'll be arrested. You broke her nose."

She snorted, then winced. "Ow. Shit, that hurts. But good. I dinged Brandon on the head with my stiletto."

Now it was his turn to laugh. "You did?"

"Yeah. I knew those damn shoes had to be good for something. They make excellent weapons."

"You did great."

"Thanks. I stayed alive long enough for you to find me." Her eyes shimmered with tears. "Thank you for finding me."

There was so much he wanted to say to her. He didn't know where to start. But the door opened and the nurse came in. "That's all. Ms. Grayson needs her rest now."

He turned back to Shadoe, didn't know what to say to her. Couldn't really say anything with the nurse tapping her impatient foot in the doorway.

Shit.

What was there left to say anyway?

Shadoe stared up at him, her brown eyes breaking him. He knew it would come to this. Best to make it clean.

He leaned over and pressed a light kiss to her lips. "You take care of yourself."

She didn't say anything, so he did.

"Bye."

She blinked, more tears falling. "Bye."

The nurse held the door for him while he walked out. He moved down the hall and out the door, climbed on his bike and started it up, then headed out on the interstate, not even sure where he was going.

Back to Dallas, he supposed. Where else would he go? He had paperwork to do, had to file his report, wrap up this assignment, and give all the details to Grange.

This case was over. Shadoe was on her way back to Washington. She'd be okay. The doctor said so.

He goosed the throttle and increased his speed, needing the wind in his face, needing to clear his head, needing something to fill the emptiness inside.

nineteen

DRIPPING WITH SWEAT, SPENCE CLIMBED OUT OF THE BOXING ring after going a few rounds with Diaz. It had been brutal, left him ringing wet and more than a bit bruised. But it had served its purpose. For a while, he'd been able to forget everything but fighting for his life.

"Jesus, Spence, are you deliberately looking for a fight?" Diaz, just as sweaty, leaned over the top rope and stared down at him.

Spence grabbed a towel and a bottle of water and shrugged. "Just staying in shape."

"Bullshit, man. Something's crawled up your ass in a major way. What's up?"

He guzzled down the bottle of water and tossed it in the recycle bin. "Nothing."

"It's not nothing," AJ said, climbing into the ring.

"It's the woman we had the assignment with a few weeks ago," Pax said, entering the ring after AJ. "He's in love with her."

Spence shot a look at Pax. "You want me to come in there and beat the shit out of you, Pax?"

Pax smirked down at him. "Is going a few rounds with me going to change how you feel about Shadoe?"

AJ leaned over the ropes. "Call her."

Pax finished tying the laces on his gloves. "Fuck that. Get on a plane or on your bike and go see her."

Spence turned away and wiped the back of his neck with the towel. "What good would that do? She has her job, and I have mine."

"You could call her," Diaz suggested.

Spence spun around. "Again. Why?"

Diaz rolled his eyes. "Because you're in love with her? Tell her you want to see her."

Spence shrugged. "She could have called me if she wanted to see me."

"Jesus, Spence. Man up. Get on your goddamn bike, take some time off, and go to her. If there's something between the two of you, figure out how to make it work. Trust me, it's worth it."

Diaz would know all about that since he'd had to make it work with Jessie. "It's different. She's in D.C."

"So you keep telling me. Quit looking for the problem and try to find a solution. If you love her, there'll be one."

Did he love her? He supposed he did. He wasn't sure he really knew what love was all about. He'd never been in love before. If love meant feeling miserable, then he supposed he was in love.

Maybe it was time to find out.

Not that he thought it would work out.

It never did.

But he was no coward. And he wanted to see if she was okay.

He flung the towel in the basket. "I'm going to talk to Grange."

Diaz smiled at him. "You do that. And have a good trip."

SHADOE PACED THE CONFINES OF HER APARTMENT, STOPPED, and stared out the window at the sunny sky, then frowned.

"This is stupid. *You're* stupid, Shadoe."

It had been four weeks. She felt fine, but was on six weeks of forced medical leave by the department until she was cleared. And she had nothing to do but sit around here and think.

Too much time to think.

About Spence. About how easily he'd just slipped out of her life with a kiss and a good-bye, and then . . . nothing.

For the first week she'd been too out of it to really notice. She'd had a killer headache and she'd slept a lot. Her body needed to heal.

But she recovered fast, and once she got home, sleeping and wandering around her apartment only lasted so many hours. She craved work, something . . . anything to occupy the long hours.

Her father had called her—not dropped by, of course, but called her. He said she'd performed adequately. In other words, she hadn't embarrassed him or the family name. That was it.

So much for love. Then again, it was about what she'd expected from him, so he hadn't hurt her. He'd long ago lost the capacity to hurt her. She was happy he hadn't come by to see her. It would have been awkward. They had nothing left to say to each other.

Which meant she was alone.

She had friends, but she begged off seeing anyone, claimed she was recovering and needed to be alone.

She didn't really want to be alone.

She wanted Spence.

She must have picked up her cell phone a hundred times, looked at his name in her address book, her finger hovering on the button. Then she'd put the phone down and walked away. If he'd wanted to contact her, he would have.

He hadn't.

She'd gotten his message loud and clear. The mission was over. They were over. She'd known it was coming, but she just hadn't wanted to face reality.

Reality had come and gone. Spence was out of her life. It didn't matter that she'd fallen in love with him. He hadn't fallen in love with her.

Time to move on.

She wrapped her arms around herself and stared out the window, where people went on with their lives, falling in love, finding that someone to share their world with. For some people it worked.

For her, it hadn't. She was just going to have to get it over it. Once she got back to work it would be easier. She'd forget.

She'd never forget. There was an ache inside her that wouldn't go away. And at night as she lay in bed, the cool sheets whispering over her naked body, she remembered his touch, his taste, his mouth on hers, and wanted what she couldn't have.

Her father was right. She wasn't tough at all. Every time she thought about Spence, tears filled her eyes. Like now. She swiped them away, angry that she'd let him occupy her thoughts again.

She turned at the sound of the doorbell, and moved to the door. When she looked through the peephole, she let out a gasp, her heart dropped to her feet, and she broke out in a cold sweat.

Spence! She looked down at her oversized T-shirt, which was all she wore. She wanted to jump in the shower and make herself presentable, do her hair, put on some makeup.

No time.

Ah, hell, it went to her knees like a dress, anyway. She pushed back her messy hair and opened the door.

His smile was brighter than the sun streaming in through her window.

"Hey." She smiled back at him.

"Hey yourself."

She wanted to throw herself in his arms, but she held back. "What are you doing here?"

"If you let me in, I'll tell you."

"Oh. Sorry." What a moron she was. She stepped back and he walked in. She closed the door, drinking in the sight of him in tight jeans, sleeveless shirt, and boots. Her throat had gone dry and she fought to swallow.

"Did you ride all the way here?"

"Yeah. Took a vacation."

"Wow." He rode from Dallas to D.C. To see her? She wouldn't begin to hope.

"Nice place." He turned to face her.

"It's small. One bedroom. Not much to it, really." She showed him her tiny kitchen and little eating area carved into the corner, then the living room with its view of Georgetown and the Potomac River. "I got it for the view, mainly."

He looked out the full-length window and nodded. "I can see that. It's nice."

He continued to stare out the window, as if he was stalling. She waited. Finally, he turned to face her.

"We . . . didn't get a chance to talk much after the mission ended. You were hurt and they whisked you away. We didn't debrief."

Debrief? He was here for a debriefing? Not for her, not because he missed her or wanted her or anything even remotely personal. Her heart sank. She lifted her chin. "I filed my report and sent a copy in to General Lee."

"I read it. I have a few more questions."

She steeled herself so he wouldn't see her hands shake, then pointed to the sofa. "Have a seat and I'll answer whatever questions you have. Would you like some tea?"

He took a seat and looked up at her, his expression unreadable. "Uh. Sure."

"I'll be right back." She hurried into the kitchen, wishing she could run to her bedroom, close the door, and burst into tears. But that would be what a female would do. That would be what her father would expect her to do—fall apart, show weakness.

She wasn't weak. She could do this. No man was going to break her, not even one she loved. She'd let her father hurt her by not loving her. She'd never let another man do it to her again. She inhaled, blew it out slow and easy, then did it again until she reined in her riotous emotions. Once she was calm enough, she grabbed the pitcher of tea and a couple of glasses and set them on the tray. Okay, now she had to think what else she'd need. Ice, lemon, and—

"I lied."

She almost dropped a glass. She spun around to find Spence in the doorway to the kitchen. "What?"

He walked toward her. "I lied. I'm not here for debriefing."

Her heart did a *thu-thump* in her chest, loud and pounding, picking up speed. "You're not?"

Closer now, he kept coming until he was right in front of her. He rested his hands on the counter, caging her between it and him. Heat roared off him, blasting her with everything that was male about him, everything she loved and wanted.

"No. I'm here because I missed you, because I wanted to see you, to touch you, to smell you." He leaned in, pressed his face against her hair. "God, I miss your smell. Miss you in my bed at night. I miss fucking you."

Oh, God. She couldn't breathe. Her hands came up to rest against his chest. She felt the fast beating of his heart, equaling the mad pulsing of her own. Her knees were weak, but then it didn't matter because Spence grabbed her around the waist and lifted her up on the counter, his lips on hers before she could take her next breath.

She melted. Right there on the kitchen counter, with Spence's lips on hers, she dissolved into a puddle of desire and need and want and happiness.

He *was* here for her. He'd come all this way to tell her he'd missed her. She didn't need or want anything else but his hands and mouth on her, his tongue sliding inside to lick at hers with velvety softness that was so unlike the steely hard feel of his body everywhere else. The incongruity of it all was such a turn on. The way his lips brushed so lightly against hers, then the way he grabbed her hips and jerked her forward so he could rest his erection against the pulsing wet core of her that screamed out for his touch.

He moved his hands down her back, lifted her T-shirt.

"You're naked under that thing, aren't you?" He leaned back to stare down at her with a look that burned her.

"Yes."

He pulled her hips forward and lifted the T-shirt, then pushed her knees apart.

"Damn."

He dropped to his knees and held on to the small of her back, coaxing her to lift for him. She leaned back on her hands and slid down to the edge of the counter, her entire body quivering in anticipation.

His mouth covered her sex, and she tilted her head back while he devoured her pussy, sucked on her clit, sending her into wild oblivion with his mouth and tongue and teeth.

This was so much a part of what she'd missed about him. Not the great sex—though it was phenomenal, but the fact that he knew her body so well—that he could take her to the peak—and over—so fast.

And he did, swirling his tongue over the knotted bud that she hadn't touched herself in weeks. Maybe she'd been subconsciously waiting for him, and now that she had, she couldn't wait any longer. She fell apart and cried out, slid her pussy along his mouth and tongue as she climaxed in a hard, blinding rainstorm of sensation that pounded her with relentless waves of wet pleasure.

She was still spasming when he stood, unzipped his pants and put on a condom in record time, then plunged inside her. His fingers dipped into her hips as he pulled out and rammed again. His face was tight as he stared down at the spot where they were joined, then cast his gaze back up at her.

"Yes. This is what I missed, too," he said. "Fucking you. Being inside you." He didn't slow the pace as he spoke to her in between ragged breaths, and that drove her crazy.

She couldn't breathe, could only hold on for this crazy ride that threatened to steal her sanity. She didn't want it to stop, but the pleasure overwhelmed her as he took her right to the pinnacle yet again with hard, slamming thrusts. He ground his shaft against her clit, swept in to take her mouth and gather her close at the same time.

Such sweet depth, such emotion that poured from him. He held nothing back this time and she knew it, and that made it all the better for her. That he looked her in the eyes, his emotions raw and exposed as he slid in and out of her, brought tears to her eyes.

"I love you, Spence."

He stilled, stared at her in wonder, then his lips curled upward in the hint of a smile.

He thrust, capturing her mouth again until she couldn't form a coherent thought, could only ride the wave as it crested, then crashed, taking her with it. She whimpered against his mouth as she came again, her orgasm making her clench around his cock. She felt it so deeply, and he cursed, feeling it, too.

He ground against her and shuddered, groaning against her lips as he came, too, every part of his body straining with the force of his orgasm. She held tight to him as he was racked with spasms, pushing against her time and time again until he finally relaxed.

She laid her head against his shoulder, felt the dampness under his shirt as she stroked his back.

"I love you, too, Shadoe."

She leaned back and searched his face. "What?"

"I love you, too."

They were still connected, intimately. She pulsed around him. He looked down where they were joined, then swept his gaze back to her face.

It was the most perfect moment ever. She couldn't have asked for a better declaration of love. In her kitchen, while he was inside her. While she sat on the kitchen counter.

He loved her. She sighed, feeling more a woman at that moment than she'd ever felt in her entire life. Somehow, this brooding, love-no-one type of man had just told a woman he loved her.

She felt rather special about that.

"Now what?" he asked.

It figured he wouldn't know what to do next.

Come to think of it, neither did she.

She let out a short laugh. "I have no idea."

THEY ENDED UP SHOWERING—AND MAKING LOVE AGAIN IN THERE. They couldn't keep their hands off each other. Then again, four weeks was a long time to be apart. They had a lot of time to make up for.

And Spence could cook! After they cleaned up he went into her kitchen and dragged out eggs, bacon, and bread and started making breakfast. He ordered her to sit at the table and do nothing.

She ignored him. She made a pot of coffee and poured orange juice into glasses, then set the table.

"You're supposed to be resting," he said, shooting her a frown over his shoulder.

"I've rested plenty. I feel great."

His expression changed, his eyes traveling up and down her body. "Yeah, you sure do."

She giggled, felt lighthearted and happier than she had since they parted four weeks ago. She slid into her chair and watched him flip eggs.

"You can cook."

He kept his back to her while he watched the stove. "Well, yeah."

"That surprises me."

"Why?"

"I don't know. You just don't seem the cooking type. I imagined you as a 'feed me, woman' type of guy."

He laughed. "When we all went to live with Grange, he taught us to cook, then left us on our own and told us if we wanted to eat, we could fix our own meals. Otherwise, we could starve. But he said he wasn't going to be our maid, cook, and housekeeper so we'd better learn to take care of ourselves. Since none of us were fond of baloney sandwiches twice a day, we figured it out."

She leaned back in the chair and grinned, imagining all those guys mucking about in the kitchen. "I'll bet that was interesting."

"It was. We barbecue a lot. Make a lot of salads."

She nodded. "As long as you make it work."

He turned and scooped out eggs onto both plates, then bacon.

When the toast popped up, he laid that on their plates, then sat at the table with her. She devoured everything on her plate, realizing she was starving and hadn't really been eating much the past few weeks.

"You've lost weight," he said, scooping up the last of his eggs with his fork.

"I wasn't hungry."

"Missed me, probably."

"Actually, I was miserable without you. I had trouble eating and sleeping."

His smile died. He laid his fork down and put his hand over hers. "I'm sorry. I should have called you."

Her heart ached at the tenderness in his voice. "I could have called you, too. I just . . . didn't think you wanted to hear from me."

His brows knit together. "Why would you think that?"

"At the hospital. You just leaned over and said good-bye, then left."

"They gave me one minute to see you, then the DOJ swept you away in an ambulance for transfer back here. I had no time with you."

"I'm sorry. I handled this all badly." She pushed away the empty plate.

"No, you didn't. I did." He took a long swallow of coffee, then set the cup aside. "I don't know how to do this, Shadoe."

"How to do what?"

"Love someone. I've never done it before."

Her heart swelled. "Me either. I haven't really had shining examples of love everlasting, you know."

"Yeah. So what do we do now?"

She shrugged. "I don't know. You have a life with the Wild Riders."

"And yours is here."

"So where does that leave us? Meeting up occasionally to have sex?"

His frown deepened. "That's not what I want."

"That's not what I want, either. But what other choice do we have?"

He pushed back from the table and stood, moving into the living room to stare out her picturesque window. She followed, coming behind him to thread her arms around his middle. He laid his hands over hers.

"I could live here," he said.

She stilled. "What?"

He pulled her around so she faced him. "Here. In D.C."

"What does that mean?"

He shrugged. "I talked to Grange. I can work for the Wild Riders out here."

The blood rushed so hard in her ears she could barely hear anything. "You'd do that. Just to be with me."

He pulled her against him, kissed her. "I've never told anyone I loved them, Shadoe. I don't intend to say those words to another woman again, except you."

Oh, God. Her eyes welled with tears. "I love you, too, Spence. And I've never said those words to another man. I don't want to ever say them to anyone but you. You make me feel more deeply than I've ever felt before. You make me think we can do anything as long as we're together."

He smiled down at her. "Nothing's impossible. Our only problem is logistics."

"What if I moved to Dallas?"

"What? Why would you do that? Your job is here."

Now it was her turn to shrug. "My job can be anywhere. The DOJ has an office there. I liked Dallas."

"I don't have roots anywhere. I'm more mobile. You grew up here."

She shook her head. "My father's home is here. My home is wherever you are."

"He's your family."

She snorted. "Not really. He never really wanted me anymore than my mother did."

"I want you."

Her heart swelled with love. "I know. We'll be family for each other. That's enough."

"Your father was wrong, you know."

"About what?"

"You're stronger than most of the men I've known."

She sucked in a breath. "That's quite possibly the nicest thing anyone's ever said to me."

"It's the truth. You have strength, Shadoe. You're a survivor."

"Like you."

He smiled. "Yeah. Like me."

It's what drew her to him in the first place. It's what would keep them together. Where they made it work didn't matter. Although, she had a thought. "You know what . . ."

He cocked his head to the side. "What?"

"What about New Orleans?"

"What about it?"

"Your brother is there. He's family, too."

He eyed her warily. "Shadoe, I haven't contacted him in years."

She wasn't going to let it go. Family was too important. At least the kind of family that counted. She knew that somewhere, Trevor was out there. And she'd bet he'd like to know about Spence. "Trevor is your brother. He's family. You and I need all the family we can get. Besides, I liked New Orleans. And the DOJ needs good agents down there."

"You would really do that. You'd relocate."

She swept her hand along his cheek, loving the feel of his beard stubble. "Of course I would. You're willing to do the same."

"Grange said I can do my job from anywhere. I just have to go into Dallas occasionally for assignments."

"Okay. I can relocate, too. And I think it's time we find your brother."

He leaned in, touched his forehead to hers. "I don't know what to do with you. I don't know what to do with all these feelings."

"Just love me."

He lifted his head, his eyes so clear, so blue, she lost herself in them. "I do."

The rest, they'd figure out later. They had the start—they had love for each other.

The rest of it was just details. It didn't matter whether they set down roots in Dallas, D.C., New Orleans, or somewhere else entirely.

As long as they were together, they'd be home.